SPLINTERED

KELLY MILLER

© 2016 by Kelly Miller

All rights reserved. No part of this book may be reproduced, stored in a retrieval system or transmitted in any form or by any means without the prior written permission of the publisher, except by a reviewer who may quote brief passages in a review to be printed in a newspaper, magazine, journal, or online medium.

The final approval for this literary material is granted by the author.

First printing

All characters appearing in this work are fictitious. Any resemblance to real persons, living or dead, is purely coincidental.

ISBN: 978-0-692-59011-9

Published by Kelly Miller
contactkelly@kellymillerauthor.com
www.kellymillerauthor.com

Printed in the United States of America
Splintered is printed in Minion Pro

Other Books by Kelly Miller

Dead Like Me
Deadly Fantasies

ACKNOWLEDGEMENTS

Thanks to everyone who participated in any way to help bring this story to life. I couldn't have done it without you. Any mistakes rest solely on my shoulders. In particular, I'd like to thank:

Jennifer Schusterman for suggesting the name Lily Eastin in my second annual Name a Character blog contest. Congratulations, Jennifer!

Officer Danny DeGrace for providing me with information on SWAT maneuvers and to Tracy DeGrace, for always having an answer to my medical questions. Officer Greg Stevanus for the ride up the Hillsborough River. You gave me the insider's look that enabled me to write my final scenes with such authenticity. For that I am truly grateful.

Patricia Stanton and all folks at the Temple Terrace Police Department, who gave me their time and imparted their wisdom. Thanks for letting me have a look around City Hall.

Carol Bright for an explanation of the inner workings of the Hillsborough County Sheriff's Office.

Alison Goins for serving as my Temple Terrace tour guide. I had a great time researching the city that would serve as the backdrop for this book.

Angie Wolters for her extensive knowledge off all things having to do with roads. She knows more about gravel than any person should.

My critique partner Chris Coad Taylor for pushing me to make my story stronger.

My beta readers Alison Goins, Stephanie Mitchell Lockett, Marie Scicchitano, Dana Miller Terrigino, and Lisa Vogt.

My cover designer, Ida Jansson of AMYGDALA DESIGN, for creating the most stunning book cover I've ever seen.

My husband and children, for putting up with the countless hours I was holed up in my office working to make this third book a reality. I know it's a hardship to have to share me with the characters in my stories.

My fans, who have always stuck by my side. I hope you like Detectives Parker and Wallace as much as you did Detectives Springer and Jessup.

This book is dedicated to all my fans. Your loyalty and enthusiasm has been the fire that's kept me motivated to write. Thank you for supporting me on this wonderful journey.

PART 1
MONDAY, SEPTEMBER 21

(1)
MADDY EASTIN

The grumble of a heavy diesel engine alerted Maddy that only two minutes separated her from either a ride to school or another lecture from her mom about missing the bus. She slammed the front door and stepped into the sticky heat of a dark September morning. The moisture in the Florida air enveloped her, its thickness slowing her down. Or maybe the lethargic pace simply matched her outlook toward this dreary school day.

The geometry book jutting out of the small hole in the bottom of her backpack cut into her ribs with every step. She yanked down the sleeves riding up her arms to hide the fresh marks. From behind her, a metallic grinding of brakes cut through the darkness. She reached the bus stop expecting to see the yellow beast that would drag her off to school. Instead, a fat guy hopped off the back of a garbage truck and lifted a recycling bin off the ground.

Dammit. I forgot to put the trash out. Something else for Mom to complain about.

The bus was late again. Maddy wondered where Sabrina was—her friend usually beat her to the bus stop, but this morning she was a no-show. Maybe Sabrina's cough had turned into something more serious.

Lucky. Now she will have an extra day to study for our geometry exam.

Maddy had thought about playing the sick card this morning, but she knew there was no way her mom would have believed the act. And the only thing Maddy dreaded more than geometric theorems was cleaning the toilet.

Bending down on one knee, Maddy swung her backpack to the ground. She squinted through the murky haze of the nearest streetlight and fumbled with its zipper.

Why we moved us to this dump of a neighborhood is beyond me.

Half the streetlights were burned out, including the one directly over Maddy's head.

The sun wouldn't rise for another hour, but she still found herself wiping away moisture collecting near her hairline.

A soft squealing noise jerked her attention away from the task of rearranging the books in her bag. A van had pulled up to the corner—a real piece of junk from the sound of the roughly idling engine. The feeling of being watched caused a crop of goose bumps to pop up on her arms.

Really? Now a van has you spooked?

Maddy blamed the paranoia on those stupid stranger-danger videos her mom had forced her to watch as a kid. She could still hear the nasally narrator's voice in her head, warning her not to get into a car with someone she didn't know, and never to accept candy from a stranger.

Duh.

Maddy zipped her backpack closed and stood, still staring at the van. It's not like work vehicles in this neighborhood were an unusual occurrence. Most days it was like playing *Mario Kart*, having to dodge all the trucks on the street. It seemed half the neighbors cut grass for a living and parked their trailers full of lawn equipment on the road every night after work.

The smell of burning rubber drifted toward her. The voice in Maddy's head morphed into her dad's and informed the idiot in the van that he should change the belts. Of course, the source of the smell could've been coming from an oil leak in the engine. Maddy couldn't decide the exact cause. She'd always hated it when her dad forced her into the garage to help him tinker with the car. Even so, she'd give anything to have him back now, to complain one more time about the grease stuck under her fingernails or how impossible it was to remove oil stains from her jeans.

A muted flash appeared behind the tinted glass of the van's passenger window. Someone still sat inside.

Probably getting his rocks off staring at my bare legs.

The window slid down a crack. A new scent skirted the air, a sweeter smell that caused a craving to wash over Maddy.

She strained her eyes, looking for writing on the side panel of the van. Nothing visible. She wondered if a workman had arrived early to a job site. The sound of a garage door opening down the street tore Maddy's attention away. She turned, hoping to see Sabrina rushing toward the bus stop. The low light of the streetlamp illuminated a dark figure pushing a garbage can to the curb.

Another rumble drew near. Maddy breathed a sigh of relief when she caught a glimpse of yellow passing between the houses and trees on the other side of the neighborhood. Her stop would be next.

She cocked her head to the side, realizing the smell of smoke was closer. Just as she turned her head, an iron hand clamped around her wrist.

(2)
DETECTIVE TERRANCE WALLACE

Detective Terrance Wallace stared at Maddy Eastin as she retold her story. Trails of tears dried on her cheeks while new tears formed in the corners of her eyes.

"The man grabbed you. Then what happened?" Wallace asked.

"I already told you." Exhaustion marked her every word. "The guy pulled me back toward the van with one hand on my left wrist and the other on my waist. When the bus turned the corner he yelled, 'Come help me, will ya?' I figured he was hollering at someone else in the van, but no one showed up. The guy kept yanking on me, trying to drag me backward. I screamed and stomped on his foot. He let go. I ran toward the bus. The pervert jumped in his van and hauled ass away from the curb. I barely escaped."

Once again, the girl broke down weeping. She had given three accounts of her story now, and each time she retold it additional details surfaced. Wallace couldn't decide if they were actually forgotten memories or new embellishments. He'd seen it before when interviewing suspects. When the believability of a story was in question, new details were often added in the hopes that the explanation sounded more plausible. Only Maddy Eastin wasn't a suspect.

The girl's jagged crying had also gotten more drawn out and over the top with each breakdown. When her tears finally slowed, she grabbed another tissue and rubbed her eyes, streaking the already-smeared mascara. The tips of her straight, strawberry-blonde hair clumped together just above her shoulders.

Perhaps I'm being too cynical.

Wallace knew his judgment had been off lately, his attitude hardened when it came to dealing with victims. Yet he couldn't afford to be burned on another case. He had to take his time uncovering all the facts before passing judgment on the veracity of this fifteen-year-old's allegation.

Dispatch had called him out on the attempted abduction earlier that morning, and he'd been sitting in the Eastins' living room for the better part of an hour going over the events with Maddy and her mother, Lily. The hysterical girl had tried relaying what had happened while she was still at the scene, but with the group of neighborhood onlookers growing in number, Wallace had decided to walk the two back to their house.

Lily and Maddy sat across from him on a tattered couch, each perched as close to their respective armrest as they could manage. The faded piece of plaid furniture leaned lower on the girl's side. A phonebook wedged underneath it made a handy-yet-unbalanced fake leg. A pillow stacked on top of folded bed sheets sat on the floor next to it.

As Maddy's latest bout of crying ended, Lily tried traversing the space between them. She took Maddy's hand and rubbed it. Lily had a faraway look in her eyes though. It seemed as if she were stroking a cat, not consoling her daughter.

Maddy jerked her hand away and shot her mother a dirty look. She turned toward Wallace. "Why don't you believe me?"

Wallace leaned in closer. He ignored the poke of the chair's spring underneath him. "I believe you, Maddy. Repeating your story helps me uncover details you may have forgotten the first time we talked about the incident. It's standard operating procedure."

"The incident? The *incident*? You mean two sickos trying to snatch me off the street. All you want to do is talk. Why aren't you out there looking for those perverts?"

"Please calm down," Lily told her daughter. "Detective Wallace is simply doing his job."

"Don't tell me to calm down, Mother. I have every right to be upset. In fact, *you* could try looking a little more distraught. Your only daughter gets attacked and you haven't shed a single tear. Have you even called Dad yet? If he were here, he'd know what to do. He'd make everything better."

Wallace saw Lily cringe at her daughter's stinging accusation.

"I left him a message," she said, "but I haven't heard anything back. He's probably on one of his business trips."

"Maddy." Detective Wallace waited until he had the girl's attention. "Maddy, I can't lie to you. This will be a difficult case to pursue. There's not much of a physical description to go on. You only saw one adult, dark-skinned male. He could have been Latino, though you're not sure. First you said he was of average height, then you said he was tall. You remembered later that he had facial hair. A scraggly beard."

"And don't forget the bad teeth," Maddy added.

"Right. Bad teeth." Wallace looked down, referring to the scant notes he'd taken. "We don't even have a concrete description of the vehicle. You thought it might have been a white van, but other than a noisy idle and bad-smelling exhaust, there's not much to go on."

Maddy looked at Detective Wallace with wide eyes brimming with new, unshed tears. She seemed to be screaming out a silent plea for someone to hold her and never let go. To show her that she was loved and that life would be worse if she'd disappeared. The sadness stretched from her down-turned face into her body; she leaned forward into her lap and slowly rocked back and forth.

Wallace looked away. He knew the girl's emotions were genuine. He just wasn't sure if her story rang true. Forcing himself to focus on the task at hand, he said, "There is one more thing I want to try. Back at the station, we have a computer program that helps us create a visual representation of a suspect. Like what a sketch artist would do, but an electronic version. Do you think you could describe your attacker to the officer who runs the program?"

Maddy slowly looked up from her tucked position. "I can try."

"Will the picture run in the newspaper?" Lily asked. "Maybe you can arrest the cretin if someone recognizes him and turns him into the authorities."

"If the newspaper decides to run an article, I'm not certain they'll include the sketch," Wallace said. "It's a bit premature to say. Let's see how this goes first."

"The paper won't use Maddy's name, will they?" Lily asked.

"No," Wallace answered. "She's a minor. It's likely the newspaper will only report an attempted abduction took place in your neighborhood. This will help inform the public, so they can be on the lookout in case these men try it again."

Maddy gave her mother a scathing look. "Great, Mom. Don't worry about me. Only think of what the neighbors will say if they see your daughter's name in the newspaper."

Lily turned away and stared at the wall.

"Maddy, you must be exhausted," Wallace said. "Why don't we take a break? Take a few moments to collect yourself before we head over to the station. I need to talk to your mother anyway."

Maddy shot Detective Wallace a skeptical look.

"Routine, I assure you," he said. "I need some information on the neighbors before I talk to them later today. Hopefully, I can find someone who saw the van. Another witness would certainly help the case."

"Maddy, why don't you go lie down in your bedroom?" Lily suggested. "I'll knock on the door when it's time to leave."

Maddy sighed loudly in the way only teenagers could. She showed her displeasure at being shooed away by stomping down the hall.

"I have to apologize for my daughter's behavior. She's had a tough go of it lately."

Wallace nodded, offering a sympathetic smile. "Maddy's experienced a very traumatic event."

Lily gave a slight eye roll and flicked her wavy hair back over her shoulder. The color was similar to Maddy's, but with a darker shade of red mixed in with the blonde.

"Don't you believe your daughter's account of the attempted abduction?" Wallace asked.

"Of course I believe Maddy. It's just . . . I don't know." Lily sighed. "How about we go into the kitchen? I'll make a pot of coffee."

"Sure."

Lily seemed the type of woman who felt more comfortable staying busy. She'd probably be more forthcoming if her hands were occupied. Wallace took a seat at a scarred kitchenette table. Everything in the house seemed secondhand, from the well-worn armchair Wallace had just vacated to the battered appliances. The cramped house was in a lower-income neighborhood of Temple Terrace, a small incorporated city adjacent to Tampa on the northeast side of Hillsborough County.

Wallace flipped to a new page in his notebook and readied his pen. "Mrs. Eastin, what did you mean by your earlier comment that Maddy's been having a tough time?"

Lily stood at the counter, her back to Detective Wallace. He waited a minute, figuring she was gathering her thoughts. When another minute went by, he knew she was somewhere else. Probably stuck in the what-if loops. What if the abductors had been successful? What would have happened to Maddy if she hadn't gotten away?

Wallace coughed, trying to reengage Lily's attention.

(3)
LILY EASTIN

Lily Eastin stood with her back to Detective Wallace, fumbling with the coffee filters.

Screw it.

She jammed two stuck-together paper cones down into the filter tray. The coffee would only work to magnify her jittery nerves, but nevertheless she wanted a cup. Maybe the steaming mug would thaw the chill that had settled into her bones the moment she'd received Maddy's frantic phone call.

Her daughter had complained she'd yet to show any emotion over the attempted abduction, that Lily hadn't cried for what Maddy had gone through. It wasn't that she didn't care—quite the opposite. Lily's tears were simply frozen, unable to flow. She'd almost lost Maddy once before, and the possibility of living through that again had paralyzed her.

Detective Wallace coughed.

The distraction reeled Lily back from the edge and deposited her firmly back in the confines of the small kitchen. She wondered how long she'd been silently standing at the counter.

She looked over her shoulder at the patient smile on Detective Wallace's face. "Do you take cream or sugar in your coffee?" she asked.

"Neither. Black is fine."

Lily stared at the man sitting at her table. A bronze glow seemed to radiate from the black hue of his skin—a color as dark as cocoa beans. Lily tried to imagine what colors she'd mix to create just the right pigment if she were to paint him on canvas. She would've enjoyed trying to capture the contradictions that defined him. Detective Wallace had an imposing presence, yet his chubby face lent him a warmth. Those cheeks looked like they could hold a dozen acorns—a real juxtaposition to his tall, athletic body.

The detective seemed nice enough, intent on helping, but as Lily prepared the two coffees she wondered how much of Maddy's recent past she should divulge. Could this be just another of her daughter's stunts? Five months ago, Lily would've said Maddy didn't have a devious bone in her body, but when her dad had walked out, it was like an injection of sneakiness had been plunged into her veins. Like Maddy's very DNA had changed. The once-sweet little girl had morphed into a deceitful young woman hell-bent on making Lily's life miserable.

Maddy blamed Lily for her dad leaving.

She'd probably felt blindsided when he walked out. Understandable, considering Maddy rarely heard raised voices in the house.

That was part of the problem. Tom and Lily had grown so far apart, they were mere roommates at the end, barely speaking to each other unless it concerned their daughter. Of course it hadn't always been like that, but even at the height of their fighting, Maddy never observed the nastiness. They'd kept it behind closed doors.

There were lots of reasons why Tom left. All of which Lily wouldn't burden Maddy with. The girl had always looked up to her father, had raised him high on a pedestal. Lily knew what it meant when a father didn't live up to a daughter's expectations. She couldn't bear to pop Maddy's bubble, even if that meant she took on the role of the bad guy.

She handed Detective Wallace his mug.

"Thank you for the coffee." He blew on it, took a hesitant sip, then a long swallow.

Lily wanted to be honest with Detective Wallace, but she didn't want to say too much and get Maddy into trouble. What happened today wasn't simply a case of ditching school. Maddy had reported a crime. If it was a lie, the possibility that she could be charged with filing a false police report would hang over her daughter's head like an executioner's ax waiting to drop.

Lily resumed her position with her back to the kitchen counter, her cup of coffee untouched.

"Mrs. Eastin, earlier you mentioned Maddy's been having a tough time. In what way?"

"Maddy's father left us in April. Our divorce should be final in a few weeks." Lily paused, looking down at her hands. She noticed they were shaking and locked them together in front of her. "My finances took a big hit when Tom walked out. I had to move us here this past summer. Maddy hasn't been taking the change or the breakup well. The real problem is that Tom's completely shut Maddy out of his life. He's always travelled a lot for business. He's a Regional Sales Manager for a food packaging equipment manufacturer. So Maddy's used to his absences, but this is different. He hasn't seen or even called her in five months. The last time he and I spoke, Tom said he had to find himself." She emphasized the last two words by making air quotes.

"Did Mr. Eastin leave because of another woman?"

Lily crossed her arms in front of her chest, as if that action could keep the words from penetrating her heart. "No."

"I'm sorry. Please don't think I'm prying. These questions are only asked in the hopes of gaining a clearer picture of the circumstances Maddy's been dealing with."

Detective Wallace didn't look sorry at all. He may have played the mock-embarrassment card well, but Lily knew it was all a tactic to try and get in her good graces.

He probably hopes I'll open up and blab the whole sob story. That's not going to happen.

Lily couldn't even trust herself to think about why her husband had left, much less relate the reasons out loud to a stranger.

She grabbed her mug of untouched coffee and slowly turned the decorative cup in circles on her palm. Tiny colorful fingerprints dabbed into the shape of a Christmas wreath adorned it. "You don't believe Maddy's account of what happened this morning, do you, detective?"

"That's not what I said." Wallace straightened his golden tie clip as he spoke. "I apologize if you think my words or actions imply I don't believe Maddy. The investigation has only begun. I don't have enough facts to form an opinion yet. I only know kids change during a divorce."

"Do you have children?"

"None of my own, ma'am, but my wife and I foster kids stuck in the system."

"Well then, I'm sure you've seen children at their worst. How they can be angry at the world because of the circumstances forced upon them. That's Maddy. When you check into her school background you'll find a history of truancy, plunging grades, marks for belligerence, and a tall stack of detentions. Last month, a store owner even caught Maddy stuffing a tube of lipstick into her purse. It took some doing, but he didn't press charges."

Lily watched Detective Wallace's eyes narrow. His face grew serious when he heard her admit to smoothing over the offense. Actually, Lily had gotten lucky because the owner was a friend of a friend. Although now she'd never be able to patronize the store or even hang out with that girlfriend again. She'd die of embarrassment if the woman found out that Lily had used her name to get Maddy out of a jam. She'd think Lily was the worst mother in the world.

"I know what you're thinking, detective. I'm one of 'those mothers.' The kind who jumps through flaming hoops to fix her daughter's mistakes rather than let the girl own up to the consequences of her actions. You're right. I am that kind of mother. I refuse to let Maddy ruin her future. Tell me, why should she have to pay for her parents' shitty decisions?"

Detective Wallace never admitted to thinking the worst of Lily. Instead, he changed the subject, asking her for the names and phone numbers of anyone who might be helpful to contact about Maddy's attempted abduction. Lily grabbed her address book, then brought it and her coffee mug over to the table. She sat and relayed the information while Detective Wallace wrote in his notebook.

Lily noticed his pen. "Makes for lovely notes," she said.

"What?"

"The purple ink you're writing with. It gives your notes some panache."

The wrinkles in Wallace's brow line softened. Smiling, he answered, "The kids love to play practical jokes on me. Most of the time, I find Little People figurines in my shoes. They can hardly contain their giggles when they watch as I pull on each shoe only to realize my foot doesn't fit. This morning, one of them got creative—my usual pen was replaced with this one. I didn't even notice until I got to here."

Wallace's last statement seemed to remind him of the task at hand. Lily watched as his smile faded.

"What do you do for a living, Mrs. Eastin?"

I used to paint breathtaking portraits.

"I'm a manager at Michaels, the chain store specializing in arts and crafts. Nothing fancy, but it pays the bills."

"Must be hard. Lots of hours, working weekends and holidays?"

Lily nodded, afraid her voice would betray her.

"Is Maddy active in any sports or extracurriculars?"

Cop talk for, "Does she have something to keep her busy while I'm at work?"

"She used to be on the middle school volleyball team, but she didn't make the high school team. She talked about starting club ball but . . . well, that never happened. She plays clarinet though."

"Did Maddy switch schools when you moved?"

"No. She's still a sophomore at King High School. We were renting a nicer house over on Leon Avenue when the family was together. I chose this place because of its proximity to our old one. I wanted to find something in the general vicinity so Maddy wouldn't feel completely uprooted. So she'd be close enough to visit her friends. However, Maddy's been so upset lately, she hasn't brought anyone over. Truth be told, I think she's ashamed of the place. Once the divorce is settled, hopefully the child support will help us move somewhere better."

Lily watched Detective Wallace take another drink of his coffee. Hers still sat untouched as she tried unsuccessfully to draw the heat away from the mug and into her hands.

"I can see what you're doing, detective."

"What do you mean?"

"All these questions. You're painting a dismal picture of my daughter's life. An unhappy girl, left home alone while her soon-to-be divorced mom works long hours. But I can tell you, Maddy wouldn't make up a story like this. She wouldn't invent two fictitious kidnappers. My daughter may have been acting out lately, but she's a good girl. She'd never take anything this far."

"Not even to get the attention she craves from a father who, by all accounts, has tossed her aside?"

(4)
DETECTIVE TERRANCE WALLACE

Terrance Wallace thought he'd found an ally in Lily Eastin. She seemed angry at the treatment her daughter had dished out. Yet it didn't take long before she started backpedaling, playing mama bear to protect her child. But then, Terrance had been on the police force for almost twenty years and had seen it all. There were plenty of times he'd watched mothers listen to their children admit to gruesome crimes only to defend them, and sometimes even create false alibis.

A parent's job was a lot like a cop's—to protect and to serve. Terrance knew it was difficult to let children make their own mistakes. Though he didn't have any biological ones, he understood the parental bond created during the simple acts of changing diapers, late-night feedings, and reading a book to a little one more interested in the whiskers on his face than the words he read aloud.

Terrance and his wife were on the front lines of the foster system, serving as emergency-placement foster parents. They took in kids who needed a safe environment immediately. Even though the children were only in the Wallaces' care briefly—anywhere from one to forty-five days—strong bonds formed quickly.

Kids would show up at their door shell-shocked, many having been traumatized by a family implosion just hours earlier. Often Terrance would be at work, so his wife, Trudy, offered triage, bandaging the kids' wounded psyches as best she could. It was her calling, one she'd discovered as a volunteer in the Guardian ad Litem program, a legal advocacy program for children in the system.

Sometimes the state would send the kids back to their parents or a close relative; other times they'd move on to a more permanent foster family. Even though the children only stayed a short time, Terrance understood the instinct to protect them at all costs. Lily Eastin was simply doing the same for her daughter. Yet, as the woman had stood in front of him pleading her daughter's case, he couldn't tell who she was trying to convince more—him, or herself.

Lily and Maddy had followed Detective Wallace back to City Hall, driving in their own car. They met up on the third floor, where the detectives' offices were. Maddy had worked with an officer to create a facial composite of the man who'd almost abducted her. The process had been painful for both of them. She gave so many contradictory descriptions, the muddled image came out looking like an angry Cheech Marin circa 1978. Except he had a scraggly beard instead of a thick mustache.

Wallace's immediate supervisor, Corporal Rhodes, walked into Wallace's cubicle after Lily and Maddy finally left. He eased into the extra chair.

"Back still bothering you?" Wallace asked him.

Rhodes shrugged almost imperceptibly, like he was trying to avoid any extra movement. "Some days worse than others. I see the girl and her mother are gone."

"Yeah, they left about ten minutes ago."

"What are you thinking on this one?"

"Don't know yet. The girl seems pretty upset, but is it because of the attempted abduction or because Daddy walked out on her? I'm not sure. Her story lacks serious credibility. Not only did it change every time she opened her mouth, it had too many specifics. You know how it goes. During an attack, victims are so pumped full of adrenaline the details are usually a blur. This Eastin girl told me how the guy grabbed her left wrist and held her around the ribs with his right arm. It sounded more like a book report than an account of a supposed abduction."

Wallace grabbed a pen off the desk and started tapping his knee with it. "But it's too soon to make a judgment call. The patrol officer canvassing the Eastins' neighborhood didn't come up with any witnesses yet. However, half of the block was away at work, so I'm going back out there this evening."

"What about the bus driver?"

"Nothing." Wallace grabbed a copy of the report Officer Santos had given him. "Says here, at approximately six thirty a.m. the driver reported seeing Maddy Eastin run down the middle of the street, waving her arms to make him stop. As the driver exited the bus, he said Maddy babbled hysterically. He finally figured out that a guy had tried pulling her into a van. The bus driver never saw the supposed vehicle."

"I've already started fielding calls about this from newspapers." Rhodes pointed at the suspect drawing on Wallace's desk. "Do you want to let them run the picture along with the story?"

Wallace thought about it, chewing on the pen's cap.

When Wallace didn't answer, Rhodes said, "Man, that Demir case really screwed you up. I've never known you to second-guess yourself like this."

You're not the only one.

Amani Demir, a sixteen-year-old Muslim girl, had reported an attempted rape a few months back. Wallace remembered how he'd fallen hard for the girl's story. It had gotten all the way to court before the defense presented a completely different version of events—as it turned out, the true version.

Amani had been getting into trouble, and her mother had threatened to send her back to Turkey to live with relatives if she didn't change her American ways. In their Muslim faith, it was forbidden for a female to be alone in a room with a male that wasn't a relative. When Amani's mother came home early one day to find Amani with her shirt ripped and a man grabbing her by the arm, the girl cried rape. Come to find out, Amani had been dating the nineteen-year-old boy, but had tried to break it off numerous times. He'd shown up at Amani's house, but when she wouldn't take him back, he got rough with her. The guy ended up almost doing time because he couldn't take a hint. And because Wallace didn't do his job.

Even though this guy had lied through every interrogation, the suspect's stupidity still hadn't gotten Wallace off the hook with his peers and supervisors. He'd lost their respect. Worse, he hadn't been able to shake the self-doubt created by the whole fiasco.

"Let's hold off on running the picture in the paper. At least for now." Wallace adjusted his tie clip, a thirtieth birthday present from his mama. The woman had a loving heart but a wicked hand. Growing up, she'd never been afraid to use it if she thought he was screwing up.

Seems like I've been doing a lot of that lately.

"Be sure and get me your preliminary report ASAP," Rhodes said. "I need to figure out what to tell the press."

Wallace wondered how the story would read, and whether it would turn out to be another complete work of fiction.

(5)
HANK FRY

The song playing out from Hank Fry's cell phone tore his thoughts away from his dad's old barn, bringing that terrified sixteen-year-old firmly back into his thirty-one-year-old body. He looked down at his blanched knuckles and forced himself to let go of the hammer. He dropped it back in his tool belt and dug the persistent phone out of his pocket.

"I need to take this," Hank said to his buddy working beside him on the bridge embankment.

Hank walked down the hill, away from the work site. He was about three weeks into the job of widening the I-75 bridge that crossed Fletcher Avenue. The ringtone continued belting out "Gangnam Style," giving him the heads-up that his younger brother Daniel was calling. Hank grimaced at the frantic beat. He couldn't understand why Daniel liked the song so much. The boy couldn't even pronounce half the words, opting to create his own instead of singing the difficult Korean lyrics. But it never failed, every time Daniel heard the song on the radio he'd jump up, laughing and clapping, and would plead for Hank to turn up the music.

Last week, Hank had finally given in and assigned the ringtone to Daniel. He couldn't help but give in since the song made Daniel so happy every time he heard it. Daniel had the matching ringtone programmed to sing out whenever Hank called him, something Hank tried to do at least once a day.

"Hey, Small Fry. This had better be good. You know you can't call me at the job site this time of day." Though Hank felt aggravated, he didn't let his voice show it. He kept a lightness in it because Daniel was overly sensitive to anger directed toward him.

"Is this Hank Fry?" a deep voice asked.

"Who the hell is this? How did you get my brother's phone?"

"Sir, this is Chad Topher of the Hillsborough County Sheriff's Office. Am I speaking to Hank Fry?"

"Yes." Hank put a hand over his ear, trying to block out the traffic noise rushing by him on the interstate.

"Sir, I picked up your brother, Daniel Fry, for indecent exposure. He claims it's all a misunderstanding, but the woman he exposed himself to gives another story. Your brother has no priors, but when I interviewed him it became apparent he is mentally challenged. Would that be accurate, sir?"

"Yes. Daniel suffered a brain injury as a kid. What's going to happen to him?"

"It all depends on the complainant. She has twenty days to file the paperwork. After that, the State Attorney will decide whether to press charges. For now, though, I think it's best to release him to a family member. Can you pick him up?"

After the cop told him where they were, Hank rushed to clear the time off with his boss. He had to promise overtime off the books, but the important thing was to get to Daniel quickly. His brother had the mental capacity of a ten-year-old, and there was no telling what would come out of his mouth if left with a cop too long.

Shit! I can't believe Daniel got caught this time.

***

Hank parked next to a police cruiser in a lot in front of the entrance to the Takomah Trail Park. Daniel stood next to the police officer, his head down, kicking at some rocks—until he heard Hank's voice.

"Are you okay, Daniel?"

"Please don't be mad, Hank. I keep saying it was all a mistake. I told that lady I was just trying to find a place to pee. I had to go real bad, Hank. I can't help she ran by when I was peeing."

Standing there pleading his case, Daniel looked younger than his twenty-six years. It was almost like his facial features had stopped maturing when his brain did. He had rusty, brown-colored hair that he kept short on the sides and back, but longer on top. It always looked mussed up—he usually forgot to comb it before going out.

Hank laid a soothing hand on Daniel's shoulder. "I'm not mad. Next time though, make sure you us a public restroom or remember to take a leak before you leave home."

"I did, but the Mountain Dew went right through me. I'm sorry."

"Where's the lady who called 911?" Hank craned his neck, looking around the parking lot.

"She left," Officer Topher said. "Like I relayed on the phone, she has twenty days to file her complaint, but I doubt she will. I explained that your brother obviously has limited mental capacity. My nephew has Down syndrome, so I understand how a simple act can turn into a big misunderstanding."

"I appreciate your help, officer." Hank shook hands with the man. "Daniel's never done nothing like this before."

Hank saw his little brother open his mouth. He moved the hand resting on Daniel's shoulder down his brother's arm and squeezed his elbow. Daniel got the hint and kept quiet. Continuing to hold him by the arm, Hank walked Daniel over to the passenger-side door of his work van and opened it.

"Make sure you talk to your brother, Mr. Fry," Officer Topher said. "He needs to understand the severity of the situation. Daniel's lucky this didn't happen with a minor, or he would have been arrested on the spot. The sheriff doesn't take kindly to men messing with little kids in his county. Doesn't matter if it was accidental or not. You get me?"

Hank closed Daniel's door. "Understood. Again, thank you for your understanding and assistance. We appreciate it. Is there anything else?"

"No. If something more comes of this, we'll be in touch."

Hank gave a quick nod and walked around to the driver's side. He clenched his fingers around the handle and drew a few deep breaths before climbing in. Once seated, he paused before turning over the engine. Daniel had a Wolverine comic book in his lap, one he'd fished out of the glove compartment. As he turned the pages, the stress of the morning instantly disappeared from his face.

Hank was only five when Daniel was born, but he remembered how his brother had arrived prematurely. His dad had said there wasn't a chance in hell the kid would even come home from the hospital, but Daniel had proven him wrong—something that had always seemed to stick in his dad's craw. Daniel was a twig of a kid, quickly earning him the nickname "Small Fry." Of the many names he'd been called, it was the only one he didn't mind. Sitting there flipping the pages of his comic book, the boy looked innocent enough, but Hank wondered if deviant thoughts jockeyed for position inside Daniel's head.

"You promised you wouldn't expose yourself in public again," Hank said. After a couple of tries, the engine finally turned over.

Daniel turned and stared at him. Every emotion crossed the boy's face, from shock to confusion to sadness.

"No, Hank. I told you it was a mistake. I just wanted to get out of the house. To go to the park and feed the ducks. Then I had to pee. Why won't you believe me?"

Hank looked into Daniel's teary eyes. He didn't have an answer for the boy.

Daniel's face flushed red. "Stupid! Stupid! Stupid!" He slammed his fist against his head with each word he yelled at himself.

"Hey, hey. Stop that." Hank shot an arm out to block Daniel's blows.

"I didn't say you were stupid. You know we don't use that word."

Daniel dropped his chin to his chest. His breath came out in ragged bursts.

Hank hated how Daniel always used his fists to deal with his emotional pain. "How about we head over to the comic store, see if we can find you something new?"

"Really?" Daniel looked up, brightening at the suggestion. "But you hate driving all the way over to Brandon."

"Well, lucky for you, my day just freed up."

(6)
LILY EASTIN

Lily left the uneaten soup in the pot on the stove. No amount of cajoling could persuade Maddy to eat once they'd gotten home from the police station. The whole process had been agonizing—she'd had to just sit by, silently watching her daughter struggle to describe the man who'd almost stolen her away. Detective Wallace had watched Maddy with a look of skepticism on his face. It had infuriated Lily.

How in the world could a fifteen-year-old be expected to remember the thickness of an attacker's eyebrows or the angle of his cheekbones?

By the end of it, both mother and daughter were emotionally spent. They didn't say a word to each other the entire drive home.

Lily wanted to rage, to scream *"Screw it!"* at the world, and hide underneath a mountain of covers for a week. But that would be too easy, more than she deserved. Maddy hadn't created this situation, at least not on her own. The girl was a victim of bad parenting. She had a mother and father who separately had deep-seated issues, but together were even more dysfunctional.

Yet, in spite of everything that had happened that day, tears still wouldn't come. Lily refused to let herself feel anything, knowing that if she cracked open her heart even the tiniest amount, emotions would come flooding in, causing its walls to crumble completely. Lily leaned into the numbness. It'd been her go-to emotion for any stressful situation ever since Maddy was a baby.

Lily couldn't help but think back to the night when Maddy was only two months old and had refused her last evening feeding. At the time, she didn't think much of it. As a first-time mother she figured it was no big deal, that a few hours later Maddy would eat again, and would be ravenous from skipping a meal. Yet, when Lily awoke around midnight not having heard the baby's cry, she got up to check on her. In the nightlight's weak glow, Lily could see Maddy lying awake, looking up at the ceiling. She picked Maddy up to breastfeed, but the baby still refused to eat.

Lily brought her back to the bedroom and frantically woke Tom, explaining Maddy's lethargic condition. Tears streamed down Lily's face as she told Tom they should rush her to the emergency room. He allayed her fears, explaining that sometimes babies were just sleepy and didn't want to eat. Lily acquiesced to Tom, even though Maddy had been waking up like clockwork to eat every three hours since the moment she'd been born. She told herself that Maddy had finally reached the age where she could go longer between feedings. Plus, she didn't want to be labeled as one of "those" first-time parents, the type that rushed her child to the ER at the first sign of a sniffle. Both she and Tom agreed that if Maddy persisted in not eating, they'd take her to the pediatrician first thing in the morning.

The next day, Tom and Lily were waiting outside the doctor's office before the staff arrived.

The pediatrician listened to Maddy's heart and said words that almost stopped Lily's: "Your daughter's heart is pumping so fast I can't count the beats. She needs to go to the hospital immediately."

Thoughts rushed through Lily's head. *This can't be happening. This isn't the way it's supposed to be.* After the doctor left to make arrangements for transport, Lily completely fell apart.

Tom glared at Lily. "Stop crying! This is no time for one of your Lily breakdowns. Get a hold of yourself. Maddy needs you."

Through blurry vision, Lily stared at Tom, shocked he could be so harsh at a time like this. Logic told her he too was barely hanging on, that he wasn't capable of comforting his wife as well as taking care of his daughter. The words sliced through her anyway.

Pushing the old memories away, Lily walked over to the end table near the couch and picked up her purse. She dug around until her fingers found what she was looking for. She dry-swallowed two pills, hoping to alleviate the pressure building in her head. The purse slipped off her bent elbow, but she left it lying on the floor. She grabbed her cell phone off its charger and punched in Tom's number.

As angry as Lily was at him, she had to admit that what he had lacked in the husband department he made up for as a dad. She'd never seen a more loving, attentive father. That's why she couldn't understand how he could suddenly shut Maddy out of his life. It wasn't like him.

"Come on ... come on," Lily said as the third ring sounded. "You can only duck my calls for so long." She started pacing. Her strides matched the fury rising up inside as she thought about the message she would leave when the call finally switched over to voice mail.

"Hello?"

Lily paused for a moment, surprised Tom had answered. "Why haven't you returned any of my messages?"

"Really? Do we have to do this now?"

"When's a better time? Next month? Next year?" Lily's grip on the phone tightened.

"I'm hanging up now."

"No. Wait." A couple slow exhales helped to stave off the impending explosion she felt. She had to remember why she'd called, not to rehash old arguments, but to plead Maddy's case. "Tom, your daughter needs you."

And so do I.

"This isn't a good time for me."

"Are you kidding me? Didn't you listen to any of my messages? Maddy was almost abducted. Nearly ripped away from us. Again. Stop thinking about yourself for one damn minute." Silence answered Lily's accusation. She thought about how Maddy's illness had changed them both. They'd put their marriage on hold to tend to their daughter's needs, but by the time she was out of the woods, they didn't know how to find their way back to each other.

"Tom? Tom?"

A sound of something hard hitting metal reverberated over the phone.

"Tom?"

"I'm here."

"What am I supposed to tell Maddy when she asks why her father hasn't called to find out how she's doing?"

"I don't know, Lily. I told you I needed space to work through some things."

"It's been five months. Hasn't it been long enough? Look, Tom, if you want to start over without me, I can deal with that. But don't cut Maddy out of your life. She doesn't deserve it."

"I'm not cutting her out. I'm just taking time to work on me. Look, I'll call her this weekend. I promise. Right now is tough though. I'm on the road and have a big presentation to get through."

"One of these days, Tom Eastin, you're going to regret not being the hero your daughter deserves."

(7)
MADDY EASTIN

Maddy watched her mom pace back and forth in front of the couch.

"I heard you talking on the phone, Mom. Was it Dad? Did he call back?"

Lily turned around when she heard her daughter's voice. "No . . . my boss called. He wanted to talk about the schedule."

Though Maddy didn't believe her, she couldn't be certain her mother was lying. Earlier, she'd been in her bedroom with the music cranked up to keep her mom away, but when she came out to go to the bathroom, she'd heard her talking on the phone. Not loud enough to make out the conversation, but loud enough that the tension in her mom's voice was obvious.

She didn't know why her mom would hide the fact that her dad had finally called. "Whatever."

Maddy stomped back to her bedroom, ignoring the rush of her mom's words trailing behind her.

If Dad had been the one sitting beside me while I described the attacker to that idiot detective, it wouldn't have been such a nightmare.

Going into the station, Maddy had had a picture of the abductor in her head, but once the officer pelted her with questions about his complexion, the fullness of his lips, and whether he had wide-set eyes, she became confused. Detective Wallace had stared at her like he didn't believe a word she'd said. And her mom was even worse, looking embarrassed to be there. Finally, Maddy had told everyone the sketch was correct just so she could leave.

Maddy slammed her bedroom door and glanced at the time on her watch—a birthday present from her dad. For weeks, she'd agonized over which watch color to choose. She'd finally settled on yellow, and her dad laughed, saying he knew that would be her choice all along. The memory caused a sudden sharpness to shoot through her chest. The waterworks threatened to start up again. For the hundredth time, Maddy told herself she should take the damn thing off her wrist. It was a constant reminder of everything she'd lost.

Why hasn't he called?

She grabbed her cell phone off the nightstand, wondering if the battery had died.

Maybe he called Mom because he couldn't get through. Then they probably got into a fight before he had a chance to talk to me. She always screws everything up.

No, the phone was fully charged.

Maddy couldn't understand why almost being kidnapped hadn't brought her dad back. *Why didn't he show up to rescue me from this pit of hell? I don't know how much more I can take of being stuck with the Ice Queen. Even this morning didn't thaw the coldness around Mom's heart.*

Ever since Maddy was little, she'd felt like her mom had kept her at arm's length. Not physically. She was always there to hug, kiss, and read her bedtime stories. But it seemed like she was only going through the motions and showing up in body, not in spirit. It made Maddy naturally gravitate toward her dad. He was everything her mom wasn't—loving, playful, silly. He had a real zest for life.

Her dad's voice played in Maddy's head now, extolling the virtues of patience, setting goals, and then working to realize them. "Maddy," he'd say. "I remember when I was a kid and every time I saw a shooting star streak across the sky, I'd wish for a pet. My friends had cats, dogs, fish, and even lizards, but Pop thought I was too immature for my age and he wanted me to learn some responsibility before entrusting me with an animal. No matter how much I cajoled and begged, he wouldn't give in. I finally realized if I wanted an animal to call my own, I'd have to do it his way. So I set a goal and made it happen. I had patience, and with a lot of hard work to prove myself worthy, eventually it paid off."

Maddy had heard her dad's stories hundreds of times. She smiled thinking about them, and how he invariably tied each to a life lesson.

Not in a preachy way though, like when Mom lectures me about how too much makeup gives boys the wrong impression or that young ladies should always have clean rooms.

Being with her dad again was Maddy's goal. No matter what it took, she'd make it happen.

(8)
DETECTIVE TERRANCE WALLACE

After Lily and Maddy left City Hall, Wallace headed back to the Eastins' neighborhood. It had been a long day, but he wanted to talk with the folks who'd gone into work and hadn't been interviewed yet. Wallace parked his sedan at the end of the street, opposite Maddy's bus stop. He walked down the broken sidewalk while checking his notebook, comparing the house numbers to the ones on his list to see who was left to interview. A couple of times, he had to step into the grass to avoid tripping over roots. Oak trees planted too close to the sidewalk were escaping their underground cement prison.

Wallace met with a few neighbors, none of whom had witnessed anything. They had been long gone by the time the ruckus had begun. Wallace continued working his way down the street while Maddy Eastin's voice played in a continuous loop in his mind. When she'd described her attempted abduction back at the station, her recollection of the crime was too precise. Wallace had interviewed enough victims to know that during an attack racing adrenaline made it nearly impossible to process what was happening, much less remember the particulars.

Two houses down from Maddy's bus stop, a white-haired old lady in a housecoat sat in a wicker chair on her front porch. The patrol cop's notes stated that he'd knocked on her door at 8:10 a.m., but that there had been no answer.

"Excuse me, ma'am."

"Oh, yes. How can I help you?" The old lady fussed with the material of her floral housecoat, straightening it at the sides. Her shoulders bowed over slightly, like the small hump on her back was too heavy to keep her petite frame upright.

"I'm Detective Terrance Wallace with the Temple Terrace Police Department. Do you mind if I ask you a few questions?"

"Surely. How 'bout you come up here and sit a spell?"

Wallace pushed open a rusty chain-link fence gate and took a seat next to the woman. She introduced herself as Mrs. Addie Alexander and insisted he call her Addie. "Earlier this morning a police officer came by, Addie, but no one answered—"

"That's right. I don't open my door for strangers," she said proudly.

"That's a good rule to live by, Addie." Wallace was glad she'd been sitting on her porch—he may never have gotten to talk to her otherwise. "This morning there was an attempted abduction of a girl at the corner bus stop. Did you happen to see anything?"

"Good gracious, an attempted abduction. Is the girl okay?"

"Yes, she broke free. Did you happen to see anyone suspicious in the neighborhood this morning or these past few days?"

"Suspicious, yes."

Wallace readied his pen over his notebook. "Can you tell me what you saw?"

Addie brought a finger to her lips, patted the wrinkled skin, seemingly searching her memory.

"Did you happen to see a vehicle parked on your street or at the corner that didn't look like it belonged?" Wallace prompted.

"A vehicle, yes. I saw a suspicious vehicle."

"Can you describe it?"

Again, Addie quieted down.

"Mom, are you still on the porch?" The screen door opened and a woman poked her head out. "Oh, I'm sorry. I didn't realize she was visiting with a neighbor."

"No, ma'am. I'm Detective Wallace. I'm asking Mrs. Alexander about an incident that happened in the neighborhood this morning. Do you live here?"

"Me? No, but I come over every evening after work to stay with her for a few hours. A hired companion stays with her during the day. She arrives at nine o'clock. Were you asking Mom about what she saw?"

"Yes, it seems she witnessed a suspicious vehicle in the neighborhood, but she can't quite remember it clearly enough to give a description."

The younger woman chuckled, but quickly stifled it with a hand to her mouth. "Sorry, but it wouldn't matter if a man came into the house with a bomb strapped to his body. She wouldn't remember it. She has Alzheimer's, detective. If you ask her about something that happened twenty years ago she can describe it in vivid detail, but inquire about an event she experienced this morning and she'll turn into a parrot."

"Excuse me? A parrot."

"When she's in this dementia state, which seems to be happening more often than not, she'll simply repeat back what you say to her." The daughter turned to her mother. "Mom, did you see a redheaded girl skiing down the sidewalk today?"

"A redhead skiing, yes."

"See? I'm afraid she wouldn't make a very reliable witness. Every once in a while she'll have a good day, but I'm afraid this isn't one of them. I'm sorry to waste your time."

Wallace said his good-byes and continued canvassing the neighborhood. No one he talked to reported seeing a white van on the street, but they provided Wallace with a list of companies that performed services regularly—everyone from exterminators to home-repair businesses. All the while, the good folks pumped him for details of the alleged crime. A crime they couldn't believe had been committed on their street. Some of the neighbors asked out of concern for their own families, while others merely displayed a morbid curiosity. The rumors swirling around the neighborhood had blown up by epic proportions. Marie

Delacroix, who lived directly across from the Eastins, spun Wallace's favorite tale: she had heard a girl had been kidnapped because her father worked for the CIA, and that the men were holding her hostage until the government released a captured terrorist from Guantanamo Bay.

Tomorrow Wallace would contact the list of local businesses the neighbors provided to create a timeline for when employees had been in the neighborhood. He'd go back at least a couple of months in case the men had been casing the house, planning the abduction. He'd also find out what personal vehicles the employees drove. Most people were immune to seeing a work van parked in the street. They hardly gave it a second glance. Especially in the daytime. He doubted if any of the neighbors would turn out to be reliable witnesses.

Wallace knocked on the front door of the house across the street from Maddy Eastin's corner bus stop. When no one answered, Wallace rang the bell a couple of times. He heard an angry male voice holler something about impatient imbeciles always trying to sell him things he didn't want.

A man swung the door open. "Whatever it is you're sellin', I'm not interested. I only got up out of my chair because it didn't sound like you was goin' away anytime soon. Now get outta here." A permanent scowl seemed etched onto the old guy's face. He had more white hair coming out of his ears than on top of his head, where a few tufts still managed to hold on.

"Pardon the interruption, sir. My name is Detective Wallace. I'm not here to sell you anything. I'm with the Temple Terrace Police Department, and I need to ask you a few questions about an attempted abduction on your street this morning."

"So that was the cause of all the commotion?"

"Yes, sir. I'm sorry, what was your name?"

"Why are you sorry? You didn't even ask me my name. It's not like you asked and then forgot what I told ya. Sheesh. George. George

Lumpkin."

The man grabbed his lower back in obvious pain. His other hand firmly gripped a cane, and was clearly balancing most of his weight on it.

"Are you okay, sir? Why don't we sit?"

"Damn sciatica. It don't matter if I'm sittin' or standin', the pain's all the same. But if you want to plop yourself down, come follow me."

George Lumpkin led Wallace deeper into his house. Once he reached a well-loved chair, he exhaled a big puff of air and fell back into it. He clicked off the television as Wallace sat in the only other chair in the room, a brown metal folding chair.

"Officer Santos told me you weren't home when he came around to talk to all the neighbors this morning."

"Nope. On Mondays I head over to Denny's to meet with my buddies. When I pulled out of the garage, I could barely make it through the throng of people millin' around."

"So you haven't talked to any of your neighbors about it?"

"Ain't none of my business."

"Mr. Lumpkin, did you happen to see any vehicles parked outside your house early this morning?"

"In front or on the side of the house?"

"Either."

"I reckon so."

Excitement built inside Wallace. He wondered if this would be 'the lead.' There was always one lead in a case, the one that started all the dominos falling. "Do you remember what time?"

"I have no idea. Not like I live my life by a watch. Not anymore. When I can't stand to be in bed any longer, I get up and have my coffee. It's impossible to sleep anymore with this damn sciatica. I remember taking the trash to the curb. Later, after I read the paper, I decided to throw it away before the truck arrived. Doctor's always bitchin' at me to move around more. It hadn't come yet, so I put the paper in the garbage can.

That's when I noticed a van, thought it was broken down. It looked like it was on its last legs."

"Do you remember the make and model, maybe the color?"

"Why would I? It had nothing to do with me. Anyway, it was still dark out."

"You have a clear view of the corner bus stop from your front door and west window. Did you happen to notice a girl waiting for her bus this morning?"

"Nope."

"Okay, Mr. Lumpkin. Can you give me a list of anyone who's done work at your house? Maybe a bug guy or a lawn service?"

"Social security don't cover none of that. A neighbor boy down the way cuts the lawn for me. Little punk's jacked up the prices twice on me. Now I gotta shell out six bucks every time he starts that piece of crap lawn mower of his. Oughta be a crime. Extortion, that's what it is. That's the crime you need to look into."

The glamorous life of a detective. Nothing like how the TV crime dramas portray it.

Wallace spent much of his time interviewing "witnesses," though he thought they should be called "people who never seem to witness anything." These people usually fell into one of two camps. The first saw the police interview as an excuse to complain about someone in their lives. A person who'd invariably committed a small infraction against them that they felt should be punishable by law. The other group was just as bad. They wanted to tell their life stories instead of answer Wallace's questions.

As he stood to leave, he glanced around the house one last time. Though run down, the place looked immaculate. "Who cleans your house, Mr. Lumpkin?"

Hopefully the housekeeper is able to squeeze more than six bucks out of the old guy.

"No one."

"Come on, now. You can barely walk. Never mind bend over to pick up something off the floor."

Lumpkin seemed on the up-and-up. He seemed like the kind of guy who would give an uncensored version even if Wallace didn't want to hear it. In an interview, Wallace always had one ear listening to the story the person told and the other trained on what the person neglected to say. An avoided topic could often be more telling than anything said aloud.

"Mr. Lumpkin, if you've got an illegal coming in here working for you, I don't want to jam her up, but I do need to talk to her. She could have seen the vehicle in question."

Or a relative of hers could have come back to the neighborhood after taking an unhealthy interest in Maddy.

Ignoring Wallace, Lumpkin started inspecting one of the many liver spots on his arm.

Wallace figured the man's hesitancy to talk might be due to his apprehension about having to find a replacement housekeeper who'd work as cheap—he doubted it had anything to do with caring about the woman's livelihood. "Mr. Lumpkin?"

George looked up and glared at him. "Juanita. Juanita Alvarez. She brings me groceries and cleans my house twice a week."

PART 2
TUESDAY, SEPTEMBER 22

(9)
MADDY EASTIN

"I'll be fine, Mom. Really."

Standing in the kitchen Tuesday morning, Maddy and her mom were engaging in a battle of wills.

Mom has that look . . .

Hands perched on her hips, head slightly cocked. Her eyes expressed skepticism—she was probably thinking Maddy was up to something.

"Are you sure?" Lily said. "Because I can stay home. After what happened yesterday, I don't want you here all by yourself."

"You need to go to work, Mom. You already missed yesterday. Mr. Fahey is a ball-breaker—"

Lily shot Maddy a new look, one that made her daughter think better of finishing her sentence.

"Your words, not mine," Maddy said. "He'll fire you if you miss too much work. Anyway, I already called Sabrina. She's on the mend, but her mom's making her stay home one more day just to make sure she's over her bug. Sabrina said she'd love it if I could come over and keep her company."

A bit of an overstatement, but her mom didn't need to know that.

Lily rubbed her temples. "That's all I need, you walking around this neighborhood by yourself."

"Sabrina only lives three houses down. I think I can make it without being kidnapped."

"Don't even joke." Practicality won out. Lily grabbed her purse and keys off the counter. When she leaned in to Maddy to give her a kiss good-bye, Maddy turned her face away.

Lily sighed and headed toward the door. "When you walk to Sabrina's, make sure you have your phone on and in your hand."

Yeah, great plan. If the bad guys show up, I'll call 911. And while I'm waiting for the cops, I'll throw the phone at them.

Maddy nodded. "Promise." After her mom left, Maddy locked the door behind her and then fell back against it with a loud exhale.

She was amazed at how smothering a parent could be—even when they were in another room. The night before, Maddy had awakened to sounds of crying coming from the living room. The pain filling her mom's cries ripped at Maddy until she finally couldn't take it anymore and she jammed earbuds in her ears. She would never understand adults. During the day, her mom acted all frosty, rarely showing any emotion. Then alone at night, the way she acted made it seem like she really was upset about the attack.

Why can't she just tell me she loves me?

Maddy putzed around the house for a few hours, not wanting to seem anxious by showing up at Sabrina's house too early. Her resolve finally broke down just before lunch and she headed out, her phone tucked into the back pocket of her jeans. She knew her mom would call to check up on her, and the last thing she wanted was for her to rush home if Maddy didn't answer right away.

Sometimes it's hard to breathe with all this hovering.

As Maddy walked down the sidewalk, warring emotions battled inside her. On one hand, she wanted her mom to grab her and wrap her in her arms so tightly that she couldn't break free. Yet when her mom did show tenderness, like this morning with the attempted kiss, Maddy felt so angry she wanted to turn away.

Why do I do that?

Maddy vaulted up Sabrina's porch steps and rang the doorbell. She tapped her foot, waiting for an answer.

Sabrina opened the door but leaned up against the frame, blocking the entrance. "Hey."

"Hey, Sabrina. You're looking better."

"Yeah, I could have gone back to school today, but I talked The Mom into one more day of rest." Sabrina let out a chest-racking cough but then smiled, letting Maddy in on the act she had played out that morning.

"I wanted to apologize—" Maddy stopped talking as a melodic beep came from the cell phone in Sabrina's hand.

Sabrina motioned for Maddy to follow her inside, all the while continuing to read the screen. She chuckled and replied to the sender at lightning speed.

Sabrina was everything Maddy wasn't but wanted to be. She had thick, raven-black hair that had a subtle wave to it, so her locks bounced when she moved. Even now, Sabrina looked like she'd stepped off the set of a shampoo commercial. No matter how much product Maddy used in her own hair, it always hung limp and lifeless. And she hated her color. There was just enough red in it to make it look like a muddied strawberry blonde.

Strolling into the kitchen, Sabrina paused long enough to gulp down some orange juice. She absently asked if Maddy wanted some, then kept texting. Maddy said no. Her nerves were already so frayed, she'd thought she'd probably drop the glass. The speech she'd practiced this morning seemed stuck in her throat. The last time the two of them had spent together hadn't gone too well.

Maddy stared at Sabrina's iPhone—the latest model in gold. Sabrina was the only one in the group who had it, causing quite the ripples of jealousy. Everything Sabrina owned was nicer than Maddy's. Her friend had explained once that even though they didn't live in the best neighborhood, her parents refused to move. They'd paid off the house, so staying allowed them the luxuries they wanted. This was clearly evident by the family's indulgences—new furniture, the latest electronics, even a swimming pool in the backyard.

Sabrina laid down her phone. "What were you saying?"

Maddy forced herself to stop biting her nails. "Nothing. Nothing important." They'd get to the uncomfortable topic soon enough. Maddy didn't see the need to speed it along. "So, you snowed your mom with that cough. Good thinking."

"It wasn't as easy as it sounds. The Mom almost didn't let me stay home after what happened around here yesterday. Did you see the paper this morning?"

"Why would I? Boring."

In truth, a newspaper subscription was an extravagance the Eastins couldn't afford.

"Yeah, I think so too, but The Mom wouldn't stop talking about it. So I had to read the story." Sabrina grabbed the newspaper off the kitchen table and tossed it over to Maddy. "I can't believe two sickos tried to nab a girl at *my* bus stop. It could have been me!"

"Right. Lucky break," Maddy mumbled.

She bent over to look at the headline: GIRL FIGHTS OFF ATTACKER AT BUS STOP.

Sabrina's eyes grew wide. She looked down at the paper, then back up at Maddy. "Wait a minute. This fifteen-year-old girl—are you the one they're talking about?"

"I don't want to talk about it."

"But you have to tell me." Sabrina walked around the table and grabbed Maddy's hand. "We're best friends, right? And best friends tell each other everything."

Maddy was surprised to hear the label. She wanted to ask Sabrina to say the words again.

Sabrina pulled Maddy in close and hugged her tightly. "I can't believe someone attacked you. Are you okay?"

Maddy felt blown away by the display of affection. The touch caused little shocks of electricity to course through her body. Her nerves were raw, and the attention Sabrina lathered on was like a salve, soothing them. Maddy leaned in to the hug and started sobbing.

After a few minutes, she finally forced herself to pull away, worried what Sabrina would think if she lingered too long. "I'm sorry. I don't mean to blubber. It's been a rough couple of days."

"I can only imagine. Come sit down."

Maddy took a chair next to Sabrina, and the girl pulled out two black cigarettes from the pack of Djarum Blacks sitting on the table. With a shaky hand, Maddy lit one, remembering the first time she'd tried them shortly after meeting Sabrina. Maddy had been surprised by the sweet smell of the smoke. The brand her grandfather smoked when she was a girl had smelled like old, musty socks. Sabrina said her dad had gotten hooked on kretek cigarettes while living in Indonesia, but that these Djarums were just knockoffs. They had flavor crystals inside the filter, not real cloves.

Maddy pulled the smoke deep into her lungs, then exhaled.

Sabrina looked at her with a mix of scientific interest and awe. "Better?"

"Yes. Thank you."

"If you don't want to talk about what happened, I totally understand. I just think it would be good for you to vent to someone. The whole situation must have been super scary. But I get it, if you don't feel comfortable confiding in me. It's not like we ended things on a good note last time we were together."

That's the understatement of the year.

When Maddy first moved into the neighborhood, everything had started off so well, but somewhere along the way it'd gone all wrong. She'd met Sabrina Marquez at the bus stop the first day of their sophomore year. She remembered walking to the corner and quietly standing behind Sabrina as she bounced to the loud music streaming from her phone. When Maddy became uncomfortable simply standing there, half-illuminated by the dim streetlight, she began shuffling her feet and accidentally stepped on a twig. Sabrina had jumped at the sound, and turned around with a hand to her throat. Her shocked expression quickly transformed into a bright smile, seemingly happy to have someone share her bus stop. Instantly, she bombarded Maddy with questions on where she'd moved from and what school she'd attended. Sabrina had been surprised that she'd never noticed Maddy in the halls at King High School even though they had both attended the year before. Their conversation continued on the bus, where Sabrina invited Maddy to sit with her group of friends.

They had all become tight for a while. The girls had accepted Maddy as one of their own. Then the wrong boy asked Maddy out, and a firestorm had erupted because he was the ex-boyfriend of one of the girls in Sabrina's gaggle. The spurned girl made it her mission to ruin Maddy's life and to poison Sabrina against her. She started rumors that Maddy slept around and had started talking about Sabrina behind her back.

"Well?" Sabrina's smile faltered. "Do you want to talk about it?"

Maddy coughed and set her cigarette in the ashtray. The smoke seemed stuck in her lungs.

When Maddy didn't immediately respond to Sabrina's impassioned olive branch, she scooted out her chair and stood. Maddy grabbed her hand, stopping Sabrina from walking away.

"Please don't go. We're best friends, right?" Maddy added a hesitant smile.

Sabrina flashed her own megawatt smile. "That's right, we are. And best friends tell each other everything."

"Will you promise not to tell anyone? I'd be absolutely mortified if the kids at school knew the story in the paper was about me."

"Not a soul. I promise."

(10)
DETECTIVE TERRANCE WALLACE

Detective Wallace knew a light hand would be needed when it came to dealing with Juanita Alvarez, George Lumpkin's housekeeper. If she were an illegal, talking to a cop would be the last thing she'd willingly do. He'd have to blindside her at Lumpkin's house.

Wallace knocked on the man's front door. A loud shout echoed from inside. A minute later, a woman opened the door. George must have been watching the Military History Channel again and couldn't be bothered to answer the door himself. No matter. Alavarez was the one he wanted.

"May I help you?" the woman asked.

"Are you Juanita Alvarez?"

"Yes. Let me get Señor—. Wait a minute. How you know my name?"

Wallace showed her his badge and introduced himself. Juanita's eyes began scanning the road behind him like she expected a line of cars from Homeland Security Investigation to show up and drag her away. He planned to play off that fear.

"Don't worry, Mrs. Alvarez, I'm not here to get you in any trouble. I just want to talk. May I come in?"

Juanita looked hesitant. She was probably deciding what would happen if she slammed the door in his face. She finally stepped aside, though she continued standing in the entryway, obviously not willing to let Wallace get too comfortable.

Juanita smoothed a few stray black hairs against her head. A tight bun kept most of them in place, but a few strands had escaped—her moist brow revealed that she had been engaged in obvious physical exertion.

"I finished my work here," Juanita said. "No time to talk. I go to my next house." She untied her apron and blotted her forehead with it. Then she nervously crossed her arms.

"I only need a minute, Mrs. Alvarez. I promise. Did you hear about the attempted kidnapping that took place right across the street from this house yesterday?"

"Yesterday? I no work here on Mondays." Juanita looked relieved, like she believed the conversation would end now that her potential witness status had been downgraded.

"I understand, but I'd like to know if you've ever seen an old white van parked at the corner outside or driving slowly around the neighborhood. Anything?"

"I see nothing."

"A young girl was nearly taken. She barely got away. It's important we try to find the bad man who did this."

From behind Wallace, a horn blasted in two long successions.

"This has nothing to do with me. I can't help you." Juanita pushed past him. "My brother is waiting for me. I have to go now." She hurried across the street toward the idling vehicle—a light-gray van.

Wallace stared at the man sitting behind the wheel. The driver's window was rolled down. The guy sat with his head back against the seat, taking a drag off a cigarette. As the beat-up van pulled away, the driver smiled at Wallace. The guy didn't match Maddy Eastin's description, but he was certainly in dire need of some serious dental work. Wallace noted the license plate—XHL279.

(11)
HANK FRY

"Thanks for catching a ride home this evening," Hank told his brother.

"No problemo." Daniel stood in the kitchen unpacking groceries at the counter—a package of Oreos, a two-liter bottle of Mountain Dew, a frozen pizza, and two bags of chips. "We needed some snackaroos for the big game tonight. Look at all this. Didn't I do good being all self-sufficy?"

"You mean self-sufficient. Yes. You did a good job, Small Fry." Hank didn't have the heart to scold Daniel for buying so much junk food. Once a week Daniel purchased groceries at the store where he worked as a bagger. It helped with his decision-making skills. Daniel usually worked from a shopping list, but with all the trouble yesterday, Hank had forgotten to make one.

"Your arm been bothering you today?" Daniel asked.

Hank stopped rubbing his left forearm and looked down at the scar stretching across it. He could still see faint markings from the twelve stitches he'd gotten when he was only fifteen. "Nah, it's just reminding me the weather's about to turn bad. My arm's more accurate than the five o'clock news."

Daniel gave Hank a knowing smile and shuffled over to give him a big hug. Hank patted Daniel on the back. He could still smell the boy's watermelon shampoo. While Daniel gathered up the plastic sacks off the counter, Hank studied the imperfection marring his arm.

He could still picture Daniel's face the day he'd rushed into their dad's bedroom to find the old man's prized guitar lying in pieces on the carpet. Daniel was on his hands and knees, cradling the wood and strings in his hands. The terror in his eyes had made Hank's legs weak.

Earl Fry must have heard the commotion from the living room. His heavy footfalls thudded on the stairs like a sledgehammer you hoped wouldn't pound you into the ground.

"What in the holy hell did you do, you little shit?" Earl had towered over Daniel, flexing his fists at his sides.

"It was an accident . . . wanted . . . to strum it . . . just once . . . but tripped."

Daniel could barely get the words out, panic had such a firm grip on his vocal cords. Both brothers knew what the guitar meant to Earl. How he'd saved up for over a year to buy it, then stood in line for three hours to have his idol—the same country and western singer he'd named Hank after—sign the instrument.

The boys weren't supposed to be in their parents' bedroom, and under no circumstance were they allowed to touch the guitar, but Hank knew no threat of violence could have been severe enough to keep Daniel away from it. The longing in his brother's eyes was too obvious as he watched Earl play each night. Like their dad, Daniel was drawn to music.

When Earl saw the guitar in pieces, he bent down and pulled Daniel up off the floor by his shirt collar. Hank had tried to push his dad away, but it would've been easier to shove a freight train down the tracks. Earl backhanded Hank across the room. Daniel's wiry body slipped out of his shirt. He lunged under the two meat hooks that grabbed at him, then scampered toward the door on his hands and knees. He almost made it to freedom. Then Earl caught him by the ankle.

Pain had shot through Hank's jaw as he tried to clear the stars from his eyes. He had propped himself up halfway against a chest of drawers and watched their dad pull Daniel back toward him—first by his ankles, then by his jeans. Hank leaped forward, grabbing at Earl's fists, trying to break his grip. Earl let go of one of Daniel's legs, but only to use his free hand to grab a piece of broken guitar and slash at Hank's arm. He had followed that up with an elbow to the ribs.

Hank writhed on the floor, crying out in pain. He remembered clutching his side with his bloody arm while holding his other hand over the bleeding wound. Through the haze of pain, Hank had watched as Earl picked Daniel up by the shoulders, like he weighed no more than a rag doll. A flash of yellow rushed by the open door—his mother's dress. She was taking cover. Hank would be the only one bearing witness that day—the day Earl Fry pounded his youngest son's head into the wall so many times it caused brain damage.

Hank shook his head, trying to clear his mind. The kitchen gradually came back into focus. Daniel was staring at him, an odd look on his face. Hank tried to divert his brother's attention, so he grabbed a beer from the fridge and asked, "Who'd you hitch a ride home with?"

Daniel blushed.

"Was it Natalie?"

"Yeah. Her car smells like oranges."

"Why didn't you ride home with George?"

"He's sick today. Anyway, Natalie's much prettier than George."

Hank choked out a laugh, barely able to keep down his swallow of beer. "I gotta give you that." When faced with the decision of accepting a ride with a twenty-year-old blonde or an overweight, middle-aged man, the choice seemed easy.

"Hank, what's fell . . . fellatio?"

"Where the hell did you hear that?"

"Natalie told me when a girl really liked a guy, she showed it by giving him fellatio. Is that some sort of gift? Like a hamster or something? Because I know Natalie likes me. Maybe she'll give me a fellatio tomorrow."

"Daniel—"

"If she does, can we keep it? Can we?"

"Listen a minute, would ya? Fellatio is not an animal, it's a blow job."

Daniel's eyes grew large.

Hank grew angry at the thought of the little tramp trying to embarrass his brother. He'd seen it before. A hypersexualized nymph getting a kick from priming "the retard" with sexual terms he wouldn't understand but that she knew he would be likely to repeat. Hank would have to keep an eye on Daniel's interest in this girl, make sure he didn't take it too far this time.

A goofy grin spread across Daniel's face. "That's even better than a hamster."

Hank clapped Daniel on the shoulder. "Come on. Let's put this pizza in the oven before the baseball game starts."

Sitting on the couch with their full plates, Hank found it difficult to keep his mind on the Rays game even though they were winning 4–3. His mind was stuck in a loop, thinking about that little grocery store blonde sucking him off. He thought maybe he should take a trip down to Nebraska Avenue, where the prostitutes hung out, and pick up a girl willing to help him out for twenty bucks.

At the moment, Hank was between girlfriends. Truth be told, he didn't have much interest in maintaining anything long term—he found women too demanding.

Always nagging about what they weren't getting, always expecting to be wooed before they'll spread their legs. Who has the time? Or the energy?

He found women his age to be master manipulators. They all seemed to either want his money or an engagement ring. And most of them weren't remotely interested in living in a house with two men. Dating Hank was a package deal. Kind of like a two-for-one, with Daniel as the bonus.

Hank had never dated much in high school either. While his buddies were out boozing it up with girls, he had stayed at home to keep one eye on Daniel and the other on his dad. Hank never resented Daniel for it—his brother had turned out to be the only person who'd ever loved him unconditionally. Hank knew he was a hero in Daniel's eyes. They shared a deep bond over their shared past. They knew each other's flaws and still loved each other anyway.

He stole a glance at his brother, who was staring at the shiny box. When the TV was turned on, nothing else could get Daniel's attention. Hank rubbed the dark hairs of his goatee, wondering again, for the thousandth time, whether he should find Daniel professional help. What Hank thought had been an innocent interest in girls seemed to have transformed over the past year.

Lord knows Daniel has lived through enough hell to need a therapist. We both have.

When they were kids, Hank tried to intercede between Daniel and their dad before the old man's temper erupted. He would watch Earl's face, could read it like it was a thermometer with a red line creeping up. The deep color would start at the base of his dad's neck, and Hank knew there'd be trouble if it reached his hairline. Even the tips of his ears seemed aflame when he was in a rage.

That was the thing about Daniel—he had never been able to read their dad's nonverbal cues. The boy would push and push until the old man exploded, turning his rage on whoever happened to be closest to him. Hank would step in the middle and force Earl's attention away. He could take the physical pain of a beating more than he could endure the emotional pain of watching his brother take any punches.

It had always surprised Hank that no one noticed the bruises on the Fry brothers. Then again, they never went to school after the worst of the beatings. The boys grew up on a farm in Plant City, about twenty miles east of Temple Terrace. It wasn't unusual for kids to miss class when parents needed help in the fields. The Frys grew fruits and vegetables that they'd sell at a large stand in the city. Of course, living in the strawberry capital of the world, their most profitable crop was their winter strawberries. Most of the other months were pretty lean.

So no one ever mentioned the black-and-blue marks on the boys' arms. Although twenty years earlier society had had more of a "don't ask, don't tell" policy when it came to parenting. Neighbors didn't stick their noses in one another's business like they do today. Back then, parents were allowed to raise their kids how they saw fit. Nowadays, Hank knew one little swat on the butt could land a parent in jail.

On one hand, Hank wanted to get his brother help. He thought if he could keep Daniel pure and innocent, something good could come out of such a bad upbringing. On the other hand, Daniel wasn't much for discretion. Hank couldn't afford for all the family skeletons to fall out of the closet. Anyway, those head doctors always wanted to bring the entire family into the sessions. Wanted to "heal the whole unit," or something like that, Hank had heard an afternoon TV shrink spouting off one day. No way in hell was Hank going to talk to some stranger about his childhood.

He could hear the snooty voice in his head saying, "Tell me about your mother."

Hank smiled, wondering if his words would shock the doctor: "She was a coward who was happy to watch her boys take a beating if it meant her husband would leave *her* alone. The woman was pathetic and weak, and chose the easy way out. I found her hanging from the ceiling fan when I was only sixteen."

(12)
LILY EASTIN

When Lily Eastin got home, she peeked in on her daughter and found her stretched out on her bed, listening to music. Maddy noticed her and, without a word, rolled over to face the wall. Lily backed away and closed the door. After such a long day at work, she almost welcomed Maddy's cold shoulder. She couldn't have handled another heated confrontation, or playing another round of "Who's the Worst Mother in the World." It had been all she could do to make it through the day's grind at the craft store.

Lily stretched her back, rubbing the sore muscles near her spine. The large garden bathtub in her old house would have been nice to slip into right about now. She nearly moaned at the thought of sinking into a steaming hot pool of water, her favorite bath beads filling the room with the scent of lavender. Their new house only had a tiny box of a shower to spray off in—not conducive to enjoying a long, leisurely soak. She'd have to settle for her footbath tonight.

It had been an anniversary present from Tom. A portable water basin with two open slots for her feet and a built-in massager. When Lily had opened the present, she'd feigned delight and gone on about how thoughtful it was, all the while silently wondering what had possessed him to buy such a ridiculous gift. It seemed indulgent, something she would never use. It had sat unopened until she came across it packed away in one of her moving boxes. Now she knew what kind of woman needed a footbath—one stuck working on her feet all day. One who lived in a house with no bathtub.

Lily decided to skip dinner. Her low-level nausea had turned into stomach cramps, and the thought of food made her belly seize. From the mess in the kitchen, Lily could tell Maddy had already heated up a Hot Pocket for herself. Not the most nutritious of dinners, but Lily could tell from the apple peel sitting beside the empty plastic wrapper that her daughter had at least had a piece of fruit. That would have to be good enough.

Standing at the kitchen sink, Lily waited for the footbath to fill up. Her thoughts drifted to Tom and the mess he'd left her with. The same thoughts that had plagued her all day. For some reason, she couldn't get her mind off the merry-go-round of negativity.

I'm tired of taking care of everyone else's needs. What about me?

Lily had no one she could turn to. She had ended up pushing all of her friends away. Instead of turning to them for support when she and Tom were having difficulties, she'd put up a wall so she wouldn't have to admit to them that she had a less-than-perfect life. An only child, she had no siblings to call, and talking to her mother was out of the question.

She yanked the footbath out from under the faucet, barely registering that she sloshed some water onto the linoleum. She walked over to the couch, set the machine on the floor, and plugged it in. It began to hum loudly.

I don't even have a proper bedroom to hide away in.

When Tom walked out, Lily and Maddy had stayed in the house until she realized the rent was too much for her meager earnings. All she could afford now was this place. Lily knew how hard the divorce had been on Maddy, so she gladly gave up the one bedroom. But Lily didn't know how much more of the lumpy couch she could take. She hadn't gotten a good night's sleep since they'd moved in. Soon even a palate of blankets on the floor would look like five-star accommodations to her.

Not for the first time, Lily wondered what the course of her life would've been if she'd turned down Tom's proposal of marriage. He'd surprised her when he bent down on one knee, asking for her hand less than a week after she'd told him about the pregnancy. Lily thought Tom truly loved her, that she'd finally found someone who would be by her side forever. But Tom had proposed out of a sense of duty. Tom's father hadn't been there for him growing up, and he had said he couldn't stand the thought of his own child growing up fatherless—the irony was not lost on her now. Lily's best friend, Emma, had begged her to wait, to see how the relationship weathered the addition of a baby before deciding.

The couple had only dated for eight months before the pregnancy stick showed two blue lines. Lily, twenty-three at the time, worried about supporting a baby on her own. Tom was financially stable and had professed his love for their soon-to-be family, something he claimed to have also always longed for. But in the end, her best friend had been right. Love hadn't sustained the marriage. It hadn't been enough to hold the already-splintered relationship together.

When's the last time I spoke to Emma?

The two girls had grown up together. They were the kind of close that can only be achieved by sharing childhood experiences. Emma had always been Lily's partner in crime. The person Lily leaned on when life got hard. They had only lived a couple of houses apart from each other, in Brandon, Florida. Just fifteen miles from where Lily now lived.

I really should let Emma know what's going on with Maddy. After all, she is her godmother.

Lily missed her friend and thought talking to her about Maddy might be the something good that could come out of this whole situation. Maybe it could be the way back into Emma's life. Lily strained to keep her feet soaking in the water while reaching for her purse on the floor. She hooked the strap with her finger and pulled the large bag up onto her lap. Her hands pushed aside wadded-up tissues and a near-empty prescription bottle and dug until they found her cell phone. Before she changed her mind, Lily dialed Emma's number from memory.

"Hello?" asked a confident but quizzical voice.

"Emma . . . Emma, this is Lily Eastin."

Silence.

"Emma, are you there?"

"I'm here."

"I know I'm probably the last person you want to talk to, but Maddy needs you."

"What's wrong?" Immediate concern broke through the coldness in Emma's voice.

"Some guys . . . they tried to kidnap her." Lily broke down crying, finally relieved to someone to open up to. She was no longer worried about appearances, or that she was gushing to a woman she hadn't spoken to in over four years. Lily let it all out in a rush.

Emma's voice broke through. "Lily. Lily. Back up. Tell me what happened."

Through long pauses and more tears, Lily managed to get the story out.

"I'm so sorry, Lily. No one told me. How is Maddy holding up?"

"She's putting on a brave face, but it's anger that's really fueling her, probably the only thing keeping her from falling apart. Most of the anger's directed toward me. She's furious because Tom walked out, and she blames me."

"Yes, I heard about the split."

"How?" Lily asked.

"Maddy's good about keeping in touch. She usually calls every couple of weeks."

"Oh yeah, right." Lily knew her daughter still kept in contact with Emma, but Maddy never talked about it.

"I haven't heard from Maddy in a month, though," Emma said. "I figured she was busy with the new school year starting. I've been meaning to call her, but work's been crazy."

"I know how that is." Lily let out a forced laugh. "We may not be close anymore, Emma, but I'd appreciate it if you could come over to see Maddy. She might open up to you. She needs someone she can confide in. I'm worried about her. Tom won't return her calls, and she won't talk to me. I'm public enemy number one."

In the silence that followed, Lily thought about all the things she wanted to say to Emma but couldn't find the courage to speak out loud. How when she was really down, memories of their friendship had helped get her through. Lily thought about all the times she would run over to her friend's house and hide out on Emma's lanai building forts, and how an afternoon together would often stretch into a weekend-long sleepover. Those nights were always such a welcome adventure for her. Lily and Emma would paint each other's nails and take turns trying out new makeup styles into the wee hours of the night. When the giggling got too loud, Emma's dad would enforce a strict lights-out policy, but even in the dark, they'd stay up braiding each other's hair.

Lily also wanted to apologize to Emma about the angry words they'd exchanged the last time they spoke. She'd accused Emma of trying to sabotage her marriage, had said Emma was jealous because she couldn't find a man of her own—at least not one who would stick around longer than a few months. Lily hadn't actually meant those venomous words. She'd only been striking out, hoping to deflect some of her own pain.

Before Lily could find the courage to verbalize her thoughts, though, Emma said, "I have somewhere to be right now, but tell Maddy I'll call her tomorrow evening."

"Thanks—" Lily didn't finish her sentence.

There was no need. Emma had already hung up.

(13)
EMMA PARKER

Emma Parker stared at her cell phone, trying to make sense of the conversation she'd just had. More than four years had passed since she'd spoken to Lily Eastin or, rather, shouted at her. The heated words, the wounded pride—neither would budge when it came to backing down. The silence between them had stretched on for so long that it was easier for Emma to continue the course rather than to attempt to bridge the distance.

She'd enjoyed keeping in contact with her goddaughter, though, by talking on the phone and occasionally meeting for lunch. They always met on neutral ground, and it was understood the sensitive subject of Lily would only be broached by Maddy. The girl vented about her mother, and Emma listened but never asked how her old friend was doing. She didn't want Maddy to feel stuck in the middle.

Emma wondered what it would take to bury all of those hurt feelings, to suck up her pride, and to go over to Lily's house. It sounded like her goddaughter could use a shoulder. It sounded like they both could.

No. Stop thinking like that. I can't let myself be pulled into Lily's drama. Not again.

Emma had begged Lily not to marry Tom. She'd told her it would end badly. Individually, Lily and Tom were complete messes. Their relationship was like a volcano always on the brink of a big eruption.

Emma remembered the first time Lily introduced her to Tom, during their last semester in college at the University of South Florida. He was all smiles, with a salesman's charm that would serve him well in his later profession. But Emma had a knack for reading people—hearing their unspoken words rather than the ones actually said. Tom's smile never extended to his eyes. They were cold, and gave away more than he realized. Emma knew the face he showed the world didn't reflect his true self.

Within a month, Lily had moved in with Tom. That's when his mask started to slide. An anger simmered just underneath his surface, like steam rising from the skin on a cold January day. Once, when Emma was visiting, she walked in on them fighting in the kitchen. She stopped dead in her tracks when she heard the stinging words Tom hurled at Lily over the simple mistake of buying the wrong toothpaste. He didn't yell. Instead, he got in her face, standing nose-to-nose with her. With a clenched jaw and as much venom as he could muster, he said, "It must suck to be you. It must suck to wake up in the morning, to look in the mirror, and know that you're you."

Those kinds of insults were launched at Lily for the tiniest of infractions—lighting the wrong scented candle in a room, adding onions to a dinner casserole, not having extra batteries when they ran out. The constant criticism got so bad Lily tried to morph into some kind of Superwoman. It seemed like she thought if she could only look pretty enough, act smarter, dress better, then she might avoid the verbal attacks.

Emma could tell the anger Tom displayed was a front for self-loathing. The hate he felt must have been immense for him to want to constantly strike out at the one person he professed to love most in the world. After the two married, the verbal abuse didn't stop. It simply went underground as Maddy grew older.

Lily made excuses for Tom, constantly extolled his virtues as a parent. As if being Father of the Year gave him a pass for being a bastard of a husband. Emma had tried to hang on to her friendship with Lily, out of a sense of loyalty, but eventually she started making excuses to avoid spending time with Lily when Tom would be home. After a while, it became difficult to even be around her.

It was as if Lily was a drowning woman desperately trying to grab on to anything around her to keep afloat. Ultimately, it was too hard for Emma to keep pulling her up. Lily wouldn't take advice, refused to fix her situation. Her problems always came first, and eventually Emma couldn't rely on her anymore. Emma had to break away from the sinking relationship before Lily ultimately dragged them both under.

How can I be there more for Maddy without letting myself get sucked into Lily's life again?

PART 3
WEDNESDAY, SEPTEMBER 23

(14)
HANK FRY

Hank grabbed a sheet of sandpaper off the workbench in his garage. He hoped the repetitive motion of manually smoothing wood might help to quiet his thoughts. He wanted to lose himself in the scratching noise as he ground down rough edges with the gritty paper.

Even though it was the middle of the week, Hank had the day off. He would work the next two nights—Thursday and Friday evenings. A day and a half of free time seemed like plenty to finish the armoire he'd been building for a local store that sold his pieces for a commission. He used to make good money selling his work, but it seemed to him these days people preferred cheap furniture they could slap together in under an hour. In today's disposable society, if something broke, no big deal, just buy another. Rarely did people search for that one-of-a-kind piece, a family heirloom to hand down to their kids.

Hank had gotten up early that morning, hoping to jump start before Daniel woke up. Quiet times like these, when the rest of the world was still sleeping, seemed to be the only time he felt at peace. When he could push ugly thoughts away and fully engage himself in a project.

He'd learned carpentry skills from his dad. The few times the old man wasn't being an asshole, he had managed to impart some useful information. Hank could hear him now: "Not every man has the patience to build something with his own two hands, son. It takes discipline and focus to take a hunk of wood and transform it into something else. Remember, you have to be meticulous in your planning or the project will come out all wrong. Ever seen a table that wasn't level?"

Hank knew not to answer. When his dad felt like sharing, it was best to simply listen.

"Once, I saw an orange roll right off a sloping table. Now tell me, son, how can a man be proud of something like that? Answer is, he can't."

Hank soon surpassed his dad's woodworking skills. When he was twelve, he made a birdhouse for his mom's birthday. He'd worked on the piece for weeks, thoughtfully overseeing every detail. It had been crafted out of oak, and he'd given it a honey-colored finish. He planned on setting it up outside the kitchen window so when his mom washed dishes, she'd always be able to see the gift.

When Hank eagerly showed off the birdhouse to his dad, he'd seen envy dance in the old man's eyes. His dad grabbed it out of Hank's hands, turned it over and over until he finally found the flaw he'd been searching for—a spot where the finish had slightly bubbled. His dad threw the birdhouse on the ground and stomped it to pieces. He could hear the old man now, the gruffness in his voice. He always sounded like he'd just woken up from a weekend bender with a dry mouth that made it hard to speak. "Inferior work won't cut it, son. You have to work harder and smarter than everyone else to get ahead. The last thing your mom deserves is a piece of shit on her birthday."

Even as a child, Hank recognized that it was simple jealousy that caused him to destroy the birdhouse. The point was hammered home when he watched his mom open his Dad's birthday gift—a mahogany chest for the foot of their bed.

Dear old Dad would never be one-upped by his son.

Discipline, focus, meticulous attention to detail—those skills had served Earl Fry well. Not only were they traits to describe a seasoned woodworker, but also a predator.

And oh, how he'd taught his sons well.

Hank threw down his sandpaper in disgust.

Dammit! Why can't I empty my mind this morning? Concentrate on the feel of the wood, the scent of the oak shavings littering the floor.

This was supposed to be his sanctuary, the one place he could escape the past.

Hank had the willpower to fight his urges, but what about Daniel, who had the mental capacity of a ten-year-old? Boys that age had no impulse control. Combine that with the body of an adult male and the consequences could be disastrous. Hank had to shield his brother, make sure their painful past didn't ruin Daniel's future. Daniel was the best part of Hank's life. He'd been protecting the boy his whole life. Hank couldn't drop the ball now.

The knowledge that he couldn't always keep an eye on Daniel ate away at Hank. When they were younger, the times Hank hadn't been around were the times Daniel had seemed to suffer the worst. Back in middle school, a teacher once kept Hank after class for beating up a kid. She didn't even care that he'd been making fun of Daniel. She just saw the boy's bloody nose and sent Hank to the principal's office. That meant extra time Daniel would be home alone with their dad. Mom would still be at the farmer's market. Not that it mattered if she was home or not. She'd never stopped her husband before. Hank had prayed his old man would stay busy in the fields that afternoon.

When the principal finally released Hank from detention, the buses had already left. Hank had run all the way home. By the time he reached the farm, he could barely stand from the stitch in his side. Then he heard Daniel cry out from inside the barn and the pain in Hank's side had shot to his heart. Another yelp from Daniel had jolted Hank out of his frozen state. He'd dashed to the barn door and yanked it open just in time to witness his dad standing face to face with Daniel.

Hank watched his dad raise an automatic nail gun. He remembered the "pop" sound it made—and Daniel's scream as the nail went through his palm. He stood pinned against the wall, arms raised like a burglar caught in the act. Dozens of nails stuck out of the wall, surrounding the outline of his body. Blood dripped from Daniel's right ear where a nail had nicked it. Another stuck through the material of his baggy hand-me-down jeans.

"Stop it, Dad. Stop it!" Hank had rushed to the outlet and jerked the nail gun's cord out of the wall.

With the fun over, his dad had merely shrugged and left.

Hank worked quickly to remove the nails holding Daniel in place. He'd never forgotten the wet, squishing sound when he eased the one out of Daniel's palm. A pile of nearby rags were pressed into service as field dressing, though it hadn't taken long before the material was soaked through.

Daniel's loud bawling turned into mournful whimpers as the two boys waited for their mom at the end of the drive. They knew dripping blood in the house might set the old man off again. When she finally pulled up, she didn't ask how Daniel was or even provide him any comfort. The first thing out of her mouth had been a sigh followed by, "What'd you do to make him mad this time?"

Hank didn't bother explaining. He just pushed his brother into the car and begged her to take Daniel to the hospital.

The beating Hank received the day the doctor's bill came in the mail was worse than any he could remember. Still, he refused his dad the satisfaction of even a single tear—no matter how many blows the old man landed.

(15)
MADDY EASTIN

Unable to talk her mom into letting her miss another day of school, Maddy kept her head down and shuffled through her morning classes until lunchtime—her most dreaded hour. The cafeteria was always a crapshoot between trying to find an open seat and looking for someone to sit by who wasn't too far down on the social ladder.

Before the whole ex-boyfriend fiasco started, Maddy used to sit with Sabrina and her friends. Today she didn't bother surveying the room for her best option. She wasn't in the mood to keep up fake chitchat anyway. She chose the closest empty seat and concentrated on trying to swallow the cardboard lunch. Even the pizza, her favorite item on the menu, tasted sour. She had to fight the bile rising in her throat.

"Lookie who we have here."

Just what I need.

Maddy looked up, expecting another insult to follow. Malik Jordan stood with his arm around Sabrina and a lunch tray in his hand. Their crew stood close behind.

"What do you want, Malik?"

"Why the long face, Eastin? You should be smiling ear to ear. Fought off a pervert, I heard. You got some real *cajones.*"

Maddy had to remind herself to close her mouth. Luckily, Sabrina chose that moment to sit down at the table. She began talking a mile a minute so Maddy didn't have to come up with a response. Malik shot the kid sitting nearby a look, and the boy quickly found another place to eat. The two others at the table followed suit when more kids from

Sabrina's group started piling around.

"That's right," Sabrina said. "My girl Maddy here beat the shit out of some meth head trying to snatch her right off the street. Ain't that right, Maddy?"

"Well—"

"Tell us what happened!" "Give us the details." "How'd you get away?" Questions were hurled at Maddy. She did her best to answer them all, forgetting about the pizza growing cold on her tray. She slowly parceled out the details, vaguely worried this all might be some kind of trick, but the more she talked, the more interested everyone became. Soon the story took on a life of its own.

Maddy couldn't help it. It was so nice to hear the concern she'd longed for spoken in words like, "How awful." "You could have been killed!" "You're so brave for fighting back." "We're glad you got away."

Maddy knew she should have been angry at Sabrina for breaking her confidence. The things she'd unloaded at Sabrina's house were personal, and she hadn't wanted them to get around. But the kids who rode Maddy's bus already knew she'd been part of something anyway. It wouldn't have taken them long to put two and two together. In the end, it seemed like things had worked out for the best. By the time the bell rang, Maddy had left her bad mood behind with the uneaten lunch.

"Some of the girls are heading over to University Mall after school," Sabrina said. "Wanna come?"

Maddy couldn't believe the fabricated story about the ex-boyfriend had been forgotten so easily. "Sure. Can I catch a ride with you?"

"No problem. Julianna's driving. Meet us in the back lot after the last bell."

All day, Maddy basked in the warmth of newfound attention. Girls stopped her at her locker to tell her how glad they were she broke free from the kidnappers. Boys offered high-fives and pats on the back. Maddy soaked it all in. The attention seeped down into the darkest recesses inside her until it finally reached the empty hole left by her dad walking out.

(16)
DETECTIVE TERRANCE WALLACE

Detective Wallace picked up the newspaper and reread the short, three-paragraph article about Maddy Eastin's attempted abduction.

"Have we gotten any leads from the public?" Corporal Rhodes asked as he leaned against Wallace's cubicle.

"Besides a couple of women turning in their no-good baby daddies? No. But there is one guy I want to look into more. Yesterday, I interviewed the Eastins' neighbor who lives across the street from the bus stop. He employs a housekeeper who gets a ride to work with her brother. Guess what he drives?"

"A shitty-ass van?"

"Yep. The brother, Franco Alvarez, doesn't resemble the eyewitness sketch much, but he does need some serious dental work."

"Guess you made the right choice not to include the picture in the paper."

Wallace hoped his streak of bad luck had finally ended. "I ran Alvarez through the system, found out he has a record. He did time for assault. A bar brawl that barely left a scratch on him but laid the other guy up in the hospital. The guy also has a sexual battery charge against him, though charges were dropped after his girlfriend refused to testify."

"Looks like Alvarez has a bit of a temper."

Wallace nodded. "But nothing in his file indicates he has a predilection for young girls."

"Could be he just hasn't been caught with his pants down. So what's your plan?"

"Alvarez is a mechanic. I'm going to show up at his work and rattle his cage. Find out if he has an alibi." He knew suspects hated cops hanging around their place of employment. It made them antsy, unprepared, and prone to saying stupid things.

"This guy must be a piss-poor mechanic if Maddy Eastin's account of his vehicle is correct." Rhodes moved his hand around to his lower back and began kneading the muscles on his right side. "Where does he work? I want to make sure I avoid the place."

"It's over on—"

Just then Wallace's phone speaker crackled to life and the receptionist's voice boomed, "Detective Wallace, you have a visitor."

Rhodes nodded toward his office. "Don't worry about it. We'll catch up later."

Wallace pushed the intercom button on his phone. "Betty, do you know what it's in regard to?"

"That attempted abduction case you're working."

"Thanks. I'll be right out."

Wallace groaned, wondering who it would be this time—the "concerned citizen" with her list of plate numbers of all the bad elements cruising around the neighborhood? Or maybe his favorite, the local psychic Madam Zora, who couldn't be any more of a cliché if she tried? Every few months the woman read an article in the newspaper and would stop by to "lend her assistance." Somehow every one of her visions involved water—not much of a stretch considering the Hillsborough River cut through the heart of Temple Terrace and Tampa Bay was only ten miles away.

Wallace opened the door to the lobby. A man paced near the elevator. He wore neatly pressed khakis and a short-sleeve polo shirt with a logo advertising a business Wallace didn't recognize. The man's graying hair was pulled back into a ponytail at the base of his neck. He had a plastic DVD case firmly gripped in his left hand.

"Hi, I'm Detective Terrance Wallace." He extended his hand and firmly pumped the man's in greeting. "I understand you have information on one of my cases."

"Yes." The man nodded, looking back over his shoulder at the empty waiting room.

"Well, Mr.—?"

"Gleason. Paul Gleason."

"Why don't you follow me, Mr. Gleason? We can sit and talk. Coffee?"

"No thanks. I've probably had enough today."

Wallace couldn't argue. The guy was a ball of nervous energy, constantly tapping the plastic case against his leg. A clinking noise sounded every time Gleason made contact with the pocket of his pants, most likely from hitting his keys.

Wallace scooted out one of the chairs surrounding a large oval table in the middle of the office. He motioned for Gleason to sit. It was loud in this open room, with detectives working in their cubicles around them, but Wallace thought Gleason might feel uncomfortable in an interrogation room. As skittish as the man was, he figured this would be the lesser of two evils.

"What can I help you with today?" Wallace plastered on his most inviting smile.

"I didn't stop the paper. So I thought what the hell, might as well read them and get caught up on what's been going on." Gleason spoke in a rush of words. "Read Sunday and Monday's paper on Tuesday, but didn't read Tuesday's paper until this morning."

"Wait a minute. Slow down. Why don't you start at the beginning, Mr. Gleason?"

"Right." The man took a deep breath. "On Sunday, I drove up to Tallahassee to celebrate my mom's eightieth birthday. I only planned on staying the day, but then I enjoyed the party a little too much and had to stay over. When I was in the shower Monday morning, mom fell. What a nightmare that was. Anyway, the doctor says she's fine. I eventually got home Tuesday afternoon. It was actually a fortunate series of events that led me to discovering it."

Trying to hide his exasperation, Wallace said, "Discovered *what*?"

"I normally stop the newspaper from being delivered to my house whenever I'm going to be out of town. Got robbed not too long ago, and don't want to make my place an easy target. Yet, when I got home from my mom's house, three newspapers were stacked in my driveway. Got lucky. No burglars this time. Anyway, I finally got to Tuesday's paper this morning and read about the attempted abduction right at my corner. I'm at 8004 Filbert Lane."

Wallace remembered knocking on the man's front door, hoping he'd witnessed the event. Neither Officer Santos nor Detective Wallace had been able to track him down for a statement. "But how can you help, Mr. Gleason? You weren't even home when it happened."

"*I* didn't see anything, but my camera did." Gleason's anxiety faded away, and he grinned like he was ready to be pinned with a hero's medal. He placed the plastic case on top of the table. Wallace could see a silver DVD inside.

"Told you I got robbed, man. Cops never found out who it was, so I installed a security system. Didn't want to be unprepared if they made a return visit. I can't afford to move, but I can surely scrape together enough cash to buy a little peace of mind."

"Can I have this?"

"Sure. It's a copy anyhow." Gleason fiddled with a tiny hoop hanging from his earlobe. He looked like an aged hippie with a white-collar job.

Wallace walked over to some video equipment set up in the corner of the room. He turned on the TV and inserted the DVD into the player. When he looked over his shoulder, he found Gleason standing right behind him.

"I appreciate you bringing this in, Mr. Gleason. Many folks in your situation would have kept quiet, not wanting to get involved."

"I didn't want an innocent man accused of a crime he didn't commit."

"What do you mean?"

"Just watch the footage, man."

Wallace hit the "Play" button on the remote control. His eyes grew large as he watched the scene unfold in front of him. All the while, Gleason babbled on about how he'd once been interrogated in connection with a convenience store robbery. The cops had wanted to pin the crime on him. They'd sweated him out for six hours. As Wallace watched Maddy Eastin frantically try to flag down the bus driver, he thought about how glad he was that he hadn't interviewed Gleason in the interrogation room after all. The guy probably would have stroked out. Then Wallace might have missed out on this lead. Wallace smiled as he heard the tap of the dominos as they started to fall.

(17)
EMMA PARKER

Emma Parker opened the door to her downtown Tampa condo. The smell of tomatoes simmering on the stove wafted out to greet her. She could set her watch by her boyfriend's schedule. At 6:05 p.m., the pasta water would be bubbling. Beef tips on Mondays. Chicken cacciatore on Wednesdays. All the other evenings belonged to Emma. Not because she enjoyed cooking, but because Ben Jacobs only knew how to prepare two meals. If Emma had to guess, she would say she'd eaten the same chicken dish thirty-two times over the last eight months since they'd been living together.

Subtle hints of recipe magazines left lying on the couch hadn't been enough to entice him to expand his culinary horizons. Eventually, she knew she'd have to tell him the hard truth. Either that or suffer the same two meals each week for the next twenty years.

"You're home early." Ben stopped chopping onions and stretched out a cheek so Emma could kiss it.

She planted an exaggerated smooch on him and then moved over to the sink to turn on the faucet. "Why are you so stubborn? You'd rather cry than admit you need running water?"

"Just showing you my sensitive side, babe." Ben looked at her, batting his eyes demurely. He looked goofy with mock tears running down his face. She couldn't help but chuckle. That was the thing she found most attractive about Ben—his sense of humor. No matter what the situation, she could always count on him for a laugh. Emma snagged a slice of red pepper that had yet to be added to the big pot. Her hand barely missed a swat.

Ben nodded his head toward the table. "I've got wine."

"There is a God."

"Rough day at work?"

Emma poured the deep red liquid into two glasses, filling hers three-quarters full. She walked back to the counter and set Ben's beside him. "Not so much work; I'm wrestling with a another kind of problem."

"Tell me."

"I got a call from Lily Eastin, Maddy's mother."

"You mean the woe-is-me whine bag? What's it been, three years?"

"Four." Emma and Ben had started dating after the best friend explosion, so he'd never met Lily but he knew the stories, both good and bad. A couple of times he'd asked to come along to lunch with Maddy, but Emma always made up one excuse after another until Ben finally got the hint. She felt guilty for not including him in that part of her life, but for some reason she was uncomfortable with the thought that Maddy might talk to Lily about Ben.

"Maddy was almost abducted on her way to school Monday morning."

"You're kidding me." Ben put his spoon down and wiped his hands on the towel resting over his shoulder. "Is she okay?"

Emma nodded. "Lily called me and completely broke down. She told me Maddy got away, but the Temple Terrace police haven't found the guy yet." She gave Ben the rest of the details, what few she knew, and added, "Lily said the girl's a complete mess. Understandable, but it's not helping that Maddy won't talk. Lily thought I might have a better chance at getting her to open up." She sighed. "You know I love Maddy and I want to be there for her, but it's . . . complicated."

"I know it is, babe, but think about it. Things must be pretty bad for Maddy if Lily swallowed her pride and called after so many years."

Emma took a sip of the wine she'd been swishing around in her glass and watched him turn back toward the stove to test the doneness of a hot spaghetti noodle. His gray army shirt was stretched across his broad chest. Muscular arms peeked out from beneath the sleeves. Even without a shirt announcing his profession, his haircut screamed "military." The high-and-tight was also cut shorter than usual these days—the thinning brown hair on top of his head looked better when it was kept trimmed.

Ben shrugged his shoulders. "But what do I know? If this is causing you so much heartache, maybe you should cut them both out of your life." He stopped stirring the sauce and looked at Emma. "Or you could send Lily a text. Something like, 'Roses are red, violets are blue, you're a whiny bitch, don't you get it, we're through'?"

Emma looked up at Ben, her mouth open. She was surprised by his callousness. Then she saw the grin spreading across his face.

"Oh, you!" Emma put down her wine glass and lunged at him, tickling him in the ribs. With a dripping spoon in one hand and a spatula in the other, he was defenseless against her attack. Ben finally called uncle and Emma sprinted toward the bedroom before he could retaliate.

She stood in front of her dresser, absently picking out a pair of pajamas and wondering if she could completely shut Maddy out of her life. Her heart answered by flooding her brain with memories of when doctors had diagnosed Maddy with SVT (supraventricular tachycardia).

Every night for two weeks straight, Emma had visited them in the hospital after work only to find Lily an emotional wreck. Lily would forego showering and eating during the day, afraid if she left the room Maddy would cry and there'd be no one there to comfort her. The nurses were stretched too thin, and Lily had no family to help. Her dad had already passed, and she had no siblings. Her mother was holed up in bed with a slipped disc, giving Lily grief for not taking care of her like a good daughter should. Tom wasn't much help either since he kept traveling for work in an attempt to keep up with their already-mounting medical bills. Although Emma suspected staying busy was more of a coping mechanism for him so he could avoid dealing with the situation.

Several times, Emma found Lily hunched over the hospital bed, silently crying. She looked so bone tired it seemed too much effort to make noise while she wept. Lily said she couldn't sleep at night, what with nurses constantly checking Maddy's vital signs, the incessant beeping of the machines, and every peep the baby made sending her into full alert. Emma pitched in where she could, spending her early evenings at the hospital to give Lily a few hours to catch up on meals, bathing, or sleep, depending on what she needed most.

The moments when Emma was alone with Maddy, rocking the three-week old baby in her arms, she felt completely at peace. Emma would close her eyes so she wouldn't have to see all the tubes and patches attached to the infant, then simply sit back and soak up the closeness. She'd never spent much time around children, had focused more on their shortcomings than the happiness they could bring. She'd always told herself she'd didn't want to be a mom, that she didn't have what it took. So on those long nights, Emma convinced herself this just might be enough for her. That loving Maddy could fill the times when those uncontrollable yearnings for motherhood would threaten to overwhelm her.

After Lily stopped speaking to Emma, the relationship with Maddy became harder to manage, but Emma never let go of that long-ago memory of the baby in her arms. She vowed to always be there for Maddy, no matter what. So Emma knew she couldn't close the door on the Eastins even if it meant keeping her distance with Lily while she maintained her relationship with Maddy.

Emma finished changing and then crouched to the floor to grab the phone clipped to the work pants she'd just shed. She dialed Maddy's cell number.

A short voice mail message played: "This is me. So talk." A long beep followed.

Emma hadn't heard this new recording. She was surprised at the lifeless tone in Maddy's voice.

"Hi, Maddy." Emma kept her voice light in the message, hoping to draw the girl in. "I want to apologize for being the *worst* godmother in the world. It's totally my fault that we haven't talked in almost a month. Why don't we have a girl's day out? Just you and me. Pick the place—whatever you want. Your mom told me what happened on Monday. I wish you would've called me. It sounds like you could use someone to talk to. I can only imagine how scared you must have been. Call me back. I miss you and love you whole big bunches. Bye."

Emma knew work would be crazy for the next few days, but she made a mental note to call Maddy back if she didn't hear from the girl. If she had to, she'd even go over to their house and get her.

(18)
MADDY EASTIN

Maddy looked out the car window and watched the city rush by. She and her mom were headed to City Hall to meet with the detective working her case. She couldn't understand why all the hurry. She doubted he had solved the case already.

After school, Maddy had spent the rest of the afternoon hanging with Sabrina and her girls. It was like the good old days, moving from store to store a part of the pack. Maddy looked down at her new shirt, smiling. At the mall, she'd held it up to her image in the mirror and loved how the golden-yellow color made her eyes shimmer in the store lights.

Sabrina had walked up behind Maddy and put her arm around her. "That's the perfect color for you. Why don't you get it?"

"You think?" Maddy's smile faltered. She'd already looked at the price tag and knew she couldn't afford it. "I didn't bring any cash. Didn't think I'd be hitting the mall this afternoon."

Maddy had stalked off to return the shirt to the clothes rack. Sabrina followed her. Maddy replaced the hanger while Sabrina looked over her shoulder at the saleslady helping Julianna at the register. Sabrina grabbed the shirt off the hanger and stuffed it inside her backpack.

"Wait!" Maddy said. "You can't do that."

"Shush! Don't be such a nerd, Eastin."

"No, that's not what I meant. I just don't want you getting into trouble on my account."

"Don't be ridiculous. It's Julianna's turn."

"What are you talking about?" Maddy asked as she followed Sabrina toward the front of the store. As they left, Maddy cringed, waiting for alarm bells to go off. She ran different scenarios through her mind, deciding which excuse would best explain how the shirt ended up in Sabrina's backpack. When no alarms sounded, she let out a long breath and dropped down on a bench, next to Sabrina.

With a devious smirk, Sabrina said, "After we find a place with some hot clothes, each girl takes a turn buying an item. It's Julianna's turn this week. If all of us walk in and just look around, the saleslady hits us with her evil eye, but if one of us makes a purchase, it distracts her while the rest of us load up."

Through the store window, Maddy watched one of the girls stick her tongue out at them. Sabrina laughed and made a face back. The girl stuffed a pair of shorts into her bag. After everyone left, they all headed to the bathroom to change into their new clothes. Lily had texted while Maddy was in the stall, saying "Detective Idiot" needed to see them. Maddy thought it sucked that her fun had to end, but she refused to let anything ruin her good mood.

Lily let out a heavy sigh, which pulled Maddy back to the present. Although her mom's eyes were focused on the traffic, she appeared deep in thought. Maddy stared at her mom, really looking at her for the first time in months. The half of her face in view revealed dark circles under her eyes, emerging from underneath makeup that had rubbed off after a long day at work. Maddy wondered when she'd gotten so many wrinkles. There had always been worry lines etched into her forehead, most likely from the scrunched-up face she wore when lecturing Maddy, but now she noticed new lines at the corners of her eyes and mouth.

Her mom absently turned the radio on without taking her eyes off the road. Maddy noticed the shaking in her hands. She seemed extra jittery. A strum of guilt vibrated through Maddy as she thought about what her mom had been going through since her dad had left: a new full-time job, a crappy house that didn't even have enough bedrooms, and a self-absorbed teenager thrown in for good measure. Maybe her mom didn't show her love in the way Maddy wanted, but at least she was still there. Her dad had bailed, but her mom kept getting up and punching the time clock every day.

If Maddy couldn't find the emotional support she needed at home, she knew she'd just have to look elsewhere.

All my friends were amazing at school today. Maybe I should cut Mom some slack and lean on them more.

Maddy made herself a promise that, after the meeting with the cop, she would apologize to her mom for her behavior and see if they could make a fresh start.

Maddy looked out the car window. Large pine trees leaned in the wind. She'd always thought they looked so sad—they seemed to sag underneath the weight of the Spanish moss hanging from their limbs. Yet today, they looked different to her. Like the pine trees were survivors. The weight of the moss tried to hold the trees down, but they refused to let anything make them break. Instead they stood fierce, swaying back and forth to a windy song.

After parking the car in the back lot of City Hall, they both walked to the door in silence. Her mom pulled on the handle, but it wouldn't budge. Then she yanked a couple more times, but it just rattled in its frame.

"You've got to be kidding me," she grumbled.

"It's after five o'clock, Mom. We have to ring the buzzer." Maddy pointed to a nearby sign.

Lily sighed, impatience written all over her face.

They were finally admitted into the building, and then Maddy's phone rang just as they were getting on the elevator. She pulled it out of her back pocket right before it went silent.

"No signal," Lily said.

Maddy stared at her phone, waiting for the elevator doors to open on the third floor. She hurried out and saw a message notification. She thought maybe one of her friends had called.

While her mom rang a bell at the deserted receptionist area, Maddy pushed her phone's touch screen and saw Aunt Emma had left a message. Maddy smiled, excited to tell her all about her day. Then Maddy realized she hadn't even told Aunt Emma about the attempted abduction. She started dialing back when her mom smacked her hands.

"Hey!"

"Put that away." Lily practically hissed the words. "This isn't the time or place."

"It's only—"

A door opened. "Ladies, thanks for coming in," said Detective Wallace as he held the door open and waved them inside.

"Detective Wallace," Lily said, a false brightness to her voice, "You have news on Maddy's case?"

"Yes, in fact. What I'd call a major break." He led them to a conference table. Next to it sat a television set and a DVD player on a media cart, like the ones they had at Maddy's school.

"Did you catch the guys?" Lily asked once they were all seated.

"No, but we got some good evidence. A neighbor caught the entire event on video."

Maddy felt the muscles in her face freeze.

"You're right, that's quite a break." Lily said. "Were you able to see who they were? Get a description of their van?"

Detective Wallace ignored Lily's questions, but turned his full attention to Maddy. "You described your would-be abductor as having a scraggly beard and bad teeth. Is there anything else you want to tell me before we watch the tape?"

Maddy couldn't find her voice. Although she didn't know what she'd say even if she could speak. She shook her head and closed her eyes, hoping for a miracle along the lines of the TV breaking or a scratched

DVD.

Lily grabbed Maddy's hand, startling her. Maddy opened her eyes, unable to look away from Detective Wallace as he pushed the remote's "Play" button.

"Won't it be too dark to see anything?" Lily asked. "The sun wasn't even up."

"Lucky for us, your neighbor invested in a high-quality night vision camera that records even in pitch blackness. That's why the picture has this green tint."

On the television screen, a picture of a front yard showed up in various shades of green. Maddy recognized the sagging chain-linked fence as belonging to the house at her corner bus stop. The camera footage captured a wide shot of a yard, the sidewalk, and part of her street. A date stamp partially obscured the picture. The time counter recorded the approach of every new second. It felt like a countdown to an explosion that would blow up Maddy's life. She'd already lived out this scene once, but now it was like she was watching an actor play her part in a horror movie.

At precisely 6:32:05, the girl enters the frame. She moves her backpack around, wrestling with the books jabbing her in the ribs. At 6:32:36, the girl kneels on the ground to rearrange the heavy load. At 6:33:14, cue the garage door down the street. The girl looks over her shoulder, then turns her concentration to her backpack once more. At 6:33:49, the girl stands up, then remains there, unmoving until 6:34:27, when she raises her hands to her face and her shoulders begin to shake violently.

Maddy's soul aches for the actress on the screen, watching her body racked with uncontrollable sobs. So much sadness, so much pain. Standing alone on the street corner, the girl could finally let it all out.

But the tears weren't enough. No, this was the morning she put her plan into action. The bus stop was empty, there were no witnesses. It was her chance.

At 6:36:09, the girl lifts her head away from her hands. Cue the bus turning into the neighborhood. At 6:37:21, the girl begins to wildly wave her hands back and forth. She runs into the street, continuing her manic arm gestures until she moves out of view of the camera.

"I don't understand." Lily blinked like she was waking from a dream. "Where is the man? The van? Why didn't the camera capture him in the shot?"

"Because, Mrs. Eastin, there was no man. No van. Your daughter lied about the attempted abduction."

Sitting there listening to the two of them, Maddy felt like she was in a bad Dr. Seuss nightmare. All these ridiculous rhyming words: "I do not see a man, I do not see a van. Where is the man in the van, Sam I am?"

A bubble of nervous laughter welled up inside Maddy. She clamped a free hand over her mouth before it could escape. Her mom and the cop wouldn't understand. They'd think she was making one big joke out of the situation.

It wasn't supposed to happen this way.

Maddy watched her mom look down at her empty hand lying in her lap, then at the hand still holding one of Maddy's. It seemed like the movements played out in slow motion. Finally Lily looked up at Maddy's face.

Maybe Mom's stuck in a nightmare she can't wake up from either.

"When the neighbor and I watched the recording," Detective Wallace told Lily, "he mentioned that a broken-down van had been sitting at the street corner for over a week before it was finally towed. A white clunker."

Wallace turned to Maddy. "Is that where you got the idea?"

When Maddy's mute spell continued, Lily yelled, "Answer him, young lady!" A hysterical tone had entered her mom's voice. She ripped her shaking hand away from Maddy's. Not seeming to know what to do with it, she stuffed both hands under her bouncing legs.

Detective Wallace sighed. "You know, Maddy, I could charge you with filing a false police report. Do you have any idea how many wasted man hours were spent on this case? And what would've happened if we'd brought in a suspect? Would you have sent an innocent man to prison just to keep up this charade?"

"I . . . I . . . " Maddy found her voice, but her vocal cords felt rusty, like they hadn't been used in years.

"Maybe you *should* arrest her, detective," Lily said.

"What?" Maddy and Wallace choked out the word at the same time.

Lily nodded her head. "Maybe if she learned that actions have consequences, she'd finally understand lying only ends in trouble. Lord knows I've tried to protect her, but maybe that's the problem. I've insulated her to the point that she thinks she's untouchable."

"You're correct in saying actions have their consequences, Mrs. Eastin, but we'll have to wait and see if the department pursues charges. For now, I think it's best to arrange some professional help for Maddy."

The two adults continued to talk about Maddy as if she weren't even there.

What does it matter anyway? There's nothing I could add to the conversation that would be of any value. I might as well have disappeared. Invisible. That's how I feel. Dad shut me out of his life, and Mom is always gone, if not physically at least emotionally. Even Aunt Emma has been absent when I needed her most.

Maddy remembered Emma's voice mail. She vowed to delete it the first chance she got. She couldn't face admitting the truth to her and hearing disappointment in the voice of one more person she loved.

PART 4
THURSDAY, SEPTEMBER 24

(19)
HANK FRY

Hank Fry woke with a start. He gathered the sheet around him and used it to wipe away the sheen of sweat covering his face. Metallica was singing an old nineties tune on his radio alarm clock. He realized the music had been playing for eight minutes while he slept through it. He found the radio a more preferable way to wake up than the sound of some obnoxious foghorn. Usually, the station's signal came in strong, but Hank figured this morning the bad weather must be keeping it from coming in full strength.

He turned over onto his back, listening in the dark to the noise of the angry rain hitting his bedroom window. It'd also been pouring in his dream. He remembered the feel of the water hitting his skin. His insides had felt cold, but his skin must have been fever warm because a mist had risen from it once the water made contact.

In the dream, the same one he'd been having for over a week, Hank's sixteen-year-old self stood outside the barn, terrified. Yet he couldn't make himself turn around and go back in the house. He knew the barn was off-limits while his dad worked inside, but his mom had made Hank go out to tell him supper was on the table.

Normally, Hank would knock and then holler his message. His dad would yell back that he'd heard, and Hank would go wait for him back at the table, his stomach rumbling as he smelled the food and stared at his empty fork. In the dream, though, his dad's radio was turned up too loud for him to hear Hank. He hollered three times, but never got an acknowledgement that his dad heard any of the shouts.

"Enter Sandman," the same song Hank had woken up to just then, had been blaring out of his dad's radio in his dream too. Hank could always tell Earl Fry's mood by the type of music he listened to. An old country ballad if he was feeling sad, bluegrass with a heavy banjo when he was feeling upbeat, and heavy metal when his darker side took control.

In the dream, Hank heard the angry singer shouting lyrics over squealing guitars. With the barn door closed, he could barely make out a muffled noise, but once he opened them, even the music couldn't drown out the sound of screaming. Hank always jolted awake the moment he heard those blood-curdling shrieks. In the dream, Hank never stepped inside the barn, but he knew the source of the screams.

He never forgot what he'd seen the day he had actually crept inside the barn.

Hank had pulled open the barn door just enough to slide his body through. Then he got low and crawled behind bales of hay. The straw tickled his nose, and he had quickly pinched it to cover a sneeze.

Gathering his courage, Hank had peered over the hay. Forty feet into the barn, he saw his dad hunched over the worktable. A naked girl was strapped down to it with leather restraints. The music still blared, but the girl's screams had quieted. He watched as his dad smacked the girl's face. She must have passed out for a minute, but then she came to and once again started crying out. His dad held a hunting knife over the girl's face so she could see it. Her panic rose as he teased her by trailing its tip across her bare skin. Though Hank couldn't see it, he knew the exact moment his old man had drawn blood because another shriek soared high above the music.

A loud bang sounded behind Hank. He jumped at the noise and turned to see that the wind had caught the barn door he'd left ajar and blown it fully open. Suddenly another violent gust whipped up and slammed the door shut again, causing another bang. Hank looked back toward his dad. Their eyes met.

Hank mentally readied himself for the beating of his life. Instead, his father motioned with his head, indicating he should approach. With each measured step forward, a war raged inside Hank. He had a desire to help the girl, but also an overwhelming curiosity to see what his dad was planning to do next. He'd only ever seen naked females in magazines. The one strapped to the table was much younger than the ones striking dirty poses for the world to see though. This girl only looked a couple of years younger than Hank.

He couldn't help getting an erection as he neared the table. The thought that he could do anything to her without her fighting back aroused him. He had stopped directly across the table from his dad. The strawberry-blonde haired girl lay between them. A dozen or so bleeding, red tracks crisscrossed her pale breasts and belly. They weren't deep, but Hank couldn't take his eyes off the blood seeping from the wounds and dripping down her side.

The girl pleaded with Hank. He couldn't hear her words over the pounding music, but he could read her lips.

Help me. Please.

Hank had licked his lips. His tongue felt as dry and rough as sandpaper.

"You're getting older now," his dad told Hank in a loud voice. "It's time I teach you what that means. You see, females need to be molded, shaped into the pliant creatures God meant for them to be. But they can't do it on their own. They need training, instruction in the art of pleasing a man. I've had this one here for three days, and she's still willful. She has to learn the lesson: defiance will not be accepted. Lucky for her I'm a patient teacher, willing to repeat the lesson as many times as needed."

His dad had nodded toward the tools lying near the girl's feet. "Pick one, son."

Hank remembered shuffling his weight from one foot to the other, fidgeting with the front pocket of his jeans. He knew what would happen if he refused. It would be seen as the ultimate cowardly gesture. With a shaky hand, Hank had picked up a long-barreled lighter, the one he always used to light logs in the fire pit behind the house. He handed it to his dad and listened to the click of its ignition button and the *whoosh* of the flame. His dad placed the lighter against the screaming girl's flesh. A nauseatingly sweet smell wafted up from the burned patches of skin. A smell so strong Hank could almost taste it.

Over the years, his dad had taught him many lessons in that barn. How to choose the right piece of wood for a building project, how to strip paint from a piece of furniture, and ultimately, how to inflict the maximum amount of pain a person could tolerate without dying. Hank was an excellent student.

(20)
LILY EASTIN

Lily unlocked the craft store's two front doors, then stood aside to allow a couple of impatient women to enter.

Gotta get your early morning scrapbooking fix, don't you, ladies?

She forced the biting retort to stay firmly in her mind. Outwardly, she smiled, greeting the women, who were already racing down the center aisle.

When did I become so bitter?

Lily had always thought of herself as a pleasant person, the type to consider another person's feelings over her own. She believed she was the sort of friend others wanted in their corner. One who would roll up her sleeves and jump in during the tough times. So how was it that she could deal with other people's problems so well, yet completely fall apart during the rough patches in her own life?

It seemed to her that having single-mom status thrust upon her had been the tipping point. She didn't know how other women did it. There was no time to grieve over a spouse walking out when every waking moment was either spent trying to earn enough income to keep their whole house of cards from crashing down or being an emotional cheerleader for Maddy in order to get her through.

When Tom had still been part of the family, at least there had been someone else to pass the baton to once in a while. He may have travelled a lot with his job, but whenever he was home, he and Maddy were always together. Those were the times Lily could take a break. Take time for herself, to recharge and in turn have something to offer back to her family. Lily had been running on empty for so long now, she had nothing left to give.

At least I don't have to listen to someone constantly belittle me anymore.

She was glad for that, but still felt sad when she thought about no longer having a man in her life who loved her. She didn't know which was worse—Tom's stinging verbal attacks or being alone.

What would happen if I just sat in the middle of this store and refused to move?

Lily cracked a smile as she pictured herself plopping down on the floor in full tantrum mode.

Maddy got to do it, why can't I?

"What's so funny?" Holly, one of her employees, asked. She'd walked up beside Lily, probably wondering why her crazy boss was still standing at the front door.

"Oh, just daydreaming. Can you take the counter this morning?"

"Sure, boss. Do you—"

Lily suddenly felt a wave of dizziness wash over her. She put a hand on a stack of baskets near the door to steady herself.

"You okay, boss?"

"Yeah." Lily took a couple of deep breaths. "I guess skipping breakfast wasn't such a good idea."

Just then, Lily's phone vibrated in her back pocket.

A skeptical look flitted across Holly's face as she turned and walked toward the register. Lily ignored it and pulled out her phone. It was Maddy's school calling.

Now what?

Lily listened to a recorded message that announced her daughter's absence. Maddy had left the house with her backpack early that morning.

If she didn't go to school, where is she?

Lily disconnected the call and dialed Maddy's cell phone. No response. After the beep, Lily said in a low, angry voice, "I got a call from the school's absentee line this morning. What do you think you're doing, young lady? Did nothing about last night's conversation sink in? You promised you'd get your shit together. Were those words just something you said to shut me up? Call me back as soon as you get this."

Lily regretted leaving such a harsh message as soon as she hung up. The logical mom in her knew the angry words would only have the opposite effect from what she was trying to achieve, but as she thought back to the heated battle that had taken place in her living room the previous night, Lily told that know-it-all bitch yakking in her head to mind her own business.

The entire car ride home from City Hall had passed in silence. Lily had been lost in her thoughts, trying to figure out the best course of action for dealing with her daughter's deception with the police. Maddy had stared out the window sullenly. But once the front door to the house closed, the dam of silence broke. Both were armed with mental battle plans by then, and neither wanted to listen to what the other had to say. They lobbed insults back and forth like cannon fire until Maddy finally surrendered and stormed off to her bedroom.

After a long cooling-off period, Lily had gone to her daughter's room and sat beside her on the bed. She wanted to reach out and stroke Maddy's hair like she used to when she was little. Instead, she spoke to Maddy's back. Lily talked about how she was trying her best where Maddy was concerned, how she approached their conversations with the best of intentions. Lily didn't understand why she always let her anger get the best of her. She told Maddy how it seemed like her pot of emotions was always set on a low simmer and any problem made her boil over.

It was easier to open up to Maddy when she didn't have to look her in the eyes. When she didn't have to see that accusatory glare. Lily knew she had let her daughter down, and the crushing guilt was more than she could bear. She talked about how her emotions were all out of whack and how no matter which path she started down, they all ended in anger. It was the one emotion that had become her constant companion over the past year. It was easier to feel outrage than the debilitating sadness that followed her like a shadow. Lily told Maddy she was afraid that once she gave in to tears, there'd be no stopping them.

She'd hoped opening up to Maddy would get her talking. She couldn't help her daughter if she didn't know the girl's struggles. In a robotic voice, Maddy had said she would stop causing trouble. She hadn't even rolled over to look at Lily when she said it. Thinking back now, Lily realized Maddy hadn't meant a word she'd said. She'd only spoken so Lily would leave the room.

"Bonnie! Bonnie!" A woman rushed down the aisle past Lily and soon ran back up again. "Bonnie!"

"Ma'am, can I help you?" Lily placed a gentle hand on the frantic woman's shoulder as the lady continued looking around the store.

"I can't find my daughter. She's four. She's in red dress. I only turned my back for a second, but then she was gone."

Lily hadn't even noticed them enter the store.

They must have walked in while I was having my mental pity party.

"I told my husband we should buy one of those harnesses. Bonnie's a runner. But *nooo*, he said only bad parents use them. He said we were raising a child, not a dog."

A giggle echoed across the large, open store. The patter of shoes sounded to their left.

"Bonnie!"

"Ssshh," Lily told the woman. "She'll keep running if you call her name. All this is a game to her. She wants mommy to find her."

Lily crept down the center aisle, checking each side aisle for the little girl. Four rows away, she saw her crouching down, peeking around a display. Her back was to them. Lily looked over her shoulder at the woman and pointed down the aisle, then put a finger to her lips.

The woman snuck up on her daughter and scooped her up. "Gotcha, you little munchkin."

The girl squealed in delight, happy her mother had won the game.

"You know you're not supposed to run off, little one."

Lily thought of her own daughter at that age. Of Maddy's strawberry-blonde hair up in pigtails, half her lunch smeared across her face. She could still hear Maddy's sing-song voice as clearly as if she'd been standing beside her. "Bet you can't find me, MomMom." A wave of sadness crashed over Lily as she remembered the name Maddy had always called her, a name that had only hung around until the middle of first grade.

I miss being MomMom.

Lily accepted the woman's thanks on her way toward the checkout line. Lily wished she could figure out a way to help her own daughter as easily.

Pulling the phone out of her pocket again, she dialed Maddy's number and left a different type of message. "Hi, Maddy. It's Mom. I can only imagine how rough last evening must have been for you. First at the police station, then at home. I'm sure you were emotionally spent and just needed time to recharge this morning. I'm not mad you skipped school. If anything, I'm envious. How about this weekend we splurge and have a mother-daughter day? We'll talk, really talk. In the meantime, though, will you please text me back? You know how I worry about your safety . . . I love you."

(21)
MADDY EASTIN

After suffering the humiliation at the police station the previous night and dealing with the subsequent blowup at home, Maddy knew there was no way her mom would let her bad behavior continue by letting her stay home from school. But she couldn't face her friends. Not yet. So she got ready like usual but instead of stopping at her bus stop, she kept walking.

Huddling underneath her umbrella, she didn't stop until she reached the golden arches of a McDonald's. She sat there for a couple of hours, but she couldn't handle the smell of frying foods any longer. She'd only had enough change on her for a small soda, which she kept refilling at the drink station. Her empty stomach gurgled in protest as she left and headed toward the library.

Once there, she shrugged off the questioning looks from moms with toddlers in tow. She figured their parent radar probably honed in on the fact that she'd skipped school. Maddy kept her head down until she reached her favorite table—the one in the back near the adult reference section. She dropped off her stuff to save the spot and headed for the shelves of fiction novels.

She'd always enjoyed books, but had become a hard-core reader over the last year. It was a way to escape the confines of her bedroom, to transport herself to another time. A chance to become someone else. Her favorite novels were dystopian fantasies with badass girls who saved the day. Whether it was Katniss, who fought through the games to become a victor, or Tris, who battled the Erudites to save her family, she liked smart, tough girls. None of them needed a guy to feel complete.

Maddy was sick to death of that message being crammed down her throat, the one where the princess needed to be saved by a handsome prince in order to live happily ever after. She couldn't understand all the hoopla surrounding boys. They were gross, always trying to play grab-ass in the hallways at school. Anyway, she had learned they couldn't be counted on to stick around.

When Maddy hung around Sabrina and her friends, boys were the usual topic of conversation. Who liked who, which were good kissers, who had big peckers. To go along with the group, Maddy had lied and told everyone she'd lost her virginity the previous year. Some of the girls didn't believe her, and she had been forced to describe her fictional encounters to save face. The only thing that had saved her was the fact she'd stumbled upon a website full of stories about sexual encounters when she had been researching a paper for school. Maddy usually stayed away from online porn sites. She found the pictures disgusting, and had quickly learned that once you saw a girl masturbating on a guitar, nothing could scrub that picture from your mind. But the site she had read only had stories about sex acts on it. Maddy's curiosity had gotten the better of her, and she'd read for hours. When the girls had pressed her for specifics, Maddy had seamlessly weaved in the details she'd read about, finally convincing them she'd had several lusty encounters.

Maddy continued strolling down the aisle between the stacks, running a finger over the book spines until she came to *H*. She selected a Margaret Haddix novel, the only one left on the shelf. It was a title she'd already read twice, but it was one of her favorites.

When her phone started vibrating in her back pocket, Maddy moved the book to the crook of her arm and pulled it out. She saw it was her mom and let the call go to voice mail.

A librarian came around the corner and glared at her when she saw that she was holding a phone. It was against the rules to use it inside the building. Maddy ducked around the back of a tall bookshelf and skulked back to her table. Once seated, she faced the wall and listened to the message.

Her mom had gotten a call from school tattling on Maddy's absence.

Uh-oh. Mom's throwing out "young lady" again.

Maddy hated being referred to that way. She tuned out the rest of her mom's rant. It was only a repeat performance of last night, so she deleted the message before it even finished playing.

A few minutes later, Maddy felt another vibration. She looked at the phone to see who it was, but ignored it when she saw that it was her mom again. She put her feet up on the chair across from her and sat back.

Time to immerse myself in the book, to step into Nina's life and take down the population police.

Maddy couldn't hold off her grumbling belly any longer. When she stood and gathered her things, she remembered the phone call she'd missed. She pulled out her cell and saw that time had flown and it was late afternoon.

***

Maddy played the second voice mail message. She couldn't stop the smile forcing its way to the surface as she listened to the rich warmth in her mom's words. She had to admit her mom was a pushover on everything except her safety.

That's one area she's an over-the-top, psycho mom.

She suddenly remembered the days when her mom would sit on the edge of her bed, trailing small circles across her back while telling her stories of exotic animals who would find themselves in the strangest situations. Her mom had finally figured out Maddy only needed some time away, some space to recharge. Missing a day of school wasn't a big deal. Nothing to throw a hissy fit about. Her mom had even suggested a girl's day out. Maddy wasn't sure about the whole talking part, but she could definitely go for a good foot massage.

The nail salon her mom used to take her to gave the best foot rubs. Mom always got the full treatment—fingers and toes painted. Maddy only got her toes done since her fingernails were habitually bitten down to the nub. Mom had promised Maddy she'd be able to get her fingernails done too if she could stop biting them. Somehow that incentive was never enough to cure the vice though.

Maddy headed toward the library's checkout counter. Even though she knew how the Haddix novel ended, she wouldn't dream of keeping Nina hanging. Maddy had to see the story through to the end so the characters could find a peace, however brief, before the next book in the series pitted them against each other once again.

She texted her mom a short message: BEEN AT LIBRARY. LEAVING NOW.

As she shuffled past the circulation desk, a folded-up copy of the *Tampa Tribune* on its corner caught her eye. A librarian stood behind the large piece of furniture, her head down, typing on a computer. A man leaned over, trying to read the screen. Maddy scootched up to the desk, then reached forward to grab a free bookmark declaring, "Reading is Remarkable." As she moved her hand away, she grabbed the newspaper and tucked it under her arm.

Maddy hurried out of the library and sat down on a bench right outside the double doors. She unfolded the paper, checking the date.

Good, it's today's copy.

The rain had stopped, but the wind had picked up and she fought it with every page turn until she found what she'd been looking for, on page five:

Attempted Abduction in Temple Terrace a Hoax

Temple Terrace police say the fifteen-year-old girl who reported an attempted abduction during the early morning hours of September 21 admitted she lied. The girl had initially reported that a man grabbed her and tried to throw her into a nearby van while she waited for her school bus. There were no eyewitnesses to the event, but a neighbor came forward with surveillance footage that proved the girl made the entire story up.

Temple Terrace resident Paul Gleason had this to say: "I'd been visiting my mother for her sixtieth birthday, so I had no idea all of this transpired right outside my front door. When I got back in town and saw the news reports, I checked my surveillance camera to find out if it had captured the guys on video. I wanted to help the poor girl out and get those savages off our streets. But the only thing I saw was the girl waving her hands back and forth to make the bus driver stop. I didn't see anyone grab her. She made the whole thing up. What kind of kid would do something like that?"

The State Attorney's office was contacted, asking if charges would be brought against the girl for filing a false police report. The SA would not comment, other than to say his office is taking the matter under consideration.

Tears welled up in Maddy's eyes as she stuffed the newspaper into the trash can. She readjusted her backpack before heading home, her hungry belly now the least of her concerns.

***

"Maddy? Maddy?"
When Maddy heard her mom's voice on the other side of her

bedroom door, she quickly pulled the covers up over her head. She burrowed deep beneath them even though the room felt like a sauna. Maddy could hear the concern in her mom's voice. Evening had arrived, and all the lights in the house were turned off. She'd probably thought the place was empty.

Maddy's door opened, and she heard a loud sigh. She waited for the explosion of rants that would almost certainly begin with "young lady." At the sound of silence, Maddy peeked out from underneath the cover. Her mom stood backlit against the open door. Her eyes were closed, and she was mouthing something to herself. Maddy had witnessed the habit numerous times and always thought it ridiculous. Counting to ten never worked—her mom's anger never went away.

"Tough day, huh?" Lily finally said. A tiredness marked each word.

"Tough year." Maddy rolled over to face the wall.

Lily grunted in agreement. She sat down on Maddy's bed and laid a hand on the blanket covering her daughter's shoulder.

Please tell me a story, MomMom. I can't handle another lecture. Let's rewind the clock, pretend Dad's away on one of his work trips, and that I can still do no wrong in your eyes.

"So you thought you'd skip school, huh?"

Maddy tensed up. Her mom dropped her hand away.

"I understand why you didn't go in," Lily said. "I don't condone the behavior, but I do understand it. Ever since your father left, we've both been spiraling out of control. Both grieving on our own instead of helping prop each other up. I'm sorry. I've been so absorbed in my own pain that I haven't been there for you. You must feel so alone, like everyone's abandoned you."

Maddy turned over and looked at her mom. Silent tears were rolling down Maddy's face.

Lily nodded. "Your father left and you were forced out of the only home you've ever known. I checked out emotionally. Even Aunt Emma has been MIA. It must feel like your entire world has flipped upside down."

"I don't know why I made up that story, Mom. I guess I felt invisible. Like if I disappeared, no one would even notice. I wanted to see if my absence would make a difference."

"It would. It so would. I'd die if anything happened to you, Maddy. I might not say it enough or show it in the way you'd prefer, but I love you dearly. You're my entire world."

"I'm sorry . . . for lying. For worrying you."

"How can we move past all this?"

Maddy shook her head.

Her mom looked equally perplexed as to how to put the pieces of their lives back together. After a few moments she said, "I think it starts with you getting back on task. That means back to school tomorrow, start—"

"I can't!" Maddy practically howled. She sat up, but kept the covers tightly bunched up underneath her armpits. "Have you seen today's paper?"

"No. What's in it?"

"There's an article saying I made the whole thing up."

"It doesn't use your name, does it?"

"No, but everyone at school knows it's me. Yesterday they were all congratulating me, giving me high-fives and pats on the back. Now they're going to know I lied. I can't face them."

"Maddy, it won't be that bad."

"Really, Mom? The whispers behind my back, the pointing and laughing? How can I ever show my face at school again?"

"You can't stop going to school. You're only fifteen." Lily sighed.

Maddy couldn't stand that noise. She flopped back on the bed and stared at the ceiling.

"Do you think I like going to work every day? Do you think I enjoy waiting on rich women who can't decide whether to pick striped or paisley scrapbook paper to use to show off their latest Caribbean vacation? No. But I still get up every morning and I do it. Just like you will get up tomorrow morning and go to school."

Maddy continued glaring at the cracked lines above her. She bit her lip, refusing to talk so she wouldn't say the thoughts really racing through her mind.

"You made up this fantastical lie, Maddy. What did you think would happen? There are consequences to our actions, young lady."

Maddy turned her head and glared at her mom. She'd had enough. "You're such a bitch sometimes. No wonder Dad left you."

Lily gasped. Her head snapped sideways, as if the words had been a physical slap.

Maddy couldn't stop herself. The anger boiled up from a pit deep inside her, and she spewed words out with the force of a volcanic eruption. "You're a frigid, cold-hearted woman. You never showed Dad any affection. No wonder he walked out. You didn't love him, so he went looking for it somewhere else. I'm telling you right now, I won't go back to that school! I'm going to go live with Dad."

In a measured voice, Lily said, "You will go back to school tomorrow, and the next day. Even the day after that. If you think you had a horrible life before, young lady, just you wait. Miss one more day of school and I'll take away the computer, your phone—anything that gives you even the smallest amount of pleasure."

"That's bullshit! I'm calling Dad."

"Go right ahead." Lily got up and walked over to the door. She stood halfway out of the room with one hand gripping the doorknob. "He dumped you, just like he did me. Tell me, Maddy, how do you plan on convincing your father to come to the rescue when he won't even return your phone calls?"

Lily turned and quietly closed the door behind her.

(22)
EMMA PARKER

"Haven't you left yet?" Ben asked Emma over the phone.

"I'm walking out right now," Emma said.

"So you're telling me that you're *not* still sitting at the computer?" Ben knew her all too well. Emma stood up and grabbed her blazer off the back of her chair. She shuffled the phone from one ear to the other as she slid it on. "I'm waiting for the elevator." Emma bent over to shut her computer off and grabbed her half-empty can of Red Bull off the desk.

Ben sighed. "You've missed two dress fittings already. My sister has been extremely patient. Far more so than you deserve. Don't stand her up again."

"Please don't be a nagging wife, Ben. It's not like I ditched her on purpose. I had important cases. I couldn't leave in the middle of the day to go dress shopping." Emma pushed the down button once she reached the bank of elevators. "How in the world did you rope me into this thing anyway?"

"Come on now. Kathy's my only sister. She's excited about getting married in three weeks. Is it too much to ask for you to be a bridesmaid? Give her a break. She wants to spend more time with you, get to know you better."

Emma thought "excited" was definitely an understatement. When Kathy had asked Emma to be her bridesmaid, the woman was over the top talking about all the details of her upcoming nuptials. To Emma, it reeked of desperation.

How could all that enthusiasm be genuine?

"She'd better not put me in some pink frou-frou dress."

"Oh, stop it. Her colors are navy blue and silver, not pink. Anyway, think about how good you'll look walking down the aisle on my arm. Me in my penguin suit and you in your frou-frou *blue* dress."

Emma stepped into the elevator as the doors opened. "I can't see wasting good money on a dress I'll only wear once. It's ridiculous."

"Emma, try . . ."

What a shame, the line went dead.

***

"You made it!" Kathy clapped her hands in delight.

"I hope I didn't keep you too long," Emma said somewhat disingenuously.

Kathy waved her hand. "Don't worry about it. The clerk spent the extra time re-measuring me. I tell you, the seamstress says if I lose any more weight, I'm on my own. She refuses to make any more major alterations to my gown."

Emma had to admit Kathy looked good. She hadn't seen her in four months, but the woman had held true to her word that she'd lose weight before her wedding day. Her once-plump figure had transformed into a curvy hourglass shape.

"How much weight have you lost?"

"Sixty pounds. Can you believe it?"

"That's great."

"Look at you though. You've probably never had to worry about your weight."

Emma caught her reflection in the mirror. Though her black, pixie-styled hair was a mess, she knew she looked good for thirty-nine. Weight had never been an issue for her, and she'd always had a lean five-foot-six frame. She could eat whatever she wanted but rarely remembered to. Most days she lived off energy drinks.

"Let me show you the bridesmaid dress." Kathy took Emma's arm and led her back to the changing room. A navy dress hung on the door. "Go try it on." Kathy sat down on a couch situated near a bank of three angled, full-length mirrors. The space was large, clearly designed to cater to brides who wanted to show off their gowns to family members.

Emma grabbed the dress and stepped inside the changing room.

"So how's work going?" Kathy called out to Emma. They were the only two customers in the bridal shop.

"Busy, as always. Sorry I missed the other fittings. I wouldn't have left you hanging if I could have helped it."

"Don't worry about it. I know your job's important. Ben's always telling me how you're working late. How are things going between the two of you, anyway?"

Emma stopped unzipping the dress. "Great. Why? Has he said something to you?"

"Oh, no. Of course not. I guess it's just sisterly interest. You know, wondering how serious you guys are. All this matrimonial stuff makes me wonder when you two are going to tie the knot." Kathy laughed.

Emma thought her remark sounded forced, as if Kathy was intentionally trying to keep a lighthearted tone. The question of marriage had come up between Ben and Emma a few times. So far, she'd been able to keep him at bay, but she didn't know how long she could keep it up. He'd never been married and was itching to get her inside a church. Emma had already travelled down the aisle once before and wasn't ready for a return trip.

"I can't believe three weeks from now I'm going to be Mrs. Kathy Jenks. I only hope Andrew and I have as good of a marriage as my mother and father. Next June they celebrate their fortieth anniversary."

Must be nice when marriage vows actually last a lifetime.

With two and a half years under her belt to reflect on her broken marriage, Emma had finally come to understand she'd only accepted her first husband's proposal because she'd been afraid to lose him. Her gut had told her Mark wasn't the one, but her heart had appealed. She'd felt it would be better to be with him than be alone.

If he hadn't walked out, we'd probably still be married.

Emma had promised herself she'd work on her issues, would learn to be comfortable by herself. She hadn't been looking for love when Ben Jacobs walked into her life, had even fought the feelings. Eventually though, she had fallen hard for him. Not long after, they moved in together. But Emma felt it important to put the brakes on the fast-moving train before a ring showed up on her finger. She didn't want to repeat past mistakes.

"How's the dress look?" Kathy asked.

Emma hastily pulled up the sleeves and reached around the back to fiddle with the zipper. Walking out of the dressing room, still thinking about the not-so-subtle marriage hints Ben had been dropping, Emma heard Kathy inhale sharply.

"What?" Emma looked around to see what had caused Kathy's reaction.

"You look phenomenal."

Emma turned to gaze at her reflection in the mirror. The skintight dress hugged her in all the right places. Navy chiffon flowed down the back in two long strips attached at each shoulder.

"This is a beautiful dress, Kathy. It really is."

"Don't sound so shocked. Bridesmaids shouldn't be forced to buy a dress they'll never wear again. I wanted to pick out something elegant but fashionable—a dress to wear at any upscale event. Of course, we'll have to get yours hemmed."

Emma looked down. The dress was meant to fall just over the top of her shoes, but the extra fabric gathered on the floor, encircling her.

"I'm glad you agreed to be my bridesmaid, Emma. I never had a sister. And I know your job doesn't leave a lot of wiggle room for get-togethers, so maybe we can use this time to have some fun and . . . grow closer."

Emma saw the wistful look in Kathy's eyes. She decided to cut her some slack, to unwind and enjoy the moment. Maybe absorb some of Kathy's contagious happiness. After all, one day she *might* become her sister-in-law.

Emma nodded, smiling at Kathy's reflection over her shoulder in the mirror. "That sounds nice."

Kathy snapped her fingers. "I know. Let's have a glass of champagne while the seamstress pins your dress. Then we can talk about the bachelorette party."

PART 5

FRIDAY, SEPTEMBER 25

(23)
LILY EASTIN

Lily dropped Maddy off at school Friday morning. She watched as her daughter broke into a light jog on her way inside, darting around slower students then finally slipping in a side door. Uncomfortable silence had hung between them in the car like a heavy blanket, making Lily want to jump out and run away herself. She'd never seen Maddy in such a hurry to get to class. Lily couldn't blame her.

During the drive, Lily had thought of opening lines. How she should place her hand lovingly on top of her daughter's and say, "You have every right to be upset with me." Yet every word Lily practiced in her head sounded like an empty platitude, more insincere bullshit. How could a mother express a lifetime of regret in a twenty-minute car ride?

Lily knew she had screwed up again. She'd lost her temper last night when all she had wanted to do was talk to Maddy. The conversation had started out fine. She knew she'd gotten through when Maddy rolled over to face her. Maddy had finally started opening up, but somewhere along the way a switch had flipped. Lily couldn't figure out what wrong thing she'd said to make Maddy lash out.

That morning, Lily had been surprised to be awakened by the sounds of Maddy making herself breakfast. Then her daughter had asked for a ride to school. With the guilt of the previous night still weighing her down, Lily had agreed, though inwardly groaned at the thought of getting up so early. Yet, losing sleep would be a justified penance for what she'd said about Tom wanting nothing to do with his daughter.

As Lily stopped at a red light, she remembered one of the books she'd received at her baby shower, *What to Expect When You're Expecting*. At the time, it was considered *the* bible on the subject of pregnancy. She wondered bitterly why there wasn't a party thrown for mothers when their children turned into teenagers.

Now's the time when I really need advice. Maybe a book to explain how to raise a defiant daughter, one who's furious at the world because her father dumped her and ran out on his family. Or what about a book that discusses waking up one day to find your entire life turned upside down. Abandoned by a husband and friends; forced into a new job, a new home; alone with a teenager who's acting out, unable to fix her or myself. Where's the book containing those answers?

Lily knew if she didn't fix the problems plaguing her family soon, the situation would become broken beyond repair. She had watched enough daytime talk shows to know fifteen was old enough to find drugs, or even worse, to find the bad boy with drugs. Next in line would be an unwanted pregnancy or Maddy running off with a boy.

If only there was a way to fix her like when she was a baby.

Lily didn't know which was worse, then or now. She remembered every detail of that terrible day when her daughter was rushed from the doctor's office to the local ER. The staff had decided Maddy would receive the best care in the NICU at All Children's Hospital in St. Petersburg. Once there, she was quickly diagnosed with SVT. In simple terms, a fast heartbeat. At one point during the day, Lily saw the monitor record Maddy's heart rate at over three hundred beats a minute—much faster than a normal baby's rate of 160. Maddy had been in tachycardia for so long her organs had enlarged to twice their normal size.

Lily felt like she'd been kicked in the gut, and knew her daughter's worsening health was her fault. If she'd just trusted her motherly instincts and taken Maddy to the ER when she first felt the nudge, the doctors would have caught the condition before her health had deteriorated so far. If Lily had waited even a few more hours, her daughter would have likely died.

Over a stretch of two weeks, doctors had worked at finding the right combination of medications to control Maddy's SVT. Those fifteen days when she'd sat by her newborn's bedside had been the longest of Lily's life. Maddy looked so tiny with an IV tube coming out of her head—her skull had been the only place nurses could find a vein big enough to tap. To save her sanity, Lily had remained emotionally shut down. How could she not when she watched a nurse roll a heart defibrillator into the room on the off chance it might be needed to restart her daughter's heart?

Lily had readied herself to lose Maddy. She thought if she could just put enough emotional distance between the two of them that if Maddy died, Lily just might make it through somehow. But Maddy fought her way back. She stayed on medication for eighteen months until the doctor weaned her off it, saying Maddy's condition would either self-correct and go away or come back sometime after puberty started. The SVT had never returned, but Lily hadn't stopped waiting for something to take Maddy away.

She thought again about taking Maddy to see a psychologist, but asking for help seemed like admitting defeat. Like Lily didn't have her house in order, couldn't deal with the pressures of raising a child by herself.

What kind of person would the doctor think I was? What kind of mother? A failure, that's what.

Lily couldn't deal with one more person labeling her a failure. She vowed to figure out a way to turn the situation around on her own.

(24)
MADDY EASTIN

Maddy may have given in and agreed to go to school that morning, but there was no way she was going to ride the bus. The day was going to be tough enough without having to sit through thirty extra minutes of torture. She could picture the scene as clearly as if she were walking up the steps of the bus: the kids shooting her hateful glances, moving toward the aisle in their seats to block her from sitting down. The old fart that drove the bus wouldn't hear the foul words slung at her—he could barely even hear the honking horns whenever he swerved into neighboring lanes. He'd never notice the legs shooting out to trip her or the smacks to the head as she faced forward, counting the minutes until the bus made its final stop at school.

Maddy knew how vicious kids could be, had witnessed it rain down on other students who'd popped up on their radar for far lesser offenses. The girls were definitely more ruthless than the boys. She'd once watched Sabrina and a couple of her friends hold down a girl and chop the back of her hair off as a punishment for spreading rumors. They'd threatened to do worse if the girl ratted them out. It was a threat Maddy knew Sabrina would follow up on without a moment's hesitation.

That had been part of the awe surrounding Sabrina. Maddy knew she wouldn't hesitate to charge into battle for those lucky enough to be on her good side. Sabrina was fiercely protective and loyal, with a no-man-left-behind kind of code. Yet make the mistake of tripping into her crosshairs and there was no telling what the repercussions might be. Maddy could only hope the kids at school hadn't heard the news of her deception. If she could just reach Sabrina first, explain the situation, maybe the girl wouldn't feel so betrayed. Maddy would've ridden the bus just to plead her case with her at the bus stop that morning, but Sabrina had stopped riding once the story of the attempted abduction broke. A friend's parent had been giving her a ride.

So Maddy had asked her mom to drive her to school. That way she could arrive before Sabrina and be sure to catch her. But after standing vigil at the side door for over twenty minutes she'd chewed her nails down to the quick—and Sabrina still hadn't shown up.

Maddy looked down at her watch. She couldn't wait any longer. The first bell would ring in seven minutes. She gave one last quick glance out the door. No luck. Maddy turned and headed toward her locker.

I'll have to haul ass to get to my first class on time. I can't afford another detention.

She wrinkled her nose at the noxious smell filling the hallway.

Fabulous, the toilet in the boys' bathroom backed up again.

Maddy felt it was bad enough to have to suffer the indignity of having a lower locker, where she routinely felt the sting of a book falling on her head, but it was also located right next to the bathroom. So not only did its opening door routinely slam into her elbow, she also had to endure the stench.

Maddy crouched down to spin the combination dial. The odor intensified.

My lock's missing!

She opened her locker door. The sight made her fall to her knees. She covered her nose with the crook of her arm. A note was hanging on the hook bolted to the top of the locker: YOU'RE A LYING SACK OF SHIT! Attached to the note was a clear plastic sandwich bag full of runny dog crap. The bag had been left unsealed to ensure maximum smell.

Behind Maddy, the hallway filled with laughter. A boy walked by and pushed Maddy flat to the floor. "Get on the ground where you belong, bitch."

Maddy looked over her shoulder and saw Sabrina, Malik, and their friends crowding around her. She sat up and turned toward them.

"Sabrina, I tried to—"

Sabrina put a hand up, stopping Maddy from speaking. "You are so pathetic, Eastin. Making up a story about some guy grabbing you off the street. What—don't you get enough attention at home? Ohh, I know."

"Don't, Sabrina." Maddy tried to will the tears collecting in the corner of her eyes from falling. But she knew Sabrina wanted to humiliate her and would love to see her cry. The girl felt duped and wouldn't stop until she got her pound of flesh.

"Did Daddy leave poor wittle Maddy? Did he walk out on her and now she needs some attention?"

"He probably left because he couldn't stand the smell," another girl added.

Laughter rang out. More insults flew.

Sabrina ignored them all and walked up to Maddy. She pinched Maddy's chin between her two fingers. "Poor, pitiful, wittle girl. She wants us to feel sorry for her, making up stories to play on our sympathies. I should've known she was a lying sack of shit."

Sabrina reached over Maddy's shoulder and tore the baggie off the hook. She held it high over Maddy's head and emptied it.

(25)
EMMA PARKER

Emma Parker walked into the craft store at around noon, having decided to spend her lunch break in Temple Terrace. She hesitantly picked up a green basket only to set it down again, shaking her head.

Why even pretend I'm here for anything other than information?

Scanning the crowd, Emma found Lily helping a shopper trying to choose between two canvases. Emma thought of the oil painting hanging on her bedroom wall, a portrait Lily had painted of her. She'd always felt funny about it, like some self-absorbed foreign dictator, so she'd kept it in her bedroom. Yet even when Emma and Lily had parted ways, she had left the painting hanging up.

Lily had painted it shortly after Emma got her long locks cut off in college, opting for the type of pixie cut that was all the rage. Emma had hated her new look and wouldn't believe any of her friends who kept raving about it. So Lily sat Emma down and sketched her, then spent over a week painting. When Emma saw the portrait, she was awestruck by the way her best friend had captured her essence. The smirk like there was a secret joke, the intense eyes that displayed a depth of knowledge about life learned the hard way.

The other sketches and paintings Lily had given her since childhood stayed in a plastic tub at the bottom of her closet. Topping the stack was one of Emma's mom, Rose Parker. That was one picture Emma couldn't have handled walking by every day. By stuffing it away, she was hoping to bury all the unhappy memories of the woman with it, but it hadn't worked. The night Rose Parker stormed out of house for the last time always stuck with her. Emma knew her mother was furious that evening, had heard the nasty fight between her parents while she hovered at the top of the stairs. This wasn't the first time her mother had walked out, but she'd always come back. Only that time, she didn't.

"Emma, this is a surprise." Lily stood in front of her, a questioning smile on her face.

Emma's mind had been so entrenched in the past she hadn't noticed the customer walking off and Lily moving toward her. Emma coughed, trying to hide her surprise at being caught off-guard. "Is there somewhere we can talk?"

Lily's smile faltered. "Sure, follow me."

Lily led them through the back of the store and into a stock area. They weaved around shelving units and headed out a back door. When the bright sun smacked Emma in the face, she moved the sunglasses resting on her head down over her eyes.

A woman was already there, leaning against the building and looking down at her phone.

"Can you give us a minute, Holly?" Lily asked.

"Sure, boss." Holly threw her cigarette on the ground and snuffed it out with the toe of her shoe. She turned toward the door, but then stopped. She flashed a sheepish smile, bent over to pick up the butt, and scooted back inside.

"It's good to see you, Emma. You've hardly changed a bit."

"Neither have you."

Lily brought a hand up to her hair and blushed. They both knew Emma's comment was a lie. Lily, the one who'd always prided herself on looking perfectly put together, now stood in front of Emma a complete mess. Her once-bouncy curls hung limp, in need of a new perm. Their reddish color seemed somehow muted. However, it was all insignificant compared to the aging that had transformed Lily's face. Deep wrinkles were etched into her dry skin. Her neck lied, portraying an older age. If

Emma hadn't known better, she would have bet money Lily was almost ten years older than her true age of forty.

"What brings you by?" Lily asked.

"I wanted to find out what's going on with Maddy. She won't return any of my calls."

Lily sighed, seemingly crestfallen to hear the only reason Emma had shown up was because of Maddy. "She's going through a rough patch right now, that's all."

"What do you think I am, some moron? Christ Lily, I'm a detective. I may not be stationed in Temple Terrace, but that doesn't mean I don't know what's going on in the surrounding precincts. This is no little white lie about skipping school. We're talking about a crime here. What's going on with her? There has to be more to it than *a rough patch*."

Lily ignored Emma's question and decided to ask one of her own. "Have you heard whether the State Attorney will file charges?"

Emma shook her head. "I'm not privy to that kind of information. What does the Temple Terrace police force have to say?"

"That Maddy could be charged with filing a false police report."

Emma hit her fist up against the door. "Dammit, what was she thinking? When you called and told me Maddy was the girl who was almost abducted, I did a little digging of my own. I wanted to make sure the case was being handled right. Terrance Wallace will give you a fair shake. Back in the day, we went to the academy together. We still run into each other once in a while. I can't see him pressuring the state to file."

Lily let out a loud exhale.

"I only heard from you that one time," Emma said. "Why hasn't anyone called me? I left messages for Maddy, but she's ignoring me."

"Welcome to the club."

"I had to read that the police discovered the abduction was a hoax in the newspaper."

"It's not like you've been super-involved in our lives."

"That's not fair, Lily."

"Fair? You want fair? Tom walked out on us, Emma. He left me holding the bag while he up and started a new life. Do you think that's fair? I'm doing the best I can to keep it all together, to help Maddy. What can I do if she won't listen to me?"

Emma gritted her teeth.

Why does Lily always make every situation about her? Obviously, Maddy is in so much pain she resorted to making a false allegation to get her parents' attention. Can't she see that Maddy only wants to know she matters? Lily is so blinded by her own pain, she can't see past it to the daughter standing right in front of her falling to pieces.

Emma took a deep breath. "I haven't been there for Maddy. I own that, but I want to do better. Please ask her to answer my calls?"

"You can come over anytime, you know."

"If Maddy keeps avoiding me, I will."

"She might open up to you."

Emma nodded. "Sometimes it's easier for teenagers to talk to someone else. Anyone other than their own mother."

Lily looked past Emma. Her eyes seemed to be watching a different scene play out in front of her. Maybe she was looking back to a time when they were both kids. When they were best friends, like their moms had been. Rose Parker and Jackie Gordon would get together most afternoons, have an early bottle of wine, and feed off each other's negativity. Jackie was a drunk. Rose was just plain angry—about every break that hadn't come her way, every slight shown to her, that fact that she was stuck in a loveless marriage with a kid she never wanted.

Emma pushed the old memories aside. "I'll keep calling Maddy. Maybe I'll discover something to help you break through to her."

Emma didn't think Lily was listening anymore. "Lily?" Emma put her hand on her shoulder.

Startled, Lily shook her head. "What?"

"I have to get back to work. I'll keep in touch. Call me if anything else happens."

Lily nodded and smiled. Emma knew that look, had seen it on Lily's face enough times to easily recognize it. It was the plastered-on smile of someone sinking but unable to find a life preserver. Emma ignored the waves of guilt splashing over her; she knew she could throw Lily a line, but she was still unwilling to do so.

(26)
MADDY EASTIN

Maddy walked the two miles home from school, preferring the intense heat of the Florida sun to the searing heat of stares from bus riders. Each step forward seemed harder than the last, as if the flip-flops the school nurse gave her were made of weights rather than cheap plastic. She'd already ditched the large bags holding her ruined clothes. She'd kept the shoes though. Since she didn't have the luxury of buying a replacement pair, she'd have to figure out a way to salvage them.

Once she reached home, she got a scrub brush out from underneath the sink. Dish soap would have to do; a couple of squirts of the blue liquid, and Maddy started rubbing the soap over the canvas material. Even the shoelaces were filthy. She scrubbed and scrubbed.

Eventually Maddy gave in and threw the shoes down in disgust. "Screw it!" She stormed over to the couch and collapsed onto it. Remote in hand, she escaped through the shiny box until her mom walked through the door.

"How was your day?" Lily asked.

"My day?" Maddy knew she should stand up and head straight to her room, but rage had been building inside her all afternoon. Her body yearned to release the mounting pressure. So she turned her focus on the one target foolish enough to enter her sites.

Lily set her purse on the table. "School was that bad, huh?"

"The ultimate shitty day on top of a mountain of shitty days."

"Watch the language, young lady."

Maddy sprung up from the couch. "Do you have any idea what I've been through?"

"Actually, no, I don't. You won't talk to me, Maddy. How do you expect me to help if I don't know the challenges you're facing?"

"Challenges? You make it sound like I got a *D* on my biology exam. That if I only put more effort into my studies, I'd pull up my grade. You have no clue."

Lily walked over to her daughter. "Then tell me. You can't bitch and moan about your life yet refuse to do anything about it. Tell me what it's like to be you, Maddy. I used to know, but frankly, these days I'm baffled."

"That's the problem. When you look at me, you still see that little five-year-old begging to play hide-and-seek. I'm not that girl anymore."

"Then who are you?"

Maddy shook her head, trying to stop her mom's voice from penetrating her armor.

Lily grabbed her by the shoulders. "Who are you?"

"I'm nobody!" Maddy yelled. She shrugged her mom off. "Don't you understand? I'm worthless." She let out a sob, but tried to stifle the sound with her fist.

"Don't say that, honey."

"Then tell me this, Mom: if I'm so worthy, how could my father find it so easy to leave? If I'm so worthy, why don't I have at least one friend? Every kid at school thinks I'm a reject. You have no clue what happened to me once everyone found out I lied about the kidnapping."

"If you'd talk to me, maybe I could help."

Maddy brought her hand up to her hair, remembering the scene at the locker. The humiliation had been more than she could bear.

No way will I relive it again by telling her.

She could deal with the confused looks her mom gave her, but not pity. Maddy remained silent, a look of defeat on her face. She shook her head.

"We have options," Lily said. "If you're *that* unhappy, you can switch schools or even take the rest of the year off and enroll in online classes."

"You're not hearing me. Yes, school sucks, but what am I going to do somewhere else? The same thing will happen eventually. The kids will know I'm no good. It's as if a stink flows out from my pores. They'll smell my rankness."

"Maddy, you have got to stop speaking about yourself that way. You're not some leper to be shunned. You're a smart, beautiful girl who's extremely talented. You have so much to offer. You're just going through a rough patch right now. Your father, this place—everything's been a tough adjustment." Lily sighed. "I guess I haven't been much help either. I'm sorry for what I said last night. About your father dumping you and refusing to return your phone calls. The last thing you need is your own mother throwing something like that in your face. All I want to do is help, but I can't seem to figure out how. You've probably noticed that I'm not doing such a good job of helping myself. I don't know . . . maybe we should talk to a professional. Get help for the both of us."

Mom has no clue. She can't help me. Maybe it's an age thing, or it could be that the pile of shit she has to deal with is so high she can't see over it. Either way, if she thinks some quack head doctor can fix everything, she should start seeing one. But there's no way I'm spilling my guts to some stranger.

Maddy had had enough of conflict for the day. She took a deep breath and forced a smile. "That might be good. Thanks, Mom."

"Yeah?"

"Yeah."

Lily cupped Maddy's cheeks with her hands. "Good. I'll start making calls tomorrow. As for school—"

Maddy sighed and her whole body deflated.

"Well, we don't have to decide anything right now," Lily said. "It's

Friday, so we have a couple of days to figure it out." Lily kissed Maddy on the head. "Don't stay up too late. A good night's sleep will help everything look better in the morning. Don't forget, tomorrow's my day off. We'll go to the nail salon. I'll even splurge for your fingernails this time. How's that sound?"

Maddy nodded, afraid her voice would betray her. She walked silently back to her room, her fists shaking at her sides. She felt like she might explode, like if she didn't release all the stress building up inside she would spontaneously combust. Her mom hadn't even noticed that Maddy had come home from school in different clothes. She looked down at her mismatched outfit.

Who in the hell wears sweatpants in September?

Once in her room, Maddy yanked the shirt over her head. Then she stomped her legs to kick off the sweats until she was standing in only her bra and underwear. Thinking back on her day at school, she wanted to scream. It had only gotten worse as each hour dragged on.

There's no way I'm ever stepping inside that place again.

Maddy wanted to holler until she had no voice left, but that was out of the question because it would only bring her mom back.

The woman already wants to send me to a shrink. If I totally wig out, she'll probably commit me.

Maddy looked around wildly, scanning the room for anything that might help ease the tension. She eyed a fork sitting on a plate on top of her dresser. She grabbed hold of it with her fist and raked it down her calf muscle. Angry red marks appeared next to healing pink lines. Her mind blissfully emptied as she watched with quiet fascination scratches appear with every swipe. Tiny droplets of blood appeared—and then the pain hit. She savored it, letting it completely wash over her. In that moment, the emotional pain receded to make way for the physical pain. A numbness filled her mind. She sat on her bed, blissfully unaware.

***

Moving on autopilot, Maddy slipped on a pair of lightweight pajamas—short sleeves but long pants. She winced when the garment brushed against her legs. After a few minutes of standing indecisively in the middle of her room, she opted to check her e-mail in hopes that maybe her dad had responded to one of her messages.

She sat down at her desk and waited for the computer to boot up. Every time she turned it on, it took longer and longer to load. The piece of junk was on its last leg. One day soon, she would push the power button and nothing would happen.

Then I'll really be screwed. No TV or electronics in my room.

Maddy made herself quiet the inner dialogue. She refused to let go of the numbing high just yet.

Junk mail was the only thing littering her e-mail inbox. Since she wasn't in the market for penis-enhancing crème or weight loss supplements, she exited the mail program. She logged onto Facebook and was surprised to see twelve notifications. Her blossoming smile quickly disappeared when she saw the names of the posters. The first notification took her to Sabrina's wall. The post said: EVERY WORD OUT OF MADDY EASTIN'S MOUTH IS A LIE. SHE'S NOT TO BE TRUSTED. HAVE YOU SEEN THE PAPER, THE NEWS STORIES? SHE'S THE GIRL WHO LIED ABOUT THE TWO GUYS TRYING TO ABDUCT HER. SHE'S A PATHETIC EXCUSE FOR A HUMAN BEING. I TRUSTED HER. I TOOK HER INTO MY INNER CIRCLE AND SHE PLAYED ON MY SYMPATHIES. SHE HAS A SERIOUSLY PATHETIC NEED FOR ATTENTION!

Sabrina had intentionally tagged Maddy, to ensure she'd see the message. The post had twenty-eight comments already. Kids from school were chiming in, telling Sabrina not to be too hard on herself. That she was only trying to be a good friend, and Maddy had taken advantage of her. They were cheering Sabrina on while at the same time shredding Maddy to pieces. Words like "lying bitch" and "scamming whore" were just a couple of the many insults posted about her.

Maddy understood now that Sabrina had never truly been her friend. The girl had only "forgiven" her in the hopes of uncovering some juicy ammunition that could be fired back at her later. Sabrina was a manipulator, and she'd played Maddy like a fine-tuned instrument. In the end, Sabrina had turned this whole thing around to make it look like *she* was the victim—and in return got all the attention.

Maddy's hand hovered over the mouse as she realized her own Facebook wall would probably be plastered with similar rants. Her heart shouted at her, trying to shield itself from more piercing blows, but her hand refused to cooperate. She clicked on her name and saw message after message, one hateful word after another slamming her character. She got ready to shut off the computer when she noticed a recurring link showing up in the comments. Unable to stop herself, she clicked on the blue text.

The Channel 3 News website popped up on Maddy's screen. That was the station with the hunky anchorman she liked, Karl Hurly. The site showed an article about Maddy's attempted abduction and how it had all been a hoax. She was stunned that the story had been posted on the first page, but when she saw that it had attracted a hundred and two comments, she freaked. She scanned them but didn't see her name anywhere. Instead, hash signs replaced the letters of her name.

That's right . . . that idiot detective said news organizations can't legally print my name because I'm underage.

She scrolled to the bottom of the page to start reading the comments from the beginning. Even though they weren't full of the ugly words posted on Facebook, they hurt just as much. Things like: WHO DOES SHE THINK SHE IS? . . . IF THAT WAS MY DAUGHTER, I'D . . . WHAT IS WRONG WITH THIS GENERATION?

A longer comment caught Maddy's eye. WHO MAKES UP A STORY ABOUT BEING KIDNAPPED? THIS GIRL MUST BE COMPLETELY SELF-ABSORBED TO MAKE UP SUCH A LIE. SHE PUT HER FAMILY THROUGH

HELL. I FEEL SO SORRY FOR HER MOTHER.

The comments went on and on. With every new remark, Maddy felt like another weight had been added to her shoulders. The pressure became too much. Something inside her snapped. The idea that complete strangers were idly commenting about her suddenly infuriated her.

Who the hell are they to make assumptions about my life? They don't know me. They don't know what I've been through.

Maddy's internal dialogue went into overdrive. Nothing she could do would turn off the bickering chatter inside her head.

What are you going to do about this, Maddy? Are you just gonna take it? . . . Why bother, no one cares what I have to say . . . Stand up for yourself, girl. Tell them to go screw themselves . . . What does it matter anyway? Who would listen to my side of the story? . . . Go on, tell them. Write down everything you've been so afraid to say out loud.

Before Maddy lost her courage, she completed the website's registration form and created a username and password so she could add a comment. Once she started writing, the words seemed to gush out. Her fingers could barely type fast enough to keep up. She told her story from the beginning, explaining what had compelled her to lie and how it had ended—with all the bullying she'd endured both in the classroom and online. When she hit the "Submit" button, her inner voice finally fell silent.

(27)
HANK FRY

"Get your head outta your ass, Hank."

"What? Oh, shit! Sorry, Bill." Under bright floodlights, Hank had been using a demo saw to cut steel rebar while his coworker Bill held the metal in place. They were sitting on the bridge expansion with nothing but a line of concrete barriers separating them from the cars speeding down the interstate. Hank's mind had been wandering again, and he'd nearly taken Bill's finger off when he skipped the saw off the rebar.

"I'm takin' a break," Bill said, exasperated. "Get whatever's in that head of yours straightened out by the time I'm back. This is the second time you've almost lopped off a body part." Bill took off his work gloves and slapped them against his thighs. The air filled with dust. Then he turned and stalked off down the hill, shooting Hank a dirty look over his shoulder.

Hank shook his head, wondering why it was so hard to push away the thoughts that had taken over his mind. They seemed to not only have invaded his dreams, but also his every waking moment. For years, he'd fought against his most primal urges. What was different now? Hank had lost track of how many times in the last week one of his buddies at the job site had caught him staring off into the distance. He knew accidents wouldn't be tolerated. Hank's boss was always on the lookout for guys screwing around.

If I don't get my shit together, the guy will can my ass.

The combination of a wandering mind and cars racing by at seventy miles an hour was a dangerous mixture. Add that to the night shifts

Hank would be working through Saturday, and the possibility of an accident increased tenfold. Everyone knew working nights were more dangerous. The later the hour, the drunker the drivers. So far, they'd gone fifty-two days accident-free, but one slip up and the whole job would be shut down during the investigation that was sure to follow. No work meant no paycheck. There wasn't a guy on the line who could afford to be without steady income, and woe to the one who screwed it up for all of them.

An eighteen-wheeler rushed past. Hank tried to turn from the draft slapping his face, but a small pebble shot across his cheek with the force of a bullet exiting a gun. Hank brushed the side of his face. A thin line of blood spread across his work glove. He stared at the red color soaking into the brown material.

A vision of the gloves he wore as a kid working on the farm came back to him. He remembered how well they had absorbed blood. How, when it dried, you couldn't even tell what the substance had originally been.

"Son, make sure you take good care of your tools," Hank could still hear his dad telling him. "Always clean them after running them through a hard day's work. You be good to them, and they'll last a lifetime."

One time when Hank had forgotten to wash his gloves, his dad had smacked him across the face with them. One of the metal embellishments on the glove was bent, and its sharp edge had left a line off blood across Hank's cheek.

To hammer home the point that "a man's work gloves were his most basic but important tool," his dad had made him dig a hole in the backyard until sundown without the benefit of those gloves. For weeks afterward, it was painful to hold anything due to the infected, split blisters on Hank's palms. A hard lesson to learn, but one he never forgot. Not only were a good pair of rugged gloves a necessity in work and life but so was a keen intellect. Not book smarts though. His dad never put much value in those. But smarts that would serve a man well in life.

Hank had become a student of human behavior. He quickly discovered watching and listening to those around him was a much more useful tool than talking. Learn enough about a person, and you could work that to your advantage well before the time you needed to talk your way out of a situation. That was how he'd survived the Fry household—by adapting to every situation.

Bill climbed the steep embankment and headed back toward him. With an arched eyebrow he asked, "What's going on in that head of yours, Hank?"

Bill's face morphed into Earl Fry's before Hank's very eyes.

"What's going on in that head of yours, son?" Earl Fry asked, towering over Hank. The rushing cars disappeared. Hank was back in the barn. He looked down at his hands, expecting to see his work gloves. Instead they were bare and gripping the lock of a cage. He was crouched on the dirt floor.

"Answer me, boy."

Hank was confused. He felt himself say in a younger voice, "I just wanted a look-see."

"You sure about that? You wasn't sneaking in here to let that girl go, were you?"

Hank turned away from his dad and looked into the frightened eyes of a girl hunkered up against the far wall of the type of wire cage meant to hold a large dog. Dad had snatched her right out of a strawberry field in Plant City. With one punch, he'd knocked her out and carried her back to his truck. He'd gloated to his son that no one had seen a thing. He knew her illegal-immigrant parents would never go to the cops for fear of deportation.

The girl's name was Rosalina, but Hank couldn't understand anything else of the rapid Spanish that flew out of her mouth. He figured she was pleading with him to set her free, but he had other things in mind. This girl was older than the one he'd seen strapped down on top of his dad's table weeks earlier. This one actually had breasts instead of just nubs that barely poked out on the other girl. Hank figured she was around fifteen—only a year younger than he was.

"No, sir. I would never let her go. Promise."

Earl stared hard at Hank. "Well then, you must have been coming in here hoping to have a little fun of your own. That it, boy?"

Hank looked down, embarrassed by the thoughts swirling around in a mind he felt certain his dad could read.

"If you wanna have your own fun, find your own girl. Mine's off-limits."

"Hank? Hank?" Bill stood in front of Hank, his arms crossed in front of his barrel chest.

Hank shook his head to clear the memories playing out in front of him like a movie.

Bill clapped his hands together. "Snap out of it, man. What the hell's wrong with you?"

He stared at Bill, wanting to wipe the look of disdain off the man's face. Hank took four steps forward, until he was directly in front of the other man. The strong aroma of cigarette smoke was wafting off Bill in waves of stink.

With a low, menacing voice, Hank said, "I think you've got it all wrong, Bill. It's you that'll have the problem if you don't get off my ass."

Bill broke eye contact first. He looked down and shuffled his feet. "Come on, now. You know I was just razzing you. Don't take offense. I didn't mean nothing by it."

"I didn't think so. Now grab that damn saw. We've lost enough time 'cause of your cigs. Next time you need a smoke, don't make up some bullshit story about me almost cuttin' off your finger just so you can take a break. You hear me?"

Hank knew how others saw him. He used that to his advantage. Always a student of human behavior.

PART 6
SATURDAY, SEPTEMBER 26

(28)
LILY EASTIN

Lily Eastin inhaled the rich scent of coffee. Its warmth soothed her frayed nerves. Though she had the opportunity to sleep late, fractured dreams had woken her throughout the night. Unable to lie down any longer, she'd gotten off the couch still exhausted but determined to do something other than trace the cracked paths in the ceiling. This was Lily's one Saturday off this month. She planned on enjoying a relaxing morning, and held off on jumping right into a shower. That afternoon, she and Maddy would have their mani/pedi appointment.

Maybe hanging out in public will help grease the wheels of civil conversation.

She felt she'd made good headway with Maddy last night. It had started out rocky, but in the end, Lily got Maddy to agree to counseling. Her daughter suffered from the same negative self-esteem Lily did. Seeking professional help was the only way she could think to help her daughter.

After breakfast, Lily planned to borrow Maddy's computer to search for a list of psychologists in the area. Hopefully, the visits would be covered by her health plan. If so, she just might make an appointment for herself. The coping mechanisms she'd turned to since Tom left seemed to be making things worse, not better.

Lily turned on the kitchen radio and grabbed the egg carton out of the refrigerator. She would whip up a couple of omelets, cut some fresh fruit, and serve it all with a side of toast. Though her nausea had abated somewhat, she still wasn't very hungry. She'd force herself to eat a few bites, though, as she couldn't remember the last time she'd made a big breakfast. She and Maddy were always in such a hurry to get on their way in the morning that a Pop-Tart was the easiest thing to grab.

She gave herself a pep talk while cracking the eggs.

Today will be a great day. This will be the day I hold my temper. This will be the day I reconnect with my daughter.

"I Hope You Dance" began playing on the radio. Lily hadn't heard the song in a long time. She tried to remember who sang the melodic country tune, but couldn't. She hummed along, thinking back to the time when Maddy would follow her around the house "helping" with the chores. Maddy would turn in circles, pigtails bouncing, singing songs into a feather duster. She'd replace the lyrics with made-up words when she couldn't remember them.

Why is it no matter what age Maddy reaches, I always think it's the hardest one?

She used to say, "If only Maddy were potty trained, life would be simpler." Yet once that stage was mastered, she'd followed it up with, "When Maddy's in school for the entire day, things will finally be easier." Yet that easier time never came. Once Maddy passed one big milestone, another waited right around the corner. It seemed the hurdles only got larger the older she got.

Listening to the words of the song, Lily felt an ache surge inside. Life had never felt like much of a dance to her.

More like the slow beat of a tom-tom drum where every step forward is one more taken in drudgery.

She knew deep down that she *had* settled for the path of least resistance, sitting out most of her life instead of choosing to dance.

The house phone rang. Lily dropped two pieces of bread into the toaster and grabbed the phone off its base. She figured it was just another sales call. Only solicitors seemed to use her home number anymore. She didn't recognize the name. The caller ID read "Shantel Larson."

"Hello?" Lily said.

"Hi. May I speak to Maddy Eastin?"

"Sure. One moment." She hoped it was a school friend calling to check up on Maddy. She walked down the hall and knocked softly on her daughter's door. After waiting a few seconds, she opened it.

Maddy was awake and staring at the wall. The ceiling fan circled high above her, blowing wisps of hair against her cheeks. She was wrapped in her polka-dot sheets but had both feet sticking out from underneath. Lily smiled. Maddy had always slept with her feet uncovered. With the air-conditioner as antiquated as the house they lived in, having socks on or keeping them covered at night made her too hot. Maddy had always said her feet regulated her entire body temperature.

"There's a call for you. A Shantel Larson?"

Maddy held out her hand for the phone. Her brow furrowed.

"Is that one of your friends?" Lily asked.

Maddy ignored her question. She turned her attention to the person on the phone.

Lily bent over to pick a shirt off the floor. As a stall tactic, she continued grabbing the clothes strewn around the room. If Maddy found it hard opening up to her, maybe Lily could divine something by listening to the one-way conversation.

"Yes? This is Maddy Eastin."

Lily snuck a peek over her shoulder and watched as a smile spread across Maddy's face.

"Are you serious? . . . No . . . I mean, yes." Maddy listened intently and then said, "If you think it would help someone else, sure . . . The rules, huh?"

Maddy sat up and gave Lily a look. She always knew when Maddy was trying to figure something out. Her eyes would get all squinty and she would pull in her bottom lip with her front teeth and gnaw on it.

Maddy grabbed a pen off her nightstand. Lily saw her look around for paper to write on.

"Give me a sec," Maddy said into the phone.

Lily grabbed a piece of scrap paper off the dresser and handed it to her. Maddy took it and then frowned, shooing Lily away with a hand gesture. When Lily didn't move, Maddy stood up and walked over to the door, then opened it with a glare.

Lily slowly made her way over as Maddy turned and pressed the paper against the wall, the pen poised over it. "Okay, I'm ready." She wrote something down. "Sure, I can call you back this afternoon . . . Yeah . . . Thanks."

Maddy ended the call and yanked on Lily's arm, pulling her back into the center of the bedroom. "You won't believe who that was!" Maddy stared at the phone still cradled in her hand like it was a shining talisman.

"I'll go out on a limb and say . . . Shantel Larson?"

Maddy rolled her eyes. "Duh, obviously. Miss Larson is the executive producer for Channel 3 News. She wants to interview me! Can you believe it? She said my story could impact other kids and that—"

"Wait a minute, Maddy. Slow down and start from the beginning."

Maddy sighed. "The shit hit the fan—"

"Language."

Maddy threw her hands up in frustration, but quickly started over. "When the kids at school found out I made up the story about the attempted abduction, they turned on me. You have no idea how much Friday sucked. It was a never-ending stream of bullying, and when I got home, the harassment continued online."

"What?" Lily dropped her armload of clothes. She didn't understand why Maddy hadn't told her about it.

"Yeah. My Facebook and other social networking sites were full of threats and cruel slurs. Some kids even linked to a story about the hoax on the Channel 3 News website. You should've seen the awful things people were saying about me. I only wanted to tell my side of the story.

It wasn't fair that strangers were talking smack about me. So I posted my own comment."

"You did *what*?"

"Mom, you have no idea how hard it's been. I thought if I could just share my side of the story, explain why I made up the abduction scare, then people would get off my back. That's how the news station found out I was the girl involved in the case."

"You used your real name? Your address?"

"Only on the sign-up sheet. I had to. To post a comment, it's mandatory. Lots of sites have adopted that policy. Removing the anonymity cuts down on the number of haters. Well, in theory."

"Random commenters don't care about your side of the story, Maddy. They only want a forum to spew their own opinions. You thought a paragraph or two would change their minds?"

"Yeah, Mom. I did. It made a big impact on Miss Larson. She wants to get my story out."

"What do you mean? What kind of story?"

"Well, if you give me a second, I'll tell you."

Lily sank down on the bed and reminded herself to hold her temper.

"Thank you." Maddy sat down next to her. "Miss Larson read what I wrote online. She said it moved her. Bullying is a hot topic these days, and she thinks she can use my story to help others who are going through the same situation. Miss Larson told me she's tired of reporting on school shootings after the fact and that with my help we might be able to stop the senseless violence."

"She doesn't think you're going to turn a gun on your classmates, does she? Because if that's what she's implying—"

"No, Mom. Get real. It's just that school violence is a real threat. Putting out a story showing the effects of bullying might make kids think twice before doing it. I mean, it's worth a shot. Isn't it?" Maddy cocked her head to the side, seemingly imploring Lily to be on her side just one time.

"I don't know, Maddy. There's a reason it's against the law for the media to use a minor's name in connection with a criminal case. Don't you think all the attention might be overwhelming? Detective Wallace assured me that your name would stay out of the press, but now look at you, going and volunteering yourself like a sacrificial lamb."

"Mom, I have to do *something*. I can't sit back and simply take everything the kids at school dish out. I'm tired of being a victim. I'm tired of everyone making decisions for me. I feel like I'm just being dragged along for the ride. I'm ready to dig my heels in and say *no more*."

Lily was stirred by her daughter's impassioned words. Maddy sounded more grown-up than her fifteen years. A lot had happened these past few months, causing her to mature way too fast.

What if talking about the situation is exactly what she needs to turn everything around? It might prove empowering.

"The news segment wouldn't talk about how you made up the whole abduction, would they, Maddy? I'd hate for you to bring more unwanted attention to yourself. What if this story increases public pressure on the State Attorney to file charges against you?"

"That won't happen after they hear my side. Miss Larson said this interview will help everyone understand my motives, that they'll fall in love with me. Of course, the segment would have to *touch* on the abduction hoax, but Miss Larson assured me it wouldn't be the main focus. It would only be used for context, so people would understand why the bullying started. What if I—"

The sound of Lily's ringing phone interrupted them. She groaned and stood up. Maddy trailed behind her into the living room.

"Mom, can I do it? I have to have permission from a parent."

"One minute, Maddy. I need to take this. It could be important."

"But Mom—"

Lily picked the phone up and turned away so she could hear the caller. "Hello?"

"Sorry to bother you at home, Lily." It was her boss. "But I need you to come in today."

"Are you kidding me?"

"No. Holly and Michael went home sick, and their shifts just started."

"Can't you find someone else to cover? I'm in the middle of something here."

"I would if I could, but you're the only one left. It seems some kind of bug is going around."

"Yeah, a lazy bug," Lily mumbled.

"What?"

"Nothing. Fine. I'll be there in a half hour." Lily slammed the phone down.

"Let me guess," Maddy said, crossing her arms over her chest. "Another mother/daughter day canceled."

Lily felt like the worst parent in the world. No matter how good her intentions were, she always managed to let her daughter down. She wished that, just once, she could watch Maddy's face light up and know that she was the one who'd brought her joy.

"Two people have gone home sick," she said. "Nobody else will come in to cover the shifts. Saturday will be busy enough as it is, and with two people down it will be near impossible to run the store. I have to go in. I'll call the employees who have the late shift. Maybe one of them will do me a solid and come in early. I'll try to be home as soon as I can. We can still go out for dinner."

"Forget it. I knew you'd come up with some excuse not to spend time with me."

"Maddy, please. I'm sorry." A thought popped into Lily's head. Her instincts told her to keep her mouth shut, but the guilt weighing her down was too persuasive. "What if I give you permission to do the news segment?"

Maddy's mouth dropped open. She grabbed her mom's hands and squealed. "Really? You mean it? You'll let me do it?"

Lily nodded her head. The sheer happiness Maddy exhibited as she jumped up and down was almost enough to stamp out the guilt for taking that all-too-familiar path of least resistance.

(29)
EMMA PARKER

After a few quick kisses that Ben tried to stretch into something more, Emma jumped into the shower. It might be a Saturday, but criminals didn't take the weekend off. She was next up in the rotation and had to rush out to Valrico, a small city fourteen miles east of Tampa. There had been a shooting.

The Hillsborough County Sheriff's Office, her employer, was in charge of enforcing the law in the unincorporated areas of the county. They'd received a 911 call about a domestic disturbance from a next-door neighbor who had overheard the fight. A second, more frantic call had been made after that same neighbor heard a gunshot. The first officer to arrive on the scene had confirmed a dead body of a lone Caucasian female.

Television crime dramas always made detective work sound so glamorous, like every case required Sherlock Holmes–level skills to uncover a killer's identity. In real life, most of the time the whodunit was obvious. Not many people had the stomach to commit murder and cover it up with a deft hand. Many times weapons covered in fingerprints would be absently discarded right beside a body, or faces would be captured on security cameras. Emma usually found a perpetrator's identity easy to figure out. It was the why behind the crime that she rarely understood. Why a mother would sell her five-year-old daughter for a hit of meth. Why a father would take out his whole family after losing his job of twenty years.

Emma had been a detective for seven years now, and had worked as a patrol cop for eleven years before that. For as far back as she could remember, she had wanted to be a cop. It had been her Halloween costume four years in a row—and she had only retired it because the high-watered pants eventually started to look more like capris. As a little kid, she rarely went anywhere without a pair of plastic handcuffs clipped through her belt loops.

She knew her dad's influence had the most impact on her career choice. After fourteen years as a patrol cop he'd been involved in a bad car accident. He couldn't handle being reassigned to a desk job, so he quit, opting to start his own commercial landscaping business instead. It kept him busy working outside, which made him happy, but there was always a yearning Emma could see in him—especially when the sirens of a squad car raced past.

Now she could empathize. She didn't know what she'd do if her career was ever snatched away from her. The weight of her gun on her hip, the respect her badge brought her—these made her feel powerful, in control. Her job was important. She solved problems, brought closure to victims' families. She liked being needed.

She knew her dad had felt the same way when he was on the job. Sometime during her childhood, at what age she didn't remember, his bedtime stories had turned into cop-story time. Instead of a prince coming to save the princess, a police officer would rush in to save the day by stopping an armed robbery at a convenience store, rescuing a little girl from the clutches of a stranger, or busting an evil drug dealer in front of a school. Emma's dad had countless stories to fuel her vivid imagination.

He'd felt it was his job to prepare her for life. That meant hunting, fishing, learning her way around the undercarriage of a car, and especially self-defense. While most girls spent their free time practicing their culinary skills with their moms or going to dance camp, Emma's childhood was spent training in martial arts and competitive shooting.

She didn't mind adopting her dad's preferences in regards to her extracurricular activities.

It was better than hanging out with Mother. Don't go there, Emma. Get your mind back to the here and now.

She veered away from the familiar mental trap and instead focused on finding the crime scene's apartment building. She finally found a match to the address she'd written down and pulled into a large complex. She turned right, following the circular drive around to the back, where she saw yellow crime-scene tape.

A teenage girl walked down the sidewalk and past her car, bringing Maddy to the forefront of Emma's mind. She pulled out her cell phone and dialed her goddaughter's number.

"Hi, Maddy. I was just thinking about you and hoped you'd pick up, but I guess you're not there. Can you call me later? I'd like to chat. Okay, then . . . bye."

Hopefully, this would be an open-and-shut case so Emma could stop by Lily's house later that evening. Something serious must be going on with Maddy to make the girl constantly dodge her calls. Emma knew it was once again time to step up, to be the one person Maddy could count on.

(30)
HANK FRY

"Hank? Hank? Wake up, Hank."

Hank cracked one eye open, trying to focus on the numbers on the alarm clock. It read 9:28 am. "Give me a break, Daniel. I worked a seven to seven last night. I've been asleep for less than two hours."

"But my Pokémon league is about to start."

"Just take the van and go."

"I can't find the keys. Where'd you put them?"

"In the bowl on the kitchen counter, where they always are."

"I looked there." Daniel's face was flushed, his eyes glassy. "And I looked in the van and in your jeans and in the couch. They're not *anywhere*." Daniel turned the last word into a high-pitched squeal.

Hank knew a meltdown was looming if he didn't find the damn keys. He swore under his breath and forced his body to sit up. Daniel helped him the rest of the way out of bed by grabbing his arm and yanking him forward.

Most of the time, Daniel was a homebody. The only exception was for his Saturday morning Pokémon card game. Hank encouraged him to attend because it meant fewer games he had to play with him.

He used to haul Daniel over to the New Tampa library, but now he was comfortable letting him drive the back roads himself. Hank had spent weeks getting to know the people who regularly attended the meetings. He'd been worried the other players would make fun of his brother. As it turned out, he had nothing to worry about. They were one big group of outcasts. Sure, there were plenty of ten-year-old boys carrying armloads of photo books containing their Pokémon cards, safely protected by sheets of plastic, but there were just as many twenty-something guys simply looking for an outlet for their hobby. Anywhere else these older guys would have been teased and labeled nerds, so when they met together as a group they made it a point to help everyone who walked through the door feel welcome.

"Hurry, Hank! I'm gonna be late. I finally found a Zekrom EX card, and I want to see Bobby's face when I play it on his Gyarados card."

Hank scanned the bedroom, but didn't see his set of keys on the nightstand or dresser. He trudged into the living room with Daniel on his heels. Hank picked the newspaper up off the table, searched under the couch cushions, and even bent over to look under the couch, but he didn't find any keys.

He could feel Daniel breathing down his neck as the boy followed him from place to place. Hank knew he was about to lose his temper, so he took a couple of deep breaths, turned to Daniel, and asked, "Did you eat breakfast yet?"

"Haaaaank!"

Again with that whiny voice. I'm going to lose it if I have to hear that noise one more time.

"I can't. Especially since it's—" Daniel looked down at his watch. With a sharp intake of air, he barely managed to say the time. "Nine thirty-one."

"Well, at least grab some OJ while I'm looking around. You know how you get when you're hungry, Small Fry. It's going to hit you like a Mack truck in about an hour."

Daniel sighed heavily, displaying his real mental age. He was a boy trapped in a man's body. He stomped over to the refrigerator and opened the door. A second later, a squealing Daniel turned around, jumping in the air with jangling keys swinging from his finger. "I found them!"

He ran over to Hank and gave him a bear hug. "You're a genius, Hank."

Huh. I must have laid them down in the fridge when I grabbed that slice of pizza this morning.

He patted his brother on the back and watched him rush out the door. Daniel's books of cards were loaded in his arms, the orange juice forgotten.

Hank took a pit stop and then headed back to the sanctuary of his covers. With Daniel out of the house, he hoped to get a good chunk of uninterrupted sleep. He tried to block out the sound of Daniel's whining bouncing through his mind like a manic pinball. It was the same tone of voice his mother had used when an argument went south with his dad. Hank figured Daniel had heard the sound enough times growing up that he'd unconsciously adopted it. The boy's whines grated on Hank almost as much as his mother's had.

That bitch deserved everything she got just for making that horrible noise.

Trying to find sleep, his mind wandered back to his mom's last day on earth. He'd heeded his dad's warning and stayed away from the caged girl. For three days, at least. Like Daniel was drawn to their dad's guitar, Hank was drawn to the sight of exposed flesh.

With a plan in mind, he'd faked an illness after his dad left for the fields one morning. His mom had bought the act and tucked him in before heading to the produce stand to sell the spring's crops. When Hank heard the backfire of their old truck in the distance, he knew it was safe to get up.

He gathered his supplies and walked outside to the barn. A heavy padlock held the door handles together. The lock was covered with rust, but Hank already knew that age hadn't weakened it any. He also knew his dad kept the key hidden in a tiny, hollowed-out knot in an oak tree near the house's back door. Two nights ago, Hank's mother had asked him to get his dad for supper. Before Hank could open the back door, he saw his dad come out of the barn and lock up for the night. Instead of coming straight to the house, though, he'd detoured to the backyard, stopping at the largest oak. Hank snuck out to see what he was up to. Earl Fry had looked over his shoulder, but it was a second too late—his oldest boy had already dropped to the ground out of sight. It wasn't until the next morning, before school, that Hank found the key hidden in the tree.

With the open lock left dangling on one of the barn door handles, Hank grabbed his full basket off the ground and headed inside. When he closed the door, the sun that had followed him in disappeared. He knew he should have been scared shitless, that he should be paying heed to the adrenaline coursing through his body. It was a warning sign telling him he should turn back—but Hank wasn't afraid of getting caught. In fact, his dad was the furthest thing from his mind. When he walked into the darkness of the barn, he felt invincible. He knew his way around, didn't even need the scant amount of light that seeped through the warped boards of the walls.

Hank could hear the heavy breaths of the frightened girl off to his right. He grabbed a hanging light from a hook and continued over toward the cage. He dropped the basket on the ground. The girl sneezed, a cute little *achoo* sound that made him smile. Hank attached the light to an empty hook bolted into the wall above the cage. When he turned it on, the bright beam caused the girl to cover her eyes with the crook of her arm.

Hank stood over the cage for a few moments. Through the squares of wire, he could see the girl's naked flesh. His eyes followed the curve of her neck where it extended into her shoulder, continued on over the hill of her breasts, down her stomach, and stopped at the hands clenched in her lap. He yearned to see what was between those closed legs, wondered whether she would have hair yet.

The basket contained all the tools he'd need for the day's adventure. His dad had taught him the lesson of preparation well. Hank took a lone piece of bread out and handed it to Rosalina. When she warily glanced back and forth from the bread to him, Hank smiled and nodded. He rolled the bread up into a ball and stuck it through one of the holes. Rosalina snatched the food away from him. With a few quick bites, she devoured it. Hank knew she was starving. His dad wasn't real big on caring for the sustenance of his captives.

He took out the Spanish-English dictionary he'd borrowed from the school library. The look on Ms. Reedy's face had been priceless. In the two years he'd attended Plant City High School, she'd never seen him check out anything other than graphic novels.

"Bueno?" Hank said. Saying the Spanish word in his slight southern drawl sounded funny even to him, but he figured using Rosalina's native language would put her more at ease.

"Sí," she said, though it was a croak of a sound. "Agua, por favor."

Hank cocked his head, not understanding what she'd said.

"Agua," Rosalina repeated, pointing at the book in Hank's hand.

"Oh, right." Hank thumbed through the dictionary to discover that *agua* meant water.

He knew the bread had made her thirsty, even more so than she must have already been. Hank had counted on that. He pulled a tall, clear glass of water out of the basket. It was only a fourth of the way full, to ensure it didn't spill during the journey to the barn. Rosalina's eyes never left it.

Hank held up a finger, the international sign for "wait a minute." Rosalina licked her lips. He couldn't risk letting her out of the cage. A cornered animal would attack if it thought it'd found a way out. He was strong, built muscularly even as a teenager, but worried that if he couldn't subdue her, she might get away. If that happened, he wouldn't live to see the next day. He knew he had to have his fun while she was still caged.

"Toque chocha," Hank said. He had done his homework and consulted his dictionary earlier to find the word for "touch." The word for "pussy" had been harder to come by. He'd had to ask a guy at school for that one.

Rosalina wrinkled her brow.

Did I pronounce the words wrong, or did that asshole kid pull one over on me? For all I know, maybe I just told the girl to touch a goat.

Tossing the dictionary aside, he decided charades would work better than words. He sat on the ground facing the cage and bent his knees in a V before him. He spread his legs open wide and touched his dick, rubbing it and groaning. Then he pointed to her crotch, back at the water, and then to her again.

As understanding dawned, Rosalina puckered up her face like she'd eaten a lemon. The thought that the boy who could have been her savior was really just a boy trying to use her had probably left a sour taste in her mouth.

Hank shrugged, then slowly tipped his hand until the water in the glass lapped against the edge. Another second, and it would trickle to the ground.

"No!"

Hank smiled, righting the glass and placing it safely on the ground next to him.

Rosalina tentatively opened her legs. She stared at the glass of water while she moved her fingers, following Hank's previous directions. Hank unzipped his pants and started beating off. Just as he reached orgasm, he heard a gasp. He had been so involved in acting out his fantasy, he hadn't heard the barn door open. Afraid his dad had caught him, Hank yanked his shirt down, trying to cover himself. When he turned his head, he saw his mother standing five feet away, her hands over her mouth, her eyes large and trying to digest the scene in front of her.

Hank shoved himself back in his pants and stood up, wiping his hand on his jeans.

"How could you?" Patricia Fry finally managed to squeak out.

"No . . . it's not what it looks like . . . Dad."

He watched as the realization of the situation sunk in on his mom's face. She shook her head like she was trying to unhear what her son had just said. Covering her ears with her hands, she ran out of the barn, wailing.

"Agua, por favor."

Hank glared at Rosalina. "You disgust me."

He kicked the glass over. Rosalina started crying as she watched the wet trail of dirt rush underneath the cage. He stood there, fascinated at her desperation for water. She licked up the small pool, dirt and all.

Hank concentrated on the visual of Rosalina sitting in the cage with her legs spread open before him as he lay in bed. He ejaculated into a shirt he'd grabbed off the floor.

What I wouldn't give for one more day with her.

Hank rolled over, closed his eyes, and fell into a dreamless sleep.

(31)
MADDY EASTIN

Maddy balked at the thought of the news crew filming at her house. She'd tried talking the producer out of the idea, but the woman was adamant about getting live shots of Maddy's bus stop and of her neighborhood. Miss Larson also insisted the interview happen that same day. At least Maddy had been able to push her off until late afternoon when her mom hopefully would be home to sign the consent forms.

Although Maddy spent the entire day cleaning, no amount of elbow grease could take away the feel of poverty permeating the house. The sad, broken-down furniture still consumed the room, the patches of missing wallpaper still marred the walls. But it was better than nothing. Maybe the cameraman could take close-up shots and get more of Maddy in the frame than her surroundings.

The house's two small closets were already threatening to burst, but Maddy managed to fit her mom's bed linens and pillow on a high shelf in one. She knew Miss Larson would figure out her mom slept on the couch since there was only one bedroom in the house, but that didn't mean she had to advertise it.

For a finishing touch, she lit scented candles and placed them throughout each room, all the while going over answers to the questions she thought Miss Larson might ask. "Why did you make up the story about two men attempting to abduct you?" The answer she'd rehearsed in her head sounded sincere, yet appropriately apologetic. If she could get the delivery just right, she'd be able to sway everyone back on her side. "What do you want to say to the kids out there who are being bullied every day at school?" Maddy pictured herself sitting tall, locking eyes with the camera, and giving her most heartfelt answer.

She knew this could be a turning point. She simply had to seize the moment. She believed Sabrina, Malik, and all the other kids at school would watch the segment, or at least hear about it, and understand how much they'd hurt her. They would surely sympathize with her motives and hopefully stop harassing her.

Maddy pulled her phone out of her back pocket and sent a text to her dad. If he was in town, he might watch. Then maybe he'd see all the pain she'd been going through and rush to her side. Of course, he wouldn't deserve forgiveness for having left her in the first place, but Maddy would be the bigger person in the relationship and accept his gushing apology. She shot off another text to Aunt Emma, suggesting they watch the segment together. She wanted to share her big moment with someone she loved, and the thought of sitting next to her mom and listening to her pick apart all her answers was more than she could handle.

Maddy remembered reading about some old guy in school who said everyone would experience fifteen minutes of fame sometime in their lives. She wondered if this was her time. Sure, it wasn't on some grand scale like starring on *American Idol* or performing on *America's Got Talent*. Still, she knew fame always changed lives for the better. Ask any kid at school. None of them wanted a high-powered career. They no longer cared about working their way up to the top of any corporate ladder. It was all about who knew your name now. Baseball stats weren't the numbers discussed at the lunchroom; it was how many Instagram likes and Twitter followers you had. Maddy just knew her popularity trajectory was about to change course for the better.

She placed the last candle in her bedroom. Hopefully, the scent would mask the slightly moldy smell that seemed to linger in the house instead of turning it into one big cinnamon stink bomb. Maddy took one last look around at her well-made bed and tidy dresser.

It will do. As long as Mom gets home soon.

She looked at her watch. Through her last half-dozen texts, Mom had repeatedly promised she'd be home by three o'clock. She'd found a couple of people to cover the shift for the sick employees she was working for and said she'd leave as soon as one of them arrived.

Maddy would've rather done the interview alone, but since she was underage, Miss Larson insisted her mom be present. There were forms to sign.

Blah, blah, blah. At least I won't have to worry about Mom hogging the spotlight since she's crazy phobic about public speaking.

Maddy hoped reporter Karl Hurley interviewed her. He had a baby face with kind eyes that naturally drew people to him. Plenty of segments had showed him reaching out to the people he interviewed, resting his hands atop theirs while they related sad stories of foreclosure or chronic health problems. She wondered if his hands would be smooth or sweaty. As she wiped her palms on her pants, she decided to change clothes again.

After exchanging her print blouse for a solid green button-up shirt, Maddy smoothed out the material and looked at her reflection in the mirror. This shirt made her eyes look darker, more piercing.

Maybe it will help draw the viewer's attention away from the gigantic pimple on the side of my nose.

She wished her dad was there. He always knew what colors looked best on her. She looked down at her jeans, rethinking the choice, when the doorbell rang.

Maddy rushed to open the door and found a woman blocking her front steps.

"Hi. Are you Maddy Eastin? I'm Shantel Larson."

Maddy was surprised by how wrong she'd been about the visual she'd created in her head for this lady. With Miss Larson's young, soft voice, she'd pictured a petite woman in her early twenties. Instead, the woman was butterball-round and old like her mom.

"Yes, I'm Maddy."

Miss Larson gave Maddy's hand an enthusiastic shake. At the sound of a door slamming, Miss Larson turned sideways. Maddy saw a man out by the street taking camera equipment out of the Channel 3 News van. Another man who was sitting in the passenger seat closed the sun visor like he'd been checking his reflection. When he got out of the van, he gave Maddy a slight head nod and smiled.

Who's that guy? Definitely not Karl Hurley.

As if picking up on her slight hesitation, Miss Larson said, "Rick's our camera operator and that's Alex Sanchez. You may not recognize him yet. He's only been with the station for a couple of months."

Great, I get stuck with the newbie. Guess my story didn't rate Karl.

"Is your mom home?" Miss Larson asked.

Maddy stopped biting on her cuticle. "She should be here any—oh wait, there she is now, pulling into the driveway."

"Great. We'll get all the necessary papers signed, and Rick will set up in . . ." Miss Larson tried to look past Maddy and into the house. Maddy stepped back inside, allowing her room to maneuver in. "He'll set up in the living room. Good? Good."

The newbie anchor and her mom stood outside talking beside the car.

At least our car isn't a piece of shit.

She watched the reporter listen to her mom, a smile plastered on his face. Her mom seemed to be setting the man straight somehow before she let him walk inside the house. Maddy was mortified.

"Mom, come in the house. They need to set up."

The newbie took his cue and headed for the front steps. He shook Maddy's hand and offered her an easy smile. Somehow, though, his expression didn't match his eyes. He seemed to be sizing her up, evaluating her in some unknown way. As he headed inside, his cologne lingered, wrapping around her throat like an invisible hand.

Miss Larson returned to the living room from the back of the house. "I think we should set up the interview in here." She'd obviously scouted out the other rooms and, after her snooping expedition, decided the whole place was equally crappy.

Maddy, still unable to find her voice, could only nod.

"Sure," the newbie said, "but I want a shot of Maddy walking to the bus stop first. Maddy, grab your backpack for me. Let's give this an authentic feel."

"But it's not dark out. When I leave the house in the morning, it's always dark."

"That's okay. It's only a reenactment. Anyway, darkness won't play as well on TV."

She looked over at her mom, standing near the open door. Her mom offered her a confident smile that helped Maddy regain her own confidence.

"Rick, make sure to get some good neighborhood shots before all the looky-loos show up," Larson said.

"Right, boss."

Maddy's mom hadn't noticed the camera guy standing behind her, and she jumped when he answered the producer.

At first, Maddy felt stupid walking to the bus stop with the camera trailing her. But on the third take, Maddy noticed Sabrina's car driving by. She couldn't see through the tinted windows, but Maddy imagined Sabrina inside, watching with jealousy pumping through her veins. Maddy's smile turned megawatt, and her walk grew bolder.

Miss Larson told Maddy to go inside and freshen up while Rick filmed Alex's intro. Maddy wanted to stay and listen, but the woman's facial expression made it clear she was in desperate need of a new coat of makeup. Late-September days in Florida were killer on a girl's looks.

An extra swipe of deodorant, a fresh coat of foundation, additional hairspray, and Maddy was ready. She hurried back into the living room, where the cameraman pointed her toward the couch. She sat down and shifted around uncomfortably, wondering if she should've changed out of her damp shirt. Rick stood behind a camera situated on top of a tripod. He looked up at Maddy, then down at the viewfinder. The frown on his face deepened. He grumbled to himself as he shuffled behind the back of the couch and adjusted a light he had set up behind Maddy's left shoulder. The brightness of the room bothered her eyes, and she asked for a tissue.

Her mom handed her one and bent over to whisper in her ear. "Are you sure you want to go through with this?"

Maddy figured her mom must have misinterpreted the reason for her request. She'd only asked for the tissue so her watery eyes wouldn't mess up her makeup again. "I'm fine, Mom."

"Ma'am, you're casting a shadow. Do you mind?" Rick said.

"Oh, right." Lily brought a fluttering hand to her chest. "Sorry."

Lily resumed her place against the far wall. Maddy knew her mom was uncomfortable with the whole situation. She had her hands clasped in front of her, but kept twiddling her thumbs.

Probably stressing out about all the mess.

The camera guy had taken over the room, moving the end tables into the kitchen and scooting the couch over for better lighting. All the hard work Maddy had put into straightening up the place had gone right out the window.

Finally satisfied with the lighting, Rick said, "We're ready, boss."

The reporter sat in the chair on Maddy's right. One camera would capture both his profile and hers. A second camera was positioned to give a straight-on view of Maddy's face.

"Okay, Madison—"

"It's Maddy."

"Right, right. Maddy. I already taped the opening segment outside your front door, so now I'm going to ask you some questions. Don't worry, they're easy. Just answer them as truthfully as possible and don't worry if you make a mistake—just keep talking. We'll edit later."

Maddy couldn't help but smile. Her head was spinning from the speed at which everything was happening. She wanted to ask some questions, but didn't want to look like some dumb kid. She wanted to be taken seriously.

Then she heard Miss Larson start counting down. With every number spoken, Maddy's heart pounded faster. "In three, two, one. Go."

On cue, the reporter smiled. This time it reached into his eyes. He seemed like a whole different person. "Maddy Eastin, it is so good to meet you. I'm glad you reached out to us about your situation." Alex sat forward and took her hands in his. "I understand you want to talk about the cyberbullying attack launched against you by the kids at your school, is that right?"

Alex's hands weren't soft at all. They were cold—cold as ice. She withdrew her hands from his and cleared her throat.

"Yes, yes I do."

"We'll definitely get to that, but first I have to ask what possessed you to make up such a horrendous lie about someone trying to abduct you?"

Maddy's mouth dropped open, surprised by his nasty tone. Her mind went blank. This was nothing like how she thought it would go. She squinted through the bright lights, trying to look at her mom. Lily's fingers were pinching the bridge of her nose. She looked embarrassed. Maddy knew her mom would be no help.

As usual, I'm on my own.

PART 7
SUNDAY, SEPTEMBER 27

(32)
EMMA PARKER

Early Sunday morning, Emma rushed out the door and went back to hunting down her murder victim's boyfriend. As it turned out, the case was an easy one to solve. Witnesses saw the guy flee the apartment and bloody fingerprints at the scene matched the ex-con's. The problem was trying to apprehend him. Every time Emma showed up at a known hangout of his, she learned the guy had just left. It was like he had ESP or something—always one step ahead.

It wasn't until late that afternoon that she found him hiding out at a second girlfriend's house. The look on the woman's face when she heard what "her man" had been up to was priceless. Emma couldn't tell whether she was most angry about the fact that the guy had been stepping out on her, that he'd killed his other girlfriend, or that he'd gotten caught.

The chase and subsequent booking had kept Emma busy until after four o'clock. When she finally dragged herself back to the condo again, all she could think about was Maddy. Her goddaughter had finally texted her back yesterday, suggesting they hang out and watch the evening news together. She thought it was an odd request, but figured maybe it was just Maddy's way of trying to reconnect.

Emma had meant to return the text with a call, but by the time she broke free, it had been much too late to call a girl who should've already been fast asleep. She had settled for a quick text back, telling Maddy she loved the idea of getting together, but that she'd have to call Sunday to see if the timing could work out.

Now it would be too late to watch the five o'clock news together, but once Emma had a chance to decompress, she vowed to call Maddy with other suggestions of things they could do. When Emma finally opened her front door, she found Ben on the couch, reading his tablet.

"How can you read and have the TV on at the same time? Especially this channel," she said. "Isn't it distracting?"

"Hello to you too."

Emma sighed and plopped down on the couch next to him. "Sorry. I'm bushed. Hello. How was your day?"

"Pretty uneventful. Worked out earlier, and now I'm vegging. And no, the TV doesn't bother me. I like background noise, makes the place feel less empty. So did you get your guy—"

"Holy shit!"

Ben looked up at Emma. Her eyes were firmly focused on the TV. "What's the matter?"

"Shush! That's Lily's house."

On TV, a reporter stood outside the Eastins' house. Even though Emma had never gone inside, she'd sat in her car and waited at the curb for Maddy plenty of times. She'd know that faded Pepto-Bismol-pink house anywhere.

The camera panned around the run-down neighborhood, then went in tight on the reporter. "During the early morning hours of Monday, September twenty-first, a fifteen-year-old girl reported that two men sitting in a van near her bus stop attempted to abduct her. She told police one of the men came up behind her, covered her mouth with one hand, and scooped her up around the waist with the other. Quick wit saved the girl. She fought off the attacker by stomping on his foot and running away. Then she frantically waved down her school bus as it turned the corner onto her street. A harrowing tale . . . maybe. Or maybe not."

Emma sat on the couch, watching in quiet shock. One part of her wanted to turn away from the screen, but she couldn't quite persuade her muscles to move. Only when she saw Maddy's shocked face did she finally allow herself to close her eyes. Unfortunately, her ears couldn't block out the reporter's rapid-fire questions.

(33)
DETECTIVE TERRANCE WALLACE

"Hey, Terrance!" Trudy called out from the kitchen. "Wasn't this your case?"

When he got up off the floor, two toddlers attached themselves to his legs. They squealed in delight as he Frankenstein-walked them into the kitchen.

Trudy stood at the counter, chopping vegetables and staring at a portable TV screen sitting next to the coffee pot. Terrance came up behind her and grabbed a slice of cucumber off the cutting board. She playfully smacked his hand, then turned up the volume on the TV to drown out the pleas of the little ones begging Terrance for another ride.

"A harrowing tale . . . maybe. Or maybe not," a news reporter said. "It looks like there might be more to this case than originally thought. As it turns out, a neighbor captured the entire incident on video from the security camera mounted on his front porch. Paul Gleason lives in this corner house, right behind the girl's bus stop."

Terrance watched the camera pan wide, turning from a shot of the street corner to Gleason's house.

"The pivotal break in the case came when Gleason came forward with the recording," the reporter said. "Who could ask for better evidence to help in tracking down these monsters, right? Well . . . you be the judge. Channel 3 News has obtained a copy of the recording from Gleason, and we want you, our viewers, to be the first to see the 'crime' as it unfolds."

"Oh, no." Terrance rubbed his forehead.

"What?" Trudy asked.

He just shook his head. Trudy bent down and extricated the two kids from his legs, shooing them into the other room. The television screen went dark, and Maddy's neighborhood glowed green.

As the video ended, the reporter said, "No, folks, you didn't miss it. The men this girl reported trying to snatch her from the bus stop never showed up in the recording—because there *weren't* any men. This whole fictitious story was all one big lie. When Channel 3 News asked the Temple Terrace police spokesperson to comment, he had this to say: 'During the course of this investigation, it was discovered the minor girl fabricated the story of the attempted abduction. The case is considered closed. The State Attorney is still reviewing the possibility of bringing up charges against the girl for filing a false police report.'"

The shot cut back to the reporter walking down the sidewalk toward the Eastins' house. "Normally, that would be the end of the story," the reporter said. "The media is required by law not to disclose personal information on minors involved in a crime. However, the girl at the center of this case reached out to Channel 3 News via our website. The kids at her school discovered she was the one who had cried wolf and started cyberbullying her. In a post on our website, she wrote about the bullying. She's agreed to talk to us on camera to tell her side of the story."

Wallace cringed, waiting for the ambush. The news channel was known more for its sensationalist journalism rather than their journalistic integrity. He couldn't understand what would've possessed Maddy to willingly let herself be fed to the wolves. Then again, most sheep—especially teenagers—thought fame was the answer to all their problems. He figured in her mind a glowing news segment would be a way to get back into the good graces of her classmates. Even more inexcusable, to his opinion, was Lily Eastin's role in letting her daughter go through with it.

Wallace watched as a side shot of the reporter and Maddy appeared on the screen. When the camera panned out, it captured their meager furnishings. "Maddy Eastin. It is so good to meet you. I'm glad you reached out to us about your situation. I understand you want to talk about the cyberbullying attack launched against you by the kids at your school, is that right?"

Maddy nodded and then cleared her throat. "Yes, yes I do."

(34)
MADDY EASTIN

Maddy sat shell-shocked, watching the news story unfold on the small television set in their living room. She knew what was coming. She'd lived it only twenty-six hours earlier, but somehow watching it on the screen was like experiencing it for the first time. She watched herself walk down the sidewalk to the bus stop, and for a moment she admired the confident stride. She wanted to warn the girl on the screen to keep walking, not to come back to the house, to the ambush that was awaiting her. As the report continued, Maddy finally got her chance to hear what Alex Sanchez had said while filming outside her front door.

"Quick wit saved the girl."

Maddy liked the sound of that. Everything seemed to be working out fine—until the footage of the security recording from that nosy neighbor's house played on screen.

Miss Larson didn't tell me they would show that!

"Uh-oh." Lily placed a hand over her mouth. Her eyes were wide with disbelief.

Her mom had been the last person Maddy had wanted to share this with, but that was before the interview. Now that Maddy knew the outcome, she was glad Aunt Emma hadn't gotten back to her.

I couldn't have handled sitting beside her, watching her have the same reaction that Mom is having now.

This was the first time she felt relief that both Aunt Emma and her dad had a habit of ignoring her requests.

Maybe they won't watch the show.

Maddy turned back to the TV just as her living room filled the screen. She'd been right. No amount of scrubbing could have wiped away the house's ugliness. She bit the inside of her lip, trying to hold back her emotions.

I can't lose it now. Mom will turn off the TV and insist we discuss my feelings. I can't handle one more "pep talk."

Maddy had already endured three since the taping. She knew she had to hold it together, had to finish watching the interview to see if it would be as bad as she remembered.

"I understand you want to talk about the cyberbullying attack launched against you by the kids at your school, is that right?"

"Yes, yes I do."

Maddy was shocked at how she looked on the screen. Makeup she'd spent so much time applying looked bright and garish. Pimples she'd thought hidden seemed to scream, "Look at me!" She couldn't take her eyes off the large one planted on the side of her nose. Then Alex Sanchez's profile appeared back on the screen, discussing the issue of cyberbullying.

"We'll definitely get to that, but first I have to ask, what possessed you to make up such a horrendous lie about someone trying to abduct you?"

"What?" Maddy remembered shaking her head in disbelief at the turn the interview had taken.

"The story about two men abducting you. It was all a lie, right? Your neighbor brought video evidence forward that proves you made the entire story up. What would drive you to make a false accusation?"

"I . . . I . . ." Maddy hadn't been able to remember the words she'd so painstakingly crafted just hours earlier. This was supposed to be *her* moment, her big TV debut.

Why wasn't I able to pull it together?

"I didn't mean for it to go as far as it did. I didn't think—"

"You didn't think the police would be called? Come on, Maddy.

You ran into the street, wildly waving your arms to get your bus to stop and . . . what? You didn't think the police would get involved? You didn't think they would try to hunt down the men you described as trying to abduct you from your bus stop? Which part did you not think about?"

"Nooo." Maddy cringed as she heard the whine in her voice. It made her look like a toddler who wasn't getting her way. "My dad walked out five months ago. It's been tough not seeing him every day. I haven't even talked to him on the phone. I only wanted him to get back. I didn't think everything would snowball so fast, would blow up into such a big deal. I just thought my dad would get a phone call from my mom about it, and he would come home. You know, to see how I was doing."

"And did he?"

Maddy watched as her television double clammed up. Her vocal cords had closed off as she tried to stave off the tears. She shook her head, looking away from Alex's searing gaze.

"Tell me what happened when you found out that the Temple Terrace police discovered you made up the story."

Maddy watched herself arch an eyebrow. Dead air filled the room.

Alex jumped back in, following up with another question. "Describe the scene when you were told there was video footage of that morning at the bus stop."

"A detective showed it to me and my mom at City Hall. We'd gone for an update on the case, and that's when he told us they'd discovered a neighbor had recorded the whole thing."

"And?" Alex asked.

"And it was tough to watch. Embarrassing."

"What does your mom have to say about all this?"

Maddy had glanced over at her mom, standing against the wall. On the screen, it seemed like Maddy had just looked away, trying to think of an answer to the reporter's question. In actuality, she had stared at her mom's bowed head, feeling like such a disappointment.

"My mom understands."

Alex seemed visibly annoyed with her short answers.

Good. It serves you right.

Maddy leaned closer to the TV, knowing the next part would shine a better light on her. She had finally been able to get her bearings, remembered what she'd meant to say earlier: "I'm sorry for lying about the two men. I'm sorry that the police wasted their time looking for two fictional guys. I'd take it back if I could. I swear. I would've come clean if the police had brought in a suspect. I wouldn't have let them charge an innocent man with something he didn't do. Things never got that far though, and now, I guess, I'm asking for forgiveness. I've suffered enough at the hands of my classmates. I've been teased, taunted, and bullied enough."

Instead of airing her passionate apology, however, it just cut to Alex asking, "Tell me how the kids at your school found out you were the girl in the attempted abduction case?"

"Wait a minute!" Maddy shouted as she jumped up from the couch. "That's not what happened next! They cut my whole part out!" She looked at her mom. "Why would they do that?"

Lily sat on the couch next to her, slowly shaking her head. When she didn't answer, Maddy sank back down beside her.

The Maddy on the screen said, "I confided in a good friend who lives down the street. She was really there for me, very supportive. She told a few people at school, and it eventually got around. But the kids would've found out anyway. The ones riding the bus knew something was going on when it stayed at my stop to wait until the police arrived that Monday morning."

Even though Sabrina had betrayed Maddy's confidence, she'd answered the question in such a way that she hoped would endear her to Sabrina again, rather than make the girl angrier.

"Admit it, Maddy. Didn't you enjoy soaking up the attention everyone lathered on you? How is it you think you have the right to cry foul now that your friends are angry about being duped?"

"Wait a minute—"

"Wouldn't *you* be mad if someone played on your sympathies with a bald-faced lie?"

"No. I mean, yes. Yes, I'd be upset, but I would never bully someone because of it. The kids at school called me nasty names, tripped me in the hallway, and singled me out on the Internet. I'm sure you've read all the hateful things they said about me online. Nothing I did deserves that kind of vicious attack."

"It's true there were hundreds of comments on our website from people chiming in on this story." Alex turned to face the camera and gave the viewers the website address so they could read the comments themselves. Then he turned his attention back to Maddy. "That's why we wanted to talk to you today. To set the story straight."

Maddy couldn't understand why they'd cut another of her answers short. After talking about not deserving the vicious attacks, she had gone on to say the reason she'd agreed to the interview in the first place was to help other kids who were being bullied. She said she'd made a mistake by dreaming up the abduction story, but that it'd opened her eyes to the issues of bullying and cyberbullying. She said she'd learned just how nasty kids could be toward one another, especially in an anonymous forum. That had been the best answer she'd given all day, and none of it was shown.

The segment cut back to Alex standing outside her house again. "Maddy Eastin was upset her father had walked out on the family. She wanted him back so badly she concocted a story in the hopes he'd come running home. That didn't happen. Instead, Maddy became entangled in a web of her own lies. She's learned a hard life lesson: actions have consequences."

After a dramatic pause where Alex adjusted his tie, he said, "We wanted to find out what others thought about Maddy's deception. Her mother, Lily Eastin, declined to be interviewed, so we met with some neighbors."

The old know-it-all from down the street came on the screen next, talking into Alex's microphone after he asked her what she thought about the girl who made up the wild story. Maddy stood up to leave the room, feeling numb to everything that was playing out before her. Then Sabrina Marquez's face filled the screen. Her bouncy, shampoo-commercial hair seemed to move in slow motion.

Knowing Sabrina, she'll get her own reality TV show out of this.

"Maddy Eastin wants us to feel sorry for her," Sabrina said. "Like *she's* the victim. She's just upset everyone found out what sort of a person she really is. I'm not going to apologize for expressing my opinions online. That's what the first amendment is all about, right?"

Alex finished the report with the camera trained on him. Maddy noticed his smile once again failed to reach his eyes. She finally recognized him for the type of man he truly was—a sleazy journalist trying to build his career off the backs of regular people just trying to get their stories out there. And he had a network behind him, so he could spin his reports any way he liked.

"Viewers, tell us online what you think," Alex said. "Log on to the Channel 3 News website and weigh in or leave us a Twitter message at #News3Bullying. Did the kids at Maddy Eastin's school have a right to be angry, or has online posting of opinions gone too far, crossing the line into cyberbullying?"

In a daze, Maddy realized her mom had put her hand on her arm. She shrugged it off and stood up. She trudged down the hall, unable to comprehend the words following her as the mounting pressure in her head began to block them out.

She stopped by the bathroom. The razor in the medicine cabinet would work far better than a fork.

(35)
HANK FRY

"Hank? You okay?"

Hank felt someone shake his shoulder. The last thing he remembered was sitting down next to Daniel to watch cartoons on the couch. "What?"

"You fell asleep again. You were moaning. I thought you were having a bad dream."

Hank rubbed his hands over his face to wake himself up. He'd decided to try and stay awake after working all night Saturday. It was tough getting through the day with no sleep, but he thought it would be worth it if it allowed him to get back on schedule Monday morning. Although it seemed even Sponge Bob's annoying laugh couldn't keep him from drifting off. "I need sugar. I'm gonna grab a drink. You want something, Small Fry?"

Daniel grabbed his can of Mountain Dew. "Yeah. Mine's almost empty."

Hank looked at the two cans sitting on the end table next to Daniel. "On second thought, it looks like you've had enough, don't you think?"

"You sound like a nagging mom." Daniel laughed at his own joke.

Hank cringed, thinking that was the last comparison he ever wanted made about him. Their mom had been the queen of nags. She could get away with the bitching and moaning as long as their dad wasn't around, but if he heard her, Earl Fry would sock her one in the mouth.

Hank walked to the kitchen to grab a drink, marveling that no matter how much their mother drowned her boys in criticisms, Daniel had still loved her in the way only ten-year-old sons could. He was the only one who'd shed any tears the day they'd found her hanging in the bedroom—the same day she'd discovered Hank in the barn with Rosalina. After she had walked in on the two of them, she'd run back into the house. Hank had finished cleaning up in the barn and then had gone inside to have a talk with her. He didn't want her squealing to Earl about what she'd seen.

His mom had locked herself in her bedroom and wouldn't answer, no matter how much Hank had pleaded with her. Even when his begging turned to anger, she still wouldn't open the door. Kicking it in wasn't an option. After all, his dad slept in that room, so how could Hank have explained a cracked door? He'd eventually gone downstairs and rummaged through the junk drawers until he found a small screwdriver. Back upstairs, he was able to pop the lock.

When he opened the door, he found his mom hanging from a rope tied around the ceiling fan. Her toes barely cleared the floor. Hank stood in the doorway and watched as her body spasmed and she clawed at the rope around her neck. He felt nothing, at least no emotion that could be construed as sorrow. He was more annoyed knowing he would now be forced to pick up the slack around the house by taking over laundry and cooking meals.

A lone piece of paper sitting on the nightstand caught his attention. Hank walked around her body and picked up the note.

After what I saw today, I can no longer keep lying to myself. My oldest son, Hank, has turned into a monster. Try not to judge him too harshly, though, as it's not his fault. He's been molded into the person he is today by the Devil himself—his father. I've slept beside that savage for the last nineteen years, wondering when I'd finally succumb to death at his hands. Though my own fingers tied the knot around my neck today, he slipped the noose over it years ago.

> *I can't go on pretending not to know what's been happening inside our barn. There's a caged girl in there, a plaything for the males of this household. She wasn't the first resident of that cage either. I've heard faint screams before, only I discounted them, explained them away as sounds of wind screeching around the corners of the house.*
>
> *If there is a God, he will punish me for turning a blind eye. Yet, how can there be a greater power that allows so many girls to suffer at the hands of men? I just ask that the police find a safe home for Daniel. He's been through so much already. I tried to protect him as best I could . . .*

Hank bristled as he remembered that line in the note, once again feeling the anger at the thought that his mom had believed she ever acted as Daniel's protector.

That stupid cow! I was the one who kept him safe, the one who jumped in front of Earl Fry's fist to save Daniel's face. That woman had never taken a blow for Daniel in her sad, pathetic life.

Hank opened the fridge and grabbed a Mountain Dew. He thought about when his dad had gotten home and Hank had showed him the scene in the bedroom.

His dad's only reaction was to say, "Shit!" Then he'd rushed out to the barn. Hank had assumed he wanted to get rid of any evidence of Rosalina. It had fallen to Hank to tell Daniel about their mom's death.

He'd been the one to sit with Daniel after the cops took their mom's body away. The one to console him all the nights he woke up from nightmares of terrifying images of her trying to claw her way out of the body bag. Daniel had wasted too many tears on a woman who was never strong enough to be their savior. A woman who took the coward's way out and left her sons alone to be raised by a monster.

Only Hank had ever read his mom's suicide note. He'd stuffed it in his pocket that day, memorized each word over the next year. The letter had gone on and on about how she'd been the one trying to save her boys from the monster living in her house.

What a crock.

"Can you bring the bag of chips when you come back?" Daniel called out to Hank from the living room, forcing Hank back into the present moment.

He was still standing at the kitchen counter with the unopened soda can squeezed in his hand. He finally acknowledged the pain the cold had inflicted on his palm and set it down. "No," Hank answered. "The chips will ruin your dinner."

"Okay, Mom."

Hank tucked the can of Mountain Dew under his arm and rubbed his hands together. Heading back toward the couch, he wondered if their lives would have turned out differently if their mom hadn't committed suicide. Hank doubted he would've been any better off. He'd already been headed down the path chosen for him after witnessing one girl bound with leather and bleeding on a worktable and another caged like a wild animal.

The old memories called to him like wolves howling in his ear, begging him to let go and finally embrace his true self. How Hank wanted to shed his outer skin, the one that fit nicely into polite society, and to run with those wolves, to follow the scent of blood. The urge was growing stronger by the day.

Hank had successfully resisted his urges, but more and more often, he asked himself why. Why was he denying himself? The answer was getting harder to remember. It wasn't because he thought he'd go to hell. Church had never been a real priority in the Fry household. No, the only thing still holding Hank back was his need to preserve Daniel's innocence. And lately, it seemed that last holdout was hanging by a string—one very frayed string.

Hank sank down on the couch as another episode of *SpongeBob SquarePants* started up. Daniel sang along to the opening song.

Hank looked at the clock on the DVD player. "Aw, man. Is it five thirty already? I missed the news."

"Don't worry. I recorded it for you." Daniel grabbed the remote off the floor and pushed buttons to start the program.

"Thanks, Small Fry."

"No problemo." Daniel took a last swallow of Dew and grabbed a Superman comic book lying on the coffee table.

Hank stretched out and put his feet up. His big toe stuck out of a hole in one of his white socks. He waved it back and forth rhythmically during the musical intro to the show. Hank barely listened to Karl Hurley's first report. His mind was on Joanna Huffing. She was the reason he watched the Channel 3 News whenever he was home. He couldn't stand that pretty boy Hurley, but he could watch Joanna all day long.

He'd met her once, at a local steak place where she was waiting tables during a benefit for some cancer organization. He had paid the hostess twenty bucks to sit him and Daniel in her section. Hank couldn't take his eyes off her long, blonde locks the entire night. Much to Daniel's delight, Hank even splurged and ordered dessert for the two of them. Anything to keep them in the restaurant longer. The picture Daniel had managed to snap of him and Joanna was even in a frame on the wall.

The weather report caught Hank's attention. It highlighted a thunderstorm due to hit the area later that evening—from the sounds of it, a real doozy. Hank wondered if the job site would be a washout the next day. He could hardly wait for the rainy season to be over next month. Every year, his pocketbook took a hit when, invariably, he and his crew would be out of work for days on end.

After the weather, Joanna's image filled the screen. She seemed to smile just for Hank. Her green eyes twinkled like they held a secret she wanted to share. Too quickly she handed the broadcast over to some new guy airing a special segment. He'd just started working for the news organization, but Hank didn't care for him. He thought the guy had a look in his eyes, like he'd sell his own daughter to get ahead in the world. But at least he wasn't some pretty boy like Hurley.

Wait, what's this?

The reporter was talking to a fifteen-year-old girl who said some guys tried to abduct her from a bus stop. "She told police one of the men came up behind her, covered her mouth with one hand, and scooped her up around the waist with the other. Quick wit saved the girl. She fought off the attacker by stomping on his foot and running away. Then she frantically waved down her school bus as it turned the corner onto her street. A harrowing tale . . . maybe. Or maybe not."

Hank leaned forward, watching the screen intently as a security camera recording of the night-vision surveillance played. He was confused at first, when he didn't see any guys.

Why would this dumbass reporter broadcast the recording if it didn't capture the guys' image?

The reporter came back on the screen, standing in front of an ugly pink house. "No, folks, you didn't miss it. The men this girl reported trying to snatch her from the bus stop never showed up in the recording— because there *weren't* any men. This whole fictitious story was all one big lie."

When the face of Maddy Eastin came on the screen, Hank swallowed hard.

The girl. That's the girl.

He could feel the frayed string that had been hanging together all these years stretching, threatening to snap.

He watched as the reporter grilled her about lying.

What an asshole.

She looked crestfallen when she tried to explain why she'd made up the story. How her dad had walked out, how she hoped almost being kidnapped would get him to come home. Then she talked about being bullied by the kids at her school once they'd discovered she'd lied about the abduction story.

When Sabrina Marquez came on the screen, Hank didn't even notice. His mind's eye still held firm to the mental picture of Maddy Eastin.

It's . . . what's the word? Serendipity. Yes, that's it. Now it all makes sense. Why I've been holding out for so many years. Why I've been waiting.

Hank had never been allowed to touch Rosalina in the way he truly yearned to. And how many times had he dreamed about what he would have done to the girl on the table had he stumbled upon her alone in the barn?

Hank rewound the recording of the news report and watched it again. Maddy Eastin and the girl who'd been strapped to his dad's worktable so many years ago had the same strawberry-blonde hair color, containing a hint of red, and the same dusting of freckles across the nose.

He paused the recording so Maddy's face filled the screen. As he sat back and imagined all the fun he could have with her, Hank swore he could hear the sound of the frayed string finally snapping.

PART 8
MONDAY, SEPTEMBER 28

(36)
LILY EASTIN

The screaming match Monday morning between Lily and her daughter had gone on for what seemed like hours. It felt like one long continuation of the previous night's fight.

"You *will* go to school this morning, young lady, and that's final." Lily was done coddling Maddy. "You've got to start facing your problems. You can't run away every time the going gets tough."

"Clichés, that's what you're giving me? 'When the going gets tough, the tough get going.' Great idea, Mom. Next time the kids shout that I'm a lying whore, I'll just say, 'Sticks and stones may break my bones, but names will never hurt me.' I'm sure that'll stop them."

"It's *one* news program. At five o'clock on a Sunday night. How many teenagers are watching the news on their day off from school?"

"You can bet their parents watched. All over town, ears perked up the second they heard the teaser promoting an exclusive interview with the Temple Terrace girl at the center of a scandal. The damn station's been running promos for the spot since Saturday night."

Lily didn't have the energy to reprimand Maddy for her language. "Go to school today, and I promise . . . I *promise*, I will get a hold of your father. I'll make sure he spends time with you."

"Like that'll work."

"This time it will. I promise not to screw it up, not to say anything that will antagonize him. I realize now how much you need to see him. If he dodges my calls, I don't care if I have to fly out to Sacramento to one of his stupid meetings. I will make this happen for you."

Lily's stomach lurched when she saw the look of hope that filled her daughter's eyes.

How will I ever make good on that promise?

Lily grabbed her purse off the kitchen counter and fished out a couple of pills, swallowed them dry. She wondered if she pull this off? She didn't know how much more disappointment her daughter could take.

Without another word, Maddy turned and headed down the hallway.

"Don't think I'm going to put up with a repeat performance of last night, young lady!" The previous evening, Maddy had locked her bedroom door and turned up the stereo full blast. "You'd better be ready for school in ten minutes!"

Lily looked around the empty living room, wondering what to do next. She'd gotten up early to make sure Maddy went to school, but she didn't need to be to work for another four and a half hours. She groaned at the thought of having to get in the shower, put on a fresh pair of clothes, and head to the craft store to pretend like her life wasn't falling apart.

After the segment aired last night, Detective Wallace had called to ask what Lily had been thinking by letting Maddy appear on TV. Of course, he hadn't used those exact words, but he might as well have. It would have saved a whole lot of beating around the bush.

He'd said it was the worst thing they could have done. The case had faded from the public spotlight, so the State Attorney hadn't felt pressured to file charges against Maddy. But he couldn't promise what would happen now.

He'd demanded to know how Lily could even attempt to justify why she'd allowed Maddy to do the interview. At the time, her instincts had screamed at her, telling her what a horrible idea caving in to Maddy's pleas would be. But Lily just wanted all the months of ugly words and hateful looks to disappear and to once again make her daughter happy. To bring a smile to the face that so often wore a look of misery.

Lily knew how difficult it was when you felt like you had no control over your life. And right now, Maddy had none. Every decision her parents made had been thrust upon her.

Who am I to deny my daughter a chance at taking control back? If Maddy hadn't done it this way, she would have just found a more destructive alternative.

Lily hadn't seen the point of trying to explain herself to Detective Wallace. He already thought she was a terrible mother, so what did it matter? Since her actions had earned her the bad mother badge, she figured she might as well accept the shame of wearing it.

Harder, though, was the call that had come five minutes later from Emma Parker. The woman didn't even pretend niceties. She'd gone right for the jugular.

"How on God's green earth could you think subjecting a fifteen-year-old girl to a pack of glorified paparazzi would be a good idea?"

"Hello to you too, Emma. I take it you saw Maddy on the news."

"You bet your ass I did. So answer me. Why'd you let her do it?"

"Don't you dare judge me. You haven't been around. You don't know what it's been like. The hell Maddy's been going through. Yes, she made a mistake lying about the abduction, but you have no idea what those kids in that school have put her through because of it."

Lily had wondered if she should tell Emma about the dog shit those asshole kids dumped all over Maddy's head. The school counselor had called to inform Lily about the incident, but she knew her daughter would be mortified if she discovered her mother had found out, much less turned around and told the story to Emma.

"You should've seen how Maddy pleaded with me," Lily said. "She only wanted a chance to set the record straight. To give a word of encouragement to other kids who are getting bullied."

"I didn't see anything like that in the news report."

"Of course not. Those bastards cut out all the parts that portrayed

Maddy in a good light. They left out her heartfelt apology for making up the story, as well as her plea to all the bullies out there, asking them to stop their hurtful behavior. Instead, that damn news reporter turned it all around on Maddy and ended up *leading* the group of bullies by taking his own shots."

"I don't know what to say, Lily."

"An apologetic teenager doesn't do much for the ratings. They edited the piece to make Maddy look like a self-absorbed brat. How can they get away with this? Don't we have any recourse?"

"Sure, if you want to fight a court battle against their team of lawyers. You could sue the station for libel, but going into this thing they knew you wouldn't. I'm sorry, but one look at your house told them you didn't have the financial means to take them on. They could report anything they wanted and not worry about any blowback."

"Aarrgghh!" Lily cried out, angry at the crappy hand life had dealt her. She fought the tears welling up. "I thought I was doing what was best for Maddy. With everything that's been happening these past few months, she's been stripped powerless. She begged me to let her tell her side of the story. I thought taking control over the situation would be a good step toward rebuilding her self-esteem. Instead, it landed the final crushing blow."

She'd spent another five minutes on the phone with Emma, then begged off. Emotionally drained, she couldn't deal with person after person lining up to remind her of what she'd always feared—that she wasn't cut out to be a mother.

Lily looked at the digital clock on the end table—6:28 a.m. Almost fifteen minutes had passed since Maddy had gone back into her bedroom. Lily walked down the hallway, preparing herself for another battle when Maddy walked out of her room dressed for school and with her backpack slung over her shoulder. Without a word, she walked past Lily and out the front door.

Guess Tom was right about me.

Over the years, he'd repeatedly questioned Lily's parenting decisions. If she grounded Maddy for getting a bad grade, he'd say she was being too harsh. If she gave her a pass for coming home late, Tom would give Lily grief for letting Maddy off too easy. Lily had become so confused and self-conscious, it had been easier to step away and let him take over the discipline. The more she thought about it, the more she realized backing off had caused her to resort to her own mother's parenting style. Over the past couple of years, she'd let Maddy grow up on autopilot. Now it seemed the plane was about to crash.

(37)
EMMA PARKER

Emma wanted to get a hold of Maddy early to set up an outing for them later that evening. It might give the girl something to look forward to, make the transition of having to go back to class a little easier. She knew she had a tight window to catch her before school, so Emma had set her alarm for 6:30 a.m. She wiped the sleep out of her eyes while waiting for Maddy to answer the phone.

"Hello?" Maddy said. "Aunt Emma, is that you?"

Emma couldn't stifle the yawn rising up. Instead of saying hello, she yawned in Maddy's ear. "Sorry. I don't know how you do it, getting up this early." Emma normally didn't have to go into work until nine o'clock.

"Not willingly, that's for sure." Maddy's voice sounded sad, and there was a heavy dose of anger mixed in. "What do you need, Aunt Emma?"

"I know you're mad at me. I've been making lots of promises lately and not following through on any of them. I'm sorry we couldn't get together last night. I know you wanted to hang out and watch TV at my place." Emma thought it best to keep the conversation light. She didn't want to talk about the interview over the phone.

"Oh, that's okay," Maddy said hastily. "I know you're busy."

"I have been. But that's no excuse. Do you mind if I come over after school today? Hang out, perhaps take you out to dinner?"

Maddy didn't answer right away. Emma wondered if she was too angry to accept her apology, or if her hesitation had more to do with Maddy's reluctance to talk about the interview. Emma decided to push a little harder.

"What about Antonio's? It's your favorite."

"Okay, I guess."

"Great." Emma said with more enthusiasm than she felt. It was time they had a hard conversation. Emma was always telling herself she would've been a better mother than Lily. It was time to prove it.

"I gotta go," Maddy said. "I see my bus coming."

"Sure. See you later. And Maddy—keep your chin up."

After Emma had watched last night's television interview, she'd raged, pacing tracks into the carpet. She'd picked up the phone to call Lily, but Ben had grabbed the phone away from her.

"Hey, what'd you do that for?" she asked him.

"Take a minute to cool down first. Shouts and accusations over the phone ended your friendship in the first place."

Emma didn't want to listen to rational suggestions. She wanted Ben to jump on her bandwagon and help rip Lily apart. Emma would never have let Maddy end up in this situation.

Like a dog with a bone, Emma wouldn't let it go. She grabbed the phone back from Ben and called Lily, guns blazing. All through the conversation, Emma had held on tight to her anger. Until Lily explained Maddy's original intent about doing the news report. Emma couldn't fault the girl for trying to stop the bullying. The Eastins had never had any interaction with the media. They didn't realize what jackals they could be. She finally understood that if Lily had any inkling of what was going to happen, she would've refused Maddy's pleas to be on TV.

Emma also realized she couldn't lay the blame solely on Lily—she was also culpable. Through the whole ordeal, she hadn't been there for Maddy, hadn't been the shoulder the girl needed to lean on. Emma tried to rationalize that thought away, telling herself that Maddy had been pulling away from her ever since she'd reached thirteen, had gravitated closer to her friends and further from the adults in her life. Emma had used the excuse of normal teenage behavior to spend less and less time with the girl.

She admitted, though, that even this past week with everything that had gone on, she still hadn't put forth much effort to reach out, only a few phone calls here and there. Emma's lack of attention contributed to Maddy's current position at the center of a media circus. Channel 3 was just the tip of the iceberg. More stations would surely follow their lead, trying to get the Eastins on camera again by handing out promises of letting them set the record straight.

Emma had asked how she could help Lily last night when they talked.

"Can you come over to our house after school?" Lily asked. "I have to work until seven. With the fragile state Maddy's in, I don't want to leave her alone."

Emma had taken a quick inventory of what she'd thought her Monday might look like. She'd just finished wrapping a big red bow on her murder case, so except for some final finishing touches on paperwork, her schedule looked remarkably clear. She still had two open cases she was working on, but things could be rearranged.

"Sure. What time?"

"She usually texts me around three to tell me she's gotten home all right. Is that good for you?"

"Sure. She and I can hang out at the house and talk, then go out for dinner. If she doesn't have a ton of homework, we won't hurry home. If that's okay with you? It'll also give you time to decompress."

Emma heard the relief in Lily's sigh. She was probably thankful to finally have help, an ally in the fight to save Maddy.

(38)
HANK FRY

Hank sat in the darkness of his van, watching as the strawberry blonde left her house. Last night, he'd scrutinized the news report and researched Maddy online to find out everything he could about her. Her house hadn't been too difficult to find either—it was the only pink one on the street.

He took a swallow of his lukewarm coffee, then resumed his thumb drumming against the steering wheel. He knew he should be exhausted since he'd only gotten six hours of sleep in the last forty-eight, but he was wired. He couldn't remember when he'd felt so alive. Every nerve ending crackled with electricity. The howling of the wolves had finally stopped echoing through his mind. Hank had joined the pack and was now on the prowl.

He watched Maddy walk down her front porch steps and hop off the second-to-last step to avoid a puddle. She shifted her backpack to the other shoulder, then reached around and fished her phone out of her back pocket. Bathed in the murky glow of her front porch light, he watched her look at the phone. She eventually put it up to her ear and continued walking down the sidewalk. Shiny rhinestone hearts were emblazoned on the back pockets of her jeans. He smiled when he realized she looked even more petite in person than on camera.

He'd been sitting in his van since 5:30 a.m., watching the neighborhood. His vehicle blended in well in the blue-collar area.

Nothing to see here, folks, just another work van parked on the street.

A few neighbors had rolled out their garbage cans to the curb, then jumped in their vehicles in a morning rush. No one had even giving him a passing glance. Some had already missed the 6:15 a.m. garbage truck that had come barreling by minutes earlier. They'd have to wait until Thursday to try their luck again. Hank had researched everything, leaving nothing to chance.

Fate had been on his side today. Last night's drenching rains ensured hazardous conditions at the job site. He and his crew would be off until things dried up.

The block was quiet. Maddy stopped at the corner bus stop. She was the only one standing there, the lone student—a fact consistent with the surveillance video shown on TV the prior evening. From a distance, Hank could only make out the girl's silhouette; the two street lights closest to the bus stop were burned out.

A roar of a bus's diesel engine rushed past him. Hank checked his watch—6:34 a.m. A tight window.

Can I pull it off?

The bus opened its doors and swallowed up Maddy, shuttling her off to school. Hank continued studying the neighborhood. He couldn't risk his van's plates getting picked up on Paul Gleason's surveillance camera. He'd have to make his move before Maddy reached the perimeter of the guy's yard. That meant he'd have to swerve to the other side of the road.

From the moment he'd seen Maddy's face on his television screen, the idea running through his head had consumed him. He had to work out every minute detail, plan for every possible scenario, or he'd get caught. Yet, do it right, and no one would ever know he had the girl. Hank could do whatever he wanted to her. High risk. High reward. And Maddy Eastin was definitely one reward he'd waited fourteen years for.

(39)
MADDY EASTIN

After school that afternoon, Maddy shuffled down the center aisle of the bus, trying to ignore the names being hurled at her. She adjusted her backpack as she stepped off and trudged toward her house. When she was almost home, she lifted her head. Her Aunt Emma sat on the porch's damp concrete steps. She stopped midstride.

"You showed up," Maddy said.

"Of course I came. I told you I'd be here."

"So where were you all the other times?" Maddy defiantly crossed her arms in front of her.

"You're right. I deserve that." Emma stood up, wiping off the back of her pants. "I could tell you that I've been busy, and I have, but that would just sound like one more lame excuse. Selfishness is the only thing I can claim. I'm sorry, Maddy. I've been more concerned with my job and my own life than with what you've been going through. If you can forgive me, I promise to do better. I want you to know that when you need me, you can reach out and I'll answer. From now on, I'll be there for you."

Maddy's mouth gaped open.

Maybe I do have someone in my corner now, someone who won't let me down again.

Unable to find her voice, Maddy just smiled and nodded.

"How was school today?" Emma asked.

Maddy's stomach dropped. She'd thought the day everyone found out that she'd lied about the attempted abduction was bad, that it couldn't get any worse. She was wrong.

She hurriedly climbed the steps and unlocked the front door. "I don't want to talk about it." She dumped her backpack inside the house and spun around before Emma even had a chance to move from her step. "Let's get out of here," Maddy said, locking the door. "Home is the last place I want to be right now."

"Where do you want to go? You name it, my treat."

"What about the mall?"

"Perfect." Emma put her arm around Maddy and pulled her in close. They walked side by side until they reached the car.

Once they were both buckled in, Emma asked, "Which mall?"

Maddy was surprised to be given a choice. She'd figured they would just head over to University Mall since it was closest, but given the choice, she knew where she wanted to go. "International Mall."

She studied Aunt Emma's face, trying to read her reaction. She knew sometimes adults asked for opinions they really didn't want, but it looked like Aunt Emma was happy with her selection.

"Sounds fun. I haven't been there in a while."

The few times Maddy had been to the posh mall, she'd been awestruck at the beauty of all the expensive shops. She knew she couldn't afford to buy anything there, but she loved going and running her fingers over the soft fabrics of all the fine clothes. She and Aunt Emma could pretend to be buyers, try on their favorites.

"Mom never wants to go there. Even if she has the time, she says she hates walking around looking at everything she can't buy."

"It's tough to go from being able to afford whatever you want to pinching pennies in order to make ends meet at the end of the month. It must be hard on you too."

Maddy shrugged. She picked at a hangnail until a droplet of blood surfaced. She was mesmerized by how the rich red color contrasted with her pale skin.

"Come on," Emma said, giving her a playful elbow in the arm. "I know things have been tough, both at school and home. You can talk to me."

"What good will it do?" Maddy turned her head and stared out the side window. "You can't change anything."

"True, but I can listen. Sometimes it's nice to have someone listen."

Maddy continued looking out the window.

It would be nice. Neither of my parents want to listen, and I don't have any friends I can trust.

Maddy sighed. She decided to take advantage of riding in the car to be able to talk without having to make eye contact.

"Did you . . . did you see me on TV?" Maddy asked.

"I did."

"And?"

"I thought Channel 3 was wrong for taking advantage of you."

Maddy turned toward Emma, shocked at what she'd said.

"Your mom told me how the news station cut out the pieces where you apologized for making up the abduction story and where you made a plea for kids being bullied."

"I can't believe they tricked me like that!"

Emma glanced at her, then back at the road. "When you agreed to the interview, what did you hope to accomplish?"

Tears welled up in Maddy's eyes. "Once the kids at school found out I lied, I just couldn't take it anymore. I had to do something. I thought it was fate when Miss Larson called asking me to be on their program. Like it was a sign. I mean, how often does a kid like me get asked to do a show like that? I tried to come up with good answers, but instead I came off sounding like an idiot."

"You didn't sound like an idiot, Maddy. Cut yourself some slack. Do you have any idea what you've been through these last five months? Living through a divorce, dealing with one parent whose entire worldview has shifted, and another one who's disappeared from your life. In my job,

I've seen plenty of grown women buckle under less pressure than what you've gone through."

"Really?"

"Yes. There's always an adjustment period after a life-altering change. The trick is to learn how to talk about what you're going through, to express your feelings. Tamping them down inside won't work for long. They always find a way of leaking out. Have you talked to *anybody* about what you've been going through?"

Maddy shook her head.

"See? When you don't open up, those feelings come out in destructive ways. Hence making up stories, looking for attention in the wrong way. In the future, if things feel overwhelming, try talking to your mom."

"Seriously?"

"What?"

"The Ice Queen? She's so screwed up herself, she can't see over her own mountain of shit to even consider helping me with mine."

"Maddy . . ."

"I'm serious, Aunt Emma. Whenever I try to talk to her, it starts out good but then . . . she says something that sets me off. Her condescending attitude drives me nuts. If she calls me 'young lady' one more time, I swear I'm going to flip out."

"Try to give her a break? Her husband bailed, and now she's the sole bread winner. That's a lot of stress to shoulder. No matter what mistakes she might make, she still shows up. Every day. She's there for you, imperfect as she may be. That should count for something. Because sometimes mothers *do* leave. Sometimes the stress is so overwhelming they walk out on their own kid."

Maddy looked down in her lap. She felt bad for Aunt Emma. Maddy may not have known all the details surrounding her aunt's childhood, but she knew Rose Parker had left her daughter.

Emma cleared her throat. "Until your mom acclimates to her new life, accepts her new reality, she may not be able to be there in the way you want her to. You might have to do some accepting of your own. Learn to let her be the person she is now, and love her despite her faults."

"Easy for you to say." Maddy couldn't help the dig.

How can Aunt Emma tell me to accept Mom when the woman can't even take her own advice? Four years is a long time to hold a grudge.

"Okay, okay, you're right. I didn't say it would be *easy*, only that you'll have to try if you want to make the relationship with your mom work."

"How did you two become such close friends anyway? You guys seem so different."

Aunt Emma was quiet for a moment, seemingly lost in thought. Eventually she spoke, but her voice sounded funny. "I wish you could have met the girl your mother used to be. Her loyalty and dependability—those were the two things I valued most. You know how your Grandma Jackie is. She's a hard person to live with, but no matter how rough things got for Lily at home, she always had a sympathetic ear for me. I remember how inseparable we became the year my mother left. I wouldn't have gotten through it without her support."

"It doesn't even sound like the same person."

"Hard times have a way of changing people. You're still young, but you'll see. The year my mother walked out, my dad completely forgot about my birthday. I guess I can't blame him. I mean, that kind of thing was always mother's job—sending out birthday invitations, baking the cake.

"Lily saw how devastated I was—not only would my mother not be there to share my ninth birthday, but it had slipped Dad's mind too. After school, she gathered all the neighborhood kids and threw a surprise party for me in her backyard. Sure, we only had animal crackers instead of birthday cake and homemade gifts instead of store-bought presents, but to this day, I swear it was the best birthday I've ever had. It wasn't the details of the party that mattered. It was the effort Lily put in to make the day special. But truthfully, Maddy, there are hundreds of examples that demonstrate how much she valued our friendship."

"You sound like you still care. Why can't you take your own advice and accept Mom for the person she's become? Things would be so much better if you guys were friends again. You could hang out at the house. I'd be able to see you more."

"It's complica—"

"Just a minute, Aunt Emma." Maddy had felt her phone vibrate and took it out of her back pocket.

It was her mom. Maddy thought about ignoring the call, but noticed Aunt Emma's disapproving look. It was like she'd been reading Maddy's thoughts.

"Hi, Mom," Maddy said when she answered.

"Are you okay? You never texted me when you got home from school."

"Sorry. Aunt Emma was waiting for me at the house and I forgot. We're headed to the mall."

"That's great. You definitely sound happier than you did this morning. School mustn't have been too bad. See, I told you it would all work out."

Maddy didn't answer. She didn't want to get into another argument.

Breaking the silence first, her mom said she had some good news. "I got hold of your father this morning. He's coming over to see you tomorrow night."

"Seriously?" Maddy stomped her feet up and down on the car floor and let out a loud squeal.

"He said he'll be in town for a couple of days before he has to head off to Buffalo. He'll pick you up at seven."

"Wow, I didn't think you could pull it off. Thanks, Mom."

"Well, I'm glad you're happy. See you—"

Maddy hung up. She couldn't wait to tell Aunt Emma the awesome news. "Guess what?" Without waiting for an answer, Maddy said, "Dad's taking me out tomorrow night. I can't wait to see him. I wonder what I should wear?"

"Sounds like you need a new outfit. My treat."

"Really?"

"Of course."

Maddy felt like she was flying so high she'd need to be tethered to the car to keep from floating away. Her two most favorite people in the whole wide world had chosen to spend time with her. She just knew tomorrow was going to be the best day of her life.

PART 9
TUESDAY, SEPTEMBER 29

(40)
MADDY EASTIN

Maddy barely slept a wink. She'd kept waking up to look at the clock, hoping it was time to get out of bed. When the radio on her alarm began playing Pink's song "Blow Me One Last Kiss," she realized she must have dozed off.

She sprung out of bed, the lyrics still floating around in her mind. Normally, she'd agree with the singer's sentiment that it would be another shit day. But she vowed that nothing the kids might dish out at school would ruin her good mood. Her dad was coming to see her tonight. Maddy was certain that with enough coaxing, she'd be able to talk him into letting her live with him.

There was no time for a shower. She decided to skip it and take one later, when she got home. She'd want to look her best for tonight anyway. After brushing her teeth and then her hair, she gave herself one last look in the mirror. It'd have to do.

With no time to sit down and eat, Maddy grabbed a Pop-Tart and started searching for her backpack. She didn't want to miss her bus—it might give her mom an excuse to cancel her night out with Dad.

"Do you need help with something?" Lily asked in a sleep-filled voice.

Maddy told her she was looking for her backpack.

"Over by the door," Lily mumbled.

"Oh, right." She remembered dropping the bag on the floor yesterday before heading out with Aunt Emma.

"Do you want me to make you some breakfast?"

"Nah, I don't have time. Go back to sleep. You should get your rest."

Maddy pulled on her shoes, gathered her stuff, and opened the door.

"I love you, Maddy. I hope you know that."

"I know . . . Love you too, Mom."

Already wondering which new outfit she should wear later, Maddy shut the door behind her. When she hadn't been able to decide between two at the mall yesterday, Aunt Emma had generously offered to buy both. All four pieces mixed and matched well together, but it made the decision that much harder. Standing in front of her mirror last night, she'd tried on every combination.

As she walked toward her bus stop, Maddy noticed movement to her right. Goose bumps popped out on her arms. She swung around to see what had caught her eye—only old Miss Addie staring at her from behind the curtains.

Why is that old bat just standing there in the dark, looking out at the street? It's so creepy.

Maddy exhaled and continued walking toward her bus stop. She continued thinking about her outfit choices until she finally made a decision. The pale yellow—

(41)
LILY EASTIN

Knowing she'd be unable to fight her way back to sleep, Lily got up and started the coffee pot. She was still thinking about her conversation with Maddy.

How long has it been since I've heard those three words—I love you—come out of her mouth?

A simple sentiment, but one she'd taken for granted. She'd only missed it once her daughter had stopped saying it.

Perhaps the worst is behind us. Maybe all Maddy needs is to spend time with—

Lily turned her head at the sound of squealing tires. She rubbed the goose bumps on her forearms and walked over to the front window, pushing aside the sheer curtains. Nothing looked amiss.

Then she heard the rumble of a diesel engine. "Crap. I bet Maddy forgot to roll the trash can to the curb." Afraid she was going to miss the garbage truck yet again, she strained her head, trying to see down the street. A streak of yellow barreled by. It was only the bus.

Good, there's still time.

She slipped on her pink robe and sandals. After she bagged the overflowing trash sitting in the pantry, she headed out the front door. Normally, the garbage can sat in the garage, but when the battery had died in the automatic door opener, Lily had started leaving it outside. She made another mental note to swing by Walmart before work and pick up a new one. She knew she'd be too wiped out afterward to do it.

Might as well make the most out of getting up early.

As she tugged the one-wheeled trash can to the curb, she watched the garage door of her neighbor's house across the street open. The light illuminated Marie Delacroix coming out in her housecoat. The woman shuffled to the end of her driveway and grabbed her garbage can.

"Looks like you're a day late," she said as she began wheeling the container back toward her house.

"What?" Lily asked.

Marie looked over her shoulder. "Garbage day was yesterday, sweetie. You missed it."

Lily looked to her right, then her left. None of her neighbors' trash cans were out. "Guess you're right. Thanks."

Embarrassed, Lily turned around. She pulled the container back up her driveway and gave a look down the street toward Maddy's bus stop. She wasn't there.

Of course she's not there, dummy. The bus just picked her up.

She blamed the new crop of goose bumps on her arms on the scraping noise of the garbage can scooting along the concrete driveway.

(42)
HANK FRY

"Drive, dammit. Drive!" Hank shouted.

The van squealed away from the curb, lurching to the left and sending Hank rolling onto his back. The girl lay right where he'd left her after knocking her head against the van floor to render her unconscious.

He pulled himself up into a squatting position and looked out the window. They'd already turned off Maddy Eastin's street. "Did you do it how I told you?"

"Yeah," Daniel answered. "I drove into the other lane so the camera wouldn't pick me up. I did real good. Didn't I, Hank?"

"You sure did, Small Fry. Now remember, drop your speed. We don't want to take the chance of getting pulled over."

"Got it."

Hank hated pulling Daniel into his plan, but it was the only option. He couldn't grab the girl and drive the van at the same time. During another reconnaissance mission in the girl's neighborhood yesterday afternoon, the time when students were released from high school, he quickly realized that time of day would be too busy. Stay-at-home moms were outside watching little ones ride bikes, and older folks leisurely sat on their porches catnapping their day away.

He'd waited for Maddy to return home, but he wasn't the only one. A woman sat down on the girl's front steps about ten minutes before she arrived. The blazer in the sweltering September heat, the bulge at her waistline—he'd instantly pegged the woman for a cop. He figured she was there to discuss the false accusation Maddy had made. But when she'd put an arm around her, Hank realized they had a closer relationship.

He'd followed them to the mall, but after they parked he left for home. He needed to finish the preparations for Maddy's stay. Different scenarios about the best way to grab her had been rolling around in his head since he'd seen her on the news. He knew those few precious morning minutes between when the girl left her house and the time the bus stopped were optimal. If someone happened to see it all go down, who would believe the eyewitness when the details would so closely resemble Maddy's made-up abduction story? The plan was genius.

Mine. She's all mine now.

He looked down at Maddy's angelic face as she slumped against the van wall. He brushed away the few strands of hair covering her forehead.

Like clockwork, the plan had unfolded exactly as he'd envisioned. He thought back through each step, congratulating himself on a plan well executed. He'd sat in the van until he knew the moment was right, like a wolf down on all fours waiting to ambush his prey. Maddy had been running a couple of minutes late. Hank had sat waiting, wondering if he'd have to postpone. The last thing he wanted was a school bus full of witnesses. But lady luck had once again shined down on him and Maddy had appeared.

She was the only one moving outside on that dark Tuesday morning. Well, except the Fry brothers. Daniel had quietly inched the van up behind the girl. She didn't even notice. Didn't make a peep as Hank jumped out the already opened side door. He had clamped his hand around her mouth before pulling her inside. Then he'd smashed her head down on the van's floor. She was out before he'd even closed the door. Hank had grabbed each of her limp wrists and handcuffed them around a metal pole bolted to the interior of the van wall. He ripped off a couple of inches of duct tape and smoothed it over her mouth.

After a few minutes of admiring his prize catch—and once he was satisfied she couldn't escape—Hank climbed into the passenger seat. He buckled up but kept glancing back at his new guest. Maddy was the only thing in the back of the van. He'd already cleaned it out, not wanting to take the chance she'd be able to grab a tool and hurt one of them.

He smiled, thinking how proud his dad would've been. He could hear his old man now. "You have to be meticulous in your planning, son. Stay disciplined, focused, and keep your eye on the details." Hank had listened then, and he had gotten the job done now.

"Is she okay?" Daniel had a worried look on his face. "You didn't hit her too hard, did ya?"

"No, just a smack to keep her quiet. She'll be fine. Now keep your eyes on the road."

Hank wasn't too worried about Daniel's driving. He'd been doing it since he was eighteen. Driving wasn't the problem; it was the directions that got him confused. The first few times Daniel had driven alone after getting his license, he'd called Hank in a panic, not knowing how to find his way home.

In preparation for today, Hank had gone over the map with Daniel dozens of times. He'd told him to stay off the main roads in order to remain hidden from the ever-seeing eyes of the traffic cameras. It was a trade-off—it meant more time riding in the van, but fewer chances of the cops being able to follow their route home.

Daniel idled at the next stop sign indecisively. Then he turned left instead of right. Hank calmly told him to take a right at the next stop sign. The boy had reached his capacity for remembering the directions, so Hank continued telling him where to turn after that.

Hank felt guilty for having concocted a story about why they took Maddy, but it was the only way he could think of to get Daniel's buy-in. The previous morning, before Daniel went to work, Hank had knocked on his bedroom door. Daniel was still lying in bed, rubbing the sleep out of his eyes.

"Can I talk to you about something, Daniel?"

"What's up?"

"You want a girlfriend, don't ya?"

Daniel had sat up in his bed. His Spiderman sheets fell away from him, bunching up in his lap. "Yeah, I sure do."

"I know you've had trouble finding a girl. Trust me. I know how difficult it is to meet the right one. The problem with all the girls our own age is that they're jaded—"

Daniel squinted, furrowing his brow.

"Jaded is like . . . oh, never mind." Hank walked over and sat next to Daniel on the bed. "Girls your age are looking for guys who have important jobs, lots of money in the bank, and a nice set of wheels."

"But Hank," Daniel whined, "I don't have any of that. How am I ever gonna get a girl?"

"Well, that's what I've been thinking about. You can always count on me to have a good idea, right?"

"Yeah!"

"We should find someone younger for you. Someone who's not into all that material stuff. You remember what Dad used to say? 'A girl's gotta be trained at an early age to learn how to properly serve a man.'"

Daniel nodded.

"What if I can find a young girl that we can train? Teach her how to be a well-behaved girlfriend?"

"That sounds good." Daniel cocked his head to the side. "But who?"

"There's this girl I know. She keeps telling me how miserable she is. Her dad up and walked out on her, and now she's stuck with a mom who beats her. The girl wants to run away, but she doesn't have anywhere to go."

"What if she came to live with us? Can she, Hank? Can she?"

"Slow down, Daniel. Do you think that's a good idea? I mean, where would she sleep?"

"She can have my room, Hank. I'll sleep on the couch. I don't mind."

"You sure?"

"Yeah. I mean, if her mom's hitting her, she needs a safe place. She'd be safe here with us, right?"

When the sound of moaning emerged from the back of the van, Hank shook his head to bring himself back to the present and turned to look behind his seat.

"She sounds hurt," Daniel said. "Why'd ya have to hit her so hard? Couldn't we have just met up with her somewhere?"

"Remember, I already told you. She's afraid of her mother. We had to make it look like someone took her."

Daniel scratched his head. "Won't the police think we did something wrong?"

"If the police ask, the girl will tell them it's all pretend. Anyway, don't worry, we won't get caught."

"Can you at least take the handcuffs off her? We're almost home."

"We have to make it look real, don't we?"

Daniel shrugged.

"Quit asking so many questions, Daniel. You're the one who wants a girlfriend. I'm doing all of this for you."

The girl's moans grew louder. Then they turned into whimpers. Hank looked over his shoulder again, staring as Maddy tried to move but was stopped by the handcuffs. She rattled them back and forth, trying to break free. He watched every emotion she felt as they crossed her face. Confusion, pain, concern. And then came his favorite—terror.

(43)
MADDY EASTIN

This can't be happening!

Through bleary, tear-filled eyes, Maddy scanned her surroundings. An empty vehicle. Large, like a van. All the back windows were covered with taped-down black trash bags. The only light streaming in came from the front window. There were two men. A driver and someone in the passenger's seat.

Why is this happening to me?

Panic welled up inside her. Maddy's stomach lurched. She forced the bile back down once she realized the tape covering her mouth would block its exit. She shook her arms, trying to move them from their position over her head.

The man in the passenger seat turned to look back at her. She squirmed under his penetrating stare and yanked her wrists down harder. The metal handcuffs dug into her skin, but she ignored the pain. It wasn't the first time her skin had been cut, afer all. She continued to twist and turn her wrists, trying to free them.

Dammit!

Maddy let out a cry of frustration that only sounded like a muffled groan. Even with the slickness of blood now coating the metal, the handcuffs were too tight. Heavy, short bursts of inhales and exhales passed through her nose. Her chest felt like it was going to explode, like her heart would literally shoot through her chest any minute.

Maddy knew if she didn't slow down her breathing, she'd hyperventilate.

Breathe. Breathe.

She ignored the blood trickling down her forearms and concentrated. The exertion of all the movement made her head ache more. The throbbing pain pulsed in time with her rapid heartbeat.

How did I get here?

Maddy remembered leaving her house, running late for the bus. Someone had grabbed her from behind. She'd been thrown down and the back of her head knocked hard against something. Then everything went dark.

A sinking feeling of déjà vu settled in.

My made-up story. It's playing out this very minute. But why? Is this your idea of a joke, God? Is this some kind of karma? Because if so, it's just cruel!

When the van came to a hard stop, Maddy lurched forward and the handcuffs clanked against the pole.

"Go unlock the front door to the house," the guy in the passenger seat said to the driver as he got out of the vehicle.

The van's side door slid open. Bright sunlight framed the man standing in front of her. Her breathing accelerated again. She couldn't pull in enough air. The man moved his hands forward, and when she felt his callused fingers touch her legs, she started kicking. Strong fingers grabbed her ankles, pinning them to the floor. The man took one of her feet and twisted it down so hard with the toes toward him, that Maddy thought he was trying to rip it off. Popping noises started sounding, and she knew if he pushed any harder, something would break. She squirmed, trying to beg him to stop, but the words were swallowed by the tape.

"We can do this the hard way," the man said in a low, gravelly voice. "But I figure you're in enough pain right now, what with your head. You wanna add a broken foot?"

Maddy stopped moving. Complete stillness was the only thing she could think of to communicate that she understood.

"Good. I'm going to climb into the van and uncuff you."

That's my chance. I can—

"Stop. Get it out of your head right now. You're thinking the second you're free, you'll scramble out of the van and run away. Don't try it. The next time you defy me, the pain in your head will be the least of your worries. I know how to inflict suffering the likes of which you've never imagined. Cross me and I will show you. You're mine now. I have all the time in the world to introduce you to each and every one of the nerve endings in your body."

Fear seized Maddy. She was afraid to move a muscle. Afraid to incur his wrath. She had no doubt he'd make good on his threat. She didn't know which was more terrifying, the words he said or the confidence with which he spoke them. The man carefully stepped into the van. He hunched over and unlocked her handcuffs.

Maddy let her arms fall forward into her lap. The cramping in her shoulders eased somewhat. She looked down at her wrists, wincing as she dabbed her shirt against the open cuts.

"Put your arms behind your back."

This is all a dream. It has to be.

Maddy was afraid to look at him. She slowly leaned forward, moving her arms behind her. She heard the clink of the closing metal and felt the sting as the tight cuffs once again ground into her skin.

The man shuffled past her and jumped out of the van. "Scoot along on your butt until you reach the edge." She did as she was told. "That's right. Now stop."

The man grabbed her upper arms and pulled her out of the van. She squinted, looking around at where she was. A dark brown, one-story house stood to the right of her. Trees and thick brush lined the property on either side. She couldn't tell if neighboring houses were close or not. The van was parked beside the house, at the end of a long driveway.

The guy who'd been behind the wheel walked up and whispered something to the other man. The driver was only a little taller than Maddy. He was skinny, with messy sandy-brown hair. He smiled with a kind of a crooked grin.

Focus on his facial features.

Finally gathering some courage, Maddy tried to memorize his face. She concentrated on the type of questions the cop who'd created the sketch at the police station had asked her. The eyes were close together. He had freckles on a short stub nose, ears that jutted out a bit. He looked like a goofy kid, but older.

Maddy looked around for more details of where she was.

The second I escape, I'm going to put these bastards in jail.

As the scary man pushed her forward, she saw numbers on a stone pillar: 10309. Her footing was off from the shove, and she fell to her knees. With a firm grip, the man stood her up and led her toward a door at the side of the house. The other one ran around them and opened the door, stepping aside to hold it.

To keep the mounting panic in check, she tried to gather details of what was around her, but it was like everything was running in fast-forward. Images of a kitchen came and went, but her mind couldn't hold on to any of them. A hand pushed against the middle of her back. The scary man kept moving her forward, then told her to stop. They stood in front of what looked like a bedroom door, but the doorknob was missing. Wood plugged the hole where the knob should have been.

"Don't move," he said. The man reached up to the top of the door. He pulled a shiny, brass slide lock open. There was another at the bottom, and he opened that too. A rectangular hole had been cut out along the bottom of the door. It reminded Maddy of the movies she'd seen of prison doors that had holes cut out of the middle so guards could slide meals through.

Is that what they're going to do? Throw me in a room and keep me locked away?

Maddy felt like she couldn't breathe. She tried to sniff in as much air as she could get.

The man pulled on a makeshift door handle that had been mounted just above where the doorknob should have been. The door swung out toward them instead of into the room. He moved Maddy aside so he could open it fully. As he stood beside her, she could feel his cold stare boring into her. She tried to comprehend the bare room in front of her. It was empty of everything except a thin mattress pad in the middle of the floor and chains snaking out from a small hole in one of the walls.

Fear ripped through her. She involuntarily backed up. Her body wanted to flee from the images of her future flashing before her. She knew she'd be punished for disobeying his order to stay put, but it was like her body had a mind of its own. She couldn't stop her legs from shuffling backward. A yelp sounded behind her, and Maddy jumped. Turning around, she saw the sandy-haired man. She had backed straight into him. Her eyes locked on the door behind him. She wanted to make a run for it, but knew it was useless to try and get out with her hands bound behind her back.

"Hi, I'm Daniel. Glad to meet you. You don't have worry to anymore. Your mom can't hurt you now."

What is he talking about?

"You're going to stay in my room." He gently took her by the arm and turned her around. He tried to lead her into the room, but she refused to cross the threshold.

"I know it doesn't look like much, but Hank said we had to keep it empty. For training purposes." Daniel leaned in and whispered into Maddy's ear. "You do good in your training, and you'll earn privileges in no time."

Maddy started shaking her head back and forth. Her groans became louder.

"Daniel, why don't you go start lunch?"

Daniel hesitated, but then started walking toward the kitchen. He gave one quick glance over his shoulder. He offered up that crooked grin again, but she noticed that the concern never left his eyes.

The scary man—what was his name? Hank, that's right. Daniel and Hank.

Hank picked her up at the waist and carried her into the room. He dropped her on the mattress. The thin padding did nothing to cushion the blow of her tailbone hitting the floor.

He walked back to the door and padlocked it closed. A piece of wood was affixed horizontally over the door as was another piece next to it, on the door frame. A latch held the two pieces together and the lock went through the latch. The key was attached to a coiled, plastic green wristband Hank wore.

He turned and pulled his shirt up over his head and dropped it on the floor beside him. Maddy scooted backward until a wall stopped her retreat.

Focus and remember. Focus and remember. Like a magical chant, she kept repeating those words in her mind.

Hank had a head of thick black hair and a goatee to match. From across the room, she couldn't make out his eye color—but his eyes were small and beady and completely focused on her. Deep lines etched across his forehead, smaller ones shot out from the corners of his eyes. The white skin of his chest stood in stark contrast to his tanned arms and face. She'd thought he might be Hispanic at first, but now realized the deep brown color of his skin was probably due to being in the sun a lot.

He kicked off his shoes. Then he unbuttoned and unzipped his jeans. He yanked the pants off and threw them to the side, along with his socks. His gaze never strayed from Maddy's huddled figure against the wall. Naked and hard, he walked toward her.

This isn't happening. This can't be happening.

"Lay down," he ordered, pointing to the crumpled mattress pad.

Maddy couldn't breathe, couldn't move. Terror froze the tears that had started to flow the second she'd entered the room.

Hank grabbed her ankle and pulled her away from the wall so quickly her head banged on the floor. He backhanded her across the face. Pain ricocheted through her head.

"Do as I say, the first time I say it."

Maddy fought through the pain and scootched her body over on top of the pad. Hank bent down on all fours, hovering over her. Icy blue. That was the color of his eyes. Maddy tried closing hers. She wanted to block out what was happening, but decided the fear of not seeing what was coming next was worse, so she opened them. His face was directly over hers. His breath was hot. A foul smell escaped his mouth. She struggled for air through her nose as he roughly grabbed her breast.

This can't happen! It's not supposed to be like this my first time.

Maddy wanted the tape off her mouth so she could scream for help. Anything other than just lie here and take it. She shook her head back and forth trying to think of a way to break free.

Hank unzipped Maddy's pants and pulled them off, then he ripped at her panties. He pressed his body down on hers. She could feel his hardness against her skin. Panic caused her to start bucking under his weight.

Hank grabbed her by the throat and squeezed hard.

Stop! I can't breathe!

"Don't move again," Hank warned.

When the pressure on her throat tightened, Maddy forced her body to go limp even though every part of her wanted to fight. It was the only way she knew how to show him that she would start listening, that she'd do anything if he'd only let her live.

Hank removed his hand.

She inhaled as much air as she could get through her nose.

"Now spread your legs."

Maddy knew she had to obey. There was nothing she could do to stop him. It seemed like fighting back only made things worse.

What would Katniss do in this situation? Pull out an arrow and let it fly into the bastard's belly.

Maddy told herself to go somewhere else in her mind. If she could concentrate hard enough, she could morph into one of the heroines in her books and transport herself to another location, leaving this bedroom far behind. Because if she were firmly locked away in her mind, she wouldn't have to experience the vile things that were about to happen to her body.

(44)
LILY EASTIN

While driving into work, Lily received an automated message informing her that Maddy had missed school again. She had no idea where her daughter had gone off to this time, but with every passing hour that Maddy ignored her phone calls and text messages, Lily's temper flared. She'd been taking it out on her coworkers all day.

If that girl thinks she's going to see her father tonight after pulling a stunt like this, she's got another thing coming.

Lily slowed the car as she reached the house, wondering why all the lights were off. She pulled into the driveway and felt the anger she'd been holding onto all afternoon immediately evaporate. Worry crept in to take its place.

At the front door, she fumbled with her keys, looking for the right one. She tried to calm her racing thoughts, reminding herself the dark house wasn't so unusual. Plenty of times she had walked in to find Maddy in her bedroom reading a book, the only light shining from a reading lamp clipped to her headboard.

"Maddy? Maddy, are you home?"

Lily turned on every light she passed. The living room and kitchen were empty. She opened the bathroom door. Also empty. She'd expected to come home to find the radio blaring and Maddy trying on every outfit in her closet. Her father would be here soon. The house felt *too* empty somehow.

Lily took a deep breath and forced herself to look down at the crack along the bottom of her daughter's door. Complete darkness. She flung the door open.

Empty.

She turned on the light and darted over to the closet, only to find a pile of clothes and a stack of boxes still packed away from the move. Lily ran back to the bathroom, realizing she hadn't looked in the shower. It was also empty. She knew she was acting irrationally, but panic had set in.

The backpack.

If Maddy had ditched school and come home, her backpack would still be here. Even if she left again, she wouldn't have wanted to haul that heavy thing around. Lily searched every corner of the house a second time. Nothing.

No matter how angry Maddy had ever gotten at Lily, not once had she ignored an entire day's worth of phone messages. Something must have happened.

She's hurt. She got hit by a car. She's in the hospital. Or . . .

Lily refused to let her mind consider the other options. No matter how loudly the "what-if's" shouted, she refused to listen.

Lily shut her mind down. Only the most basic motor functions kept working. Her legs carried her into the kitchen. Her hand grabbed the phone off its base. Her fingers dialed 911. Her mouth spoke to the operator. Then she stood, paralyzed, cradling the phone against her chest. Her worst fear had finally been realized. Tuesday, September 29—the other shoe had dropped.

***

"Ma'am? Ma'am? Did you hear me? Could your daughter be over at a friend's house?"

Lily looked up at the police officer standing in front of her. She'd been patiently answering his questions. Yes, Maddy had skipped school that day. Yes, she'd done it before, but no, she never stayed out this late.

And she never ignored calls for this long. The officer—Lily struggled for the memory of his last name—Cameron, Officer Cameron didn't comprehend the direness of the situation.

"You don't understand," Lily said. "Maddy has no friends. Her bedroom is the only place she's ever at this time of night. So please, stop with all these damn questions and go find my daughter!"

"Ma'am, she hasn't even been missing for twelve hours yet. She's fifteen with a history of truancy. She probably headed over to the mall and is late getting home."

"No. She was supposed to meet her father tonight. She wouldn't be late for that. She wouldn't miss it for anything. Can't you put out an Amber Alert or something?"

"No, ma'am. I've checked the house, and there's no evidence of foul play. The only thing I can do right now is finish getting information for my report."

"How in the hell is a report going to find my daughter? You need to call Detective Wallace."

"Detective Wallace? Why, ma'am?"

"He . . . he would know what to do."

"Detective Wallace's shift already ended. He wouldn't be in the office right now. I can leave him a message if you'd like to speak—"

"That's not good enough."

"I'm going to finish getting the details I need for the missing persons report," Officer Cameron said. "Then, if further information comes to light that indicates foul play, the report will be sent to our Crimes Against Persons Division, and they'll take over the case."

"What happened to calling in the FBI, getting dogs out to search, triangulating her phone, or whatever it is you people do? Anything other than creating a file that will sit on a desk collecting dust somewhere?"

"Ma'am, the FBI is only called in on cases where there's been an abduction across state lines. Dogs are only called in on disappearance cases with a known search area. Again, your daughter's case will be investigated if evidence comes to light—"

"Yes, I know. If evidence comes to light that there's been foul play."

"As I understand, your daughter's been having trouble at school. With being bullied, is that correct?"

"How do you—" Lily didn't need to hear the answer. In fact, she didn't even need to finish her question. Everyone on the force probably knew about Maddy's made-up abduction case.

"She's received lots of media attention lately," he said. "It must be difficult what with her father's lack of attention. Have you stopped to think that it might've all been too much, that your daughter might have run away?"

"No! My daughter would never run away. You don't know her like I do. She'd be terrified of going out on her own. I don't care how much we've fought this week, she would never run away."

The officer's wrinkled brow told Lily all she needed to know. He'd already pegged Maddy as a troublemaker, unworthy of additional man hours being wasted searching for her. Nothing Lily could say would change his mind. She finally gave in and dutifully finished answering his questions.

When each line of his report was filled out to his satisfaction, Officer Cameron handed her his business card. "Please call me when Maddy resurfaces, or if you find additional information that would be helpful to the case."

Although his words said "please call me," his pinched-up mouth relayed a different message: "leave me out of your family drama, you nut bag." Lily was tired of his self-righteous, know-it-all attitude. "See here, Officer—"

Lily's phone beeped, indicating an incoming text message.

Maddy!

She grabbed her phone out of her back pocket. It was only Tom. Her stomach dropped. The sensation of tumbling off a cliff seized her. She looked over at Officer Cameron and shook her head. He quietly made his exit.

Why is Tom texting me?

She looked at the time. It was 7:43 pm. He should have already been here by now. She had to tell him about Maddy. He would help her call the hospitals. He'd help find their daughter. Then Lily read the message.

SOMETHING CAME UP. CANT MAKE IT TONIGHT. WILL CALL MADDY TOMORROW.

(45)
EMMA PARKER

Standing in front of the Eastins' front door, Emma hesitated with her hand raised. Lily had called in the middle of the night, waking her from a fitful sleep, frantically babbling. From the scant details she'd been able to make out, it'd sounded like Maddy had finally had enough and had taken off.

Emma took a deep breath and knocked. She would put away whatever feelings she had for Lily and focus on finding Maddy. When the door opened, Lily grabbed her by the arm and pulled her inside. At Emma's quizzical look, Lily looked down at her hands, and then let go of Emma's arm. She started pacing and tapping her fingers against her legs.

"Thanks for coming," Lily said. "I'm sorry I woke you, but I didn't know what else to do. That damn cop wouldn't believe me. He said Maddy ran away, but she wouldn't have. You know that—"

Emma grabbed Lily by the shoulders. "Slow down, Lily. Come over to the couch and let's start from the beginning."

"Right, sorry. It's just . . . I don't understand how Officer Cameron could think Maddy ran away. She was in a great mood this morning. She was excited about seeing Tom, didn't even make one complaint about going to school. She said . . ." Lily brought a hand to her mouth, trying to stifle a sob.

"Said what?" Emma put a kind hand on Lily's shoulder.

"Maddy told me she loved me." Lily broke down crying.

Emma leaned over, stretching for a box of tissues sitting on the corner of an end table. She set it in between them, pulled one out, and handed it to Lily.

Lily balled it up in her fist, ignoring the tears running down her face. "Do you know how long it's been since I've heard her say those words?"

"Do you think Maddy said it because she knew it was the last time she was going to see you? Did she say it as a kind of good-bye?"

"No! She was just happy. Truly happy, for the first time in a long time."

Emma thought back to the previous evening at the mall.

Was there anything Maddy said to indicate she might have been contemplating running away from home?

Emma racked her brain, reviewing each word had Maddy spoken, looking for underlying meanings. No, she was sure Maddy hadn't been planning anything.

Lily blew her nose and dropped the dirty tissue on the couch beside her. She grabbed another from the box and started wringing it in her hands.

"Do you remember that time when Maddy was six, and she got lost at Busch Gardens? She and I were playing in the kids' area when she ran off ahead. Maddy turned a different way than I did, and the crowd seemed to swallow her up. Security had to be called to help find her. She was eventually discovered hiding in some bushes. Remember how she had nightmares on and off for a year afterward? From that day on, she's never left my side when we're out in public. I know Maddy's a teenager now, but the terror of being lost has been sewn into the fabric of who she is. I don't care how much we've fought in the past. There is no way she would run away."

"Where does that leave us?"

Lily's legs bounced, shaking the entire couch.

"I thought when Maddy ditched school again, she might have gotten hurt somewhere. I called all the hospitals already. No one's been admitted under her name or with a similar description. She has no friends that she'd go to, and she's not with her father. He was supposed to come over tonight, as you know, but he cancelled last minute with a cowardly text. That only leaves one option." Lily put her face in her hands, emotion steamrolling her again.

Could it be true? Could someone have taken Maddy?

It seemed highly unlikely. The stats about stranger abductions were low, Emma knew, even if it did seem like the news was chock-full of crazies kidnapping kids. The vast majority of missing children were taken by family members—three out of every four times.

Could Maddy be that lone one-in-four statistic? Lord knows Florida seems to have a higher per capita of wackos.

Still teary-eyed, Lily collected the dirty tissues and walked over to the trash can in the kitchen. Emma looked around the living room. It was the first time she'd stepped foot in the house, always having opted to wait for Maddy in the car.

This place is a real step down from their old house. Actually, more like a giant leap.

Their previous residence was colorful and vibrant. Lily loved mixing shades of color you'd normally think would be garish, but with her skillful hand, they blended beautifully. Living in this dismal house would sap anyone of joy.

Emma looked up when she heard the faint noise of pills knocking against a container. Lily stood in the kitchen, opening an orange prescription bottle. She dumped a pill into the palm of her hand.

Emma darted toward her. "What is that?"

"Nothing."

Emma closed her hand around Lily's. "Really?" She grabbed the prescription bottle out of Lily's hand and read the label. "Adderall? Are you crazy? This is a type of amphetamine used to treat ADHD and narcolepsy."

Emma knew there had been an upswing in abuse by university

students who swore by it. They said it helped improve concentration and kept them awake longer in order to study more.

"I know what it is, Emma."

"Then you should also know the side effects—cardiovascular problems, insomnia, dizziness, nausea, and increased anxiety, to name just a few. Do you really need a drug to enhance your anxiety?"

"Don't you dare judge me! You don't know how things have been around here. How I've had to fight not only my body but my mind to get off this damn couch every morning and make it in to work. It feels like I'm wrapped in a heavy, wet blanket. I'm so exhausted, I can barely budge. The Adderall is the only thing that helps relieve my constant fatigue."

"You promised you'd never misuse drugs again." Emma pushed away the memory of finding a sixteen-year-old Lily unconscious after taking too many of her mom's Valium.

"Yeah, well, you promised to always be my friend. Looks like neither of us kept up our end of the bargain."

Emma pried Lily's fist open, and removed the little blue pill from her palm. She returned it to the bottle, noticing the prescription was written to for a Mary Klass. "Where did you even get these?"

Lily turned her head, unable to look Emma in the eye.

"Don't bother explaining. I don't want to know."

Emma shoved the bottle of Adderall into the front pocket of her jeans. She knew if Lily took them for energy, she must also have a hidden stash of sleeping pills. Lily would need something to help her come down from that high. She'd never willingly give up their location, so Emma decided to find them on her own. Allowing them to stay in the house would be like leaving a loaded shotgun behind. With the increased stress Lily was under and the depression that would hit after the Adderall left her system, Emma couldn't allow Lily access to any amount of medication. The temptation might prove to be too great.

"What are you doing?" Lily tried to snatch her purse back from Emma's grasp.

She turned to block Lily. "You can't be trusted with them. I'm going to find every single pill in this house."

"You have no right. Leave. Now."

Emma pointed to the couch. "Sit down."

Lily glared at her, but reluctantly moved over to the couch. "You should be out looking for Maddy, not digging through my stuff."

Emma ignored the comment and began searching the living room.

***

Emma looked up from the desk drawer she'd been sifting through. She'd been so focused on the task at hand, she hadn't noticed Lily leave the room. She found her standing in front of an open hall closet.

"What are you doing?" Emma asked.

Lily jumped. She yanked her hand out of the stack of folded towels and swung around to face her. "Nothing."

Emma shoved Lily aside. She felt between each towel until her fingers touched plastic. An empty bottle of Ambien. "Where are the sleeping pills?"

"I'm out."

Emma put her hands on her hips, her head cocked to the side. "Really?" She stuck her hand down the front pocket of Lily's jeans and felt a small lump of tablets.

Lily shifted her weight, trying to get away from her. "Stop it."

"Dammit, Lily. Give me the pills. I won't let you bail on your daughter. Maddy's going to need her mother when she gets home."

"She's gone, Emma. She's never coming home." Lily gave up the struggle, dropping her chin to her chest. "What am I going to do without her?"

"I'm going to find Maddy, and I'm going to bring her home to you."

Lily looked up at her. "Promise?"

"I promise."

Emma held out her open palm.

Lily reached into her pocket and grabbed the handful of pills. She dropped them into Emma's hand. Emma patted Lily's pockets to make sure they were empty.

Emma left Lily lying on Maddy's bed so she could finish searching the house. When Emma was done, she found Lily snuggled up with her daughter's red hoodie, fat tears rolling down her face.

Emma quietly backed out of the room, but before she could shut the door, Lily said, "Please don't leave."

Emma stopped. Her shoulders fell. She couldn't fathom what Lily must be going through. Emma knew she had to be strong, had to be the one to keep it together so that Lily wouldn't completely fall apart. Ignoring her own splintering heart, she nodded and sat at Maddy's desk. She turned on the computer and waited for it to boot up.

Stay busy. Focus on finding Maddy.

Emma knew that was the only way she would get through this.

PART 10
WEDNESDAY, SEPTEMBER 30

(46)
MADDY EASTIN

With every beat of her heart, Maddy could feel the movement of time marching forward, but it could no longer be measured. She had no idea what time it was or even what day, trapped in the tiny room.

Has the sun set? Or was it the middle of the afternoon?

A large piece of plywood covered what she assumed was a window. The eternal buzzing of the fluorescent light above her ensured a constant feeling that it was daytime. Another piece of wood covered the light switch, blocking her from turning it off. To what end, she had no idea.

Her ankle ached. The rusty chain dug into her skin. She'd tried to slide it farther up her leg, but it was locked so tightly in place, the links wouldn't move. Yet even that pain was no match for the throbbing between her legs.

At least when that bastard was on top of me, I was able to transport myself into the world of my books and block out what he was doing. Mostly.

Yet, with every new degradation doled out, her mind would pop back into the present momentarily. She remembered coming back once to find two wolves staring at her. She freaked until she realized she was staring at a tattoo on Hank's chest. The larger alpha wolf had a cold, hard stare. His fangs were bared like he was ready to pounce and rip Maddy's throat out at any minute. The second, smaller wolf nuzzled into the larger wolf's neck.

I thought school was hell. That my life couldn't get any worse. How wrong I turned out to be.

Maddy rubbed her neck, trying to find relief, but every swallow pained her. Not only from the choking but also because she hadn't had anything to drink since before she left for the bus stop that morning. At least the duct tape was no longer covering her mouth. Hank had told her before he left that he was testing her to see if she could remain quiet while he was gone. When he explained what he'd do to her if she ignored his directive, Maddy knew that nothing could get her to talk.

She looked down at the tan lines where her watch should have been. She'd lost it somewhere. It made her think of her dad. She pictured him knocking on her mom's door, coming to pick her up for dinner. She could see the tears rolling down his face as he got the news she was missing. He would realize how wrong he'd been to squander the last five months.

Oh, Daddy, please come rescue me.

Maddy's breaths sped up. It felt like she couldn't catch the next one. As they became shallower, her lips tingled and the room spun. She closed her eyes and concentrated on slowing her speeding heart rate down, but nothing worked.

Calm down. You'll get through this.

Finally, she was able to draw a few deep breaths into her lungs. The anxiety seemed to pass, but when she put her hand over her heart, she could feel that it continued beating faster than she could count.

Could this be the tachycardia again?

There had been plenty of bouts of racing heartbeats since she'd been thrown in the van, but somehow the rhythm had always corrected itself. Her parents had told her the stories of when she was a baby. How she'd been hospitalized for three weeks before doctors finally got the combination of medicines right to keep her heart rate in check. As a kid, she couldn't really remember being sick, but twice a year, as regular as daylight savings, her mom would discuss what to do if she ever felt her heart racing too fast.

Maddy didn't have the luxury of telling a grown-up that her heart rate wasn't slowing on its own, and she didn't think Hank would take her to a hospital. She tried to remember the trick for getting it to skip back into a normal rhythm.

Balloons. Right.

Maddy brought her thumb up to her mouth like she was a toddler sucking on it. She created a tight seal with her lips and blew. Her cheeks expanded while she held her breath, making sure none of it escaped past the sealed thumb or through her nose. She imagined her fingers were a balloon that she was inflating with one long breath. When she couldn't hold it any longer, she opened her mouth and let out a puff of air, then greedily sucked in more oxygen. It made her feel light-headed, but when she put a hand over her chest, she found that her heart had returned to its regular beat. She wiped her wet thumb on her bare leg.

Maddy wondered if the tachycardia would return again—and if, next time, it would be as easy to fix. She knew if it was left untreated, she could be dead in a few days, but given the option of what was happening to her now, that didn't seem like such a bad thing.

Hank hadn't given her so much as a blanket, not even a sheet to hide her nakedness. There was only the thin and now-bloodied mattress pad underneath her. At the thought of her bare body, goose bumps broke out on her arms.

"Hello?" said a quiet voice. A hand shot through the rectangular cut-out at the bottom of the door. The hand waved and then retreated. "Hello?" the voice said again.

Maddy tried to move closer to the door. The chain clanked and thudded against the floor. The pain shooting through her lower body halted her movement.

The voice didn't sound like Hank's, but Maddy was still too scared to respond.

What if it's a trick? What if Hank's setting a trap for me? But what if it's the younger guy and he's willing to help me?

Maddy remembered the look of concern in his eyes and knew she had to take the chance. It might be her only way out. "Hello . . ." she whispered back.

"Hi, it's me Daniel."

"Can you let me out?"

"No, that would make Hank very angry. I just want to talk to you."

Maddy looked at the dark hole, but she couldn't see him from where she was. "Where is Hank now?"

"Sleeping. My brother told me to leave you alone, but I didn't see nothing wrong with saying hi."

"You're Daniel, right?"

"Yep, that's me. I'm super glad you came to stay with us."

"Can you go tell someone I'm here? I don't want to be here. I want to be home with my dad."

"Hank said you ain't got no dad. That your mama is mean and you wanted to come live with us."

"He's lying." Maddy's voice cracked.

"No! Hank doesn't lie. You're the liar."

"Shush, please. Don't wake him. I'm sorry. I didn't mean it. Can you please get me some water?"

"Hank told me not to give you any food or water. Said you had to be trained right."

"What about some ice? I'm in a lot of pain."

"The noise would wake him up."

She heard a shuffling sound. "No, don't go. Please don't leave me." Maddy started crying.

When she heard a shuffling sound near the door cutout again, she wiped her eyes, trying to clear her vision. A hand slowly moved through the hole. It dropped a white washrag on the floor.

"Hank never said nothing about a cold cloth. Will that do?"

Maddy laboriously moved her body forward, trying to keep all her weight on her arms. The pad on the floor scooted with her, moving along the hardwood floor. She picked up the soaking wet rag and brought it up to her mouth. She wrung out all the moisture, then placed it in between her legs. "Thank you, Daniel. What's your last name?"

"Fry. What's yours?"

"Eastin. Maddy Eastin."

"No. It's Maddy Fry. You're going to be my wife. Right after you've been properly trained. Nighty-night. Don't let the bed bugs bite."

(47)
EMMA PARKER

Emma started a pot of coffee so it could brew while she took a walk in Maddy's shoes—in a manner of speaking. It was nearing 6:30 a.m., the time Maddy usually left the house to walk to her bus stop. Emma wanted to see what the neighborhood was like at that time of the morning. She'd hoped to get a cup of coffee down before it was time to leave the house, but she didn't wake up early enough.

She'd only managed to get a little sleep, mostly during the last couple hours before she got up. Once Lily had finally let go, still clinging to Maddy's sweatshirt, Emma had retired to the couch.

Spanish inquisitors would have loved that thing. It could have doubled for a fifteenth-century torture device.

Emma walked out the front door, rubbing the sleep from her eyes. She stood on the top step and looked up and down Maddy's street. A light fog added an eerie quality to the quiet street. The first day of October had ushered in cooler weather. A slight breeze blew past. She inhaled greedily, enjoying the crispness and the feel of the microscopic water droplets against her skin as she walked through the mist.

In the distance, a garage door lumbered up. A car engine fired, and she watched brake lights tap on and off as a driver backed into the street. Emma headed toward the bus stop, slowing as she got closer to Paul Gleason's house. She could just make out a security camera hanging off the corner roof of his house.

At the sound of a heavy diesel engine, she turned. A yellow bus barreled toward her. She nodded at the bus driver when he stopped at the corner. He gave her a probing look, then turned his attention back to the empty road. He turned right and disappeared behind a line of oak trees.

Emma walked back to Lily's house, continuing to study the neighborhood.

Has someone on this street taken Maddy? Could she be gagged and bound less than fifty feet away? Or did she finally reach her breaking point, opting to try life on the streets rather than deal with the pressures of her home life?

Emma initially wondered if Maddy might have hooked up with an online suitor, but last night she'd checked the girl's computer for evidence of such a relationship and didn't find anything in e-mail or her online accounts.

Movement out of the corner of her eye caught Emma's attention. When she turned her head, she noticed a woman standing in front of a large picture window, staring at her. When she saw Emma looking at her, she let the drapes fall back into place. Emma made a mental note to check back with that neighbor at a more suitable hour.

***

"Thanks for meeting me, Rocky." Emma Parker slid into a booth across from Detective Terrance Wallace at a diner not too far from the Eastins' house. He'd already ordered a cup of coffee and was adding a heaping spoonful of sugar.

Wallace smiled at the sight of Emma. "Hey, stranger. How's it going?"

She shrugged, unable to paste on a fake smile.

"You want a coffee?" He looked around for the waitress.

"No, I've had enough caffeine." A cup of coffee and two Red Bulls were plenty.

Except for the addition of a few extra pounds, Wallace looked the same as he had in their academy days. Emma remembered how, on his first day of training, a fellow cadet—one of the smallest in the group—came up to him and called him Rocky. Not because Wallace resembled the boxer in the movie, though he did have a large, imposing stature. No, the nickname was because of his large cheeks. Like a squirrel hiding away nuts, he reminded the cadet of Rocky from *Rocky and Bullwinkle*. Everyone had quieted down, waiting to see if Wallace would explode all over the guy, but his hearty laughter cut the tension. Emma knew at that moment he was a kind soul tucked inside a hard exterior.

"I was surprised to hear from you," Wallace said. "What's it been, two years?"

Emma nodded. "Something like that."

Wallace raised an eyebrow. "So what's up?"

"I appreciate you meeting me on such short notice. I know with our crazy schedules, it's sometimes hard to pull away."

"No problem. I was on my way out to conduct a few interviews on a new case I caught yesterday. Figured I had enough time for a coffee with an old friend."

"You were the detective assigned to the Maddy Eastin attempted abduction case, right?"

Wallace's eyes narrowed. "Yes, you mean the *false* accusation reported by Maddy Eastin. What of it?"

"Are you aware that she went missing yesterday morning? That she's been gone for twenty-seven hours?"

He nodded. "Officer Cameron left me a note and a copy of the report he took from Lily Eastin last night. What's it have to do with you?"

"Are you going to work it like a missing persons case?"

Wallace exhaled, kneading the skin on his forehead. "To be honest, my sergeant has had enough of this girl. He thinks we've wasted enough man hours on her, and until additional information comes to light that indicates foul play, we're labeling Maddy Eastin a runaway."

Emma looked down at her hands, folded in front of her on the table.

She was trying to figure out the best way to play this.

"You never answered my question, Emma. How are you involved?"

Best to be honest with him. If he smells even a hint of insincerity, he'll shut me out.

"Maddy Eastin is my goddaughter."

Wallace stopped drinking midsip. "What?"

"Lily Eastin and I have been friends since elementary school. We grew up on the same street. When she gave birth to Maddy, she named me godmother. But a few years ago, Lily and I had a falling out. I've stayed in touch with the girl, though obviously not often enough, what with the stunt she pulled making up that story about the two abductors. I'm sorry you had to deal with that, Rocky. I take partial responsibility. But now Maddy's disappeared. I don't know whether someone really has snatched her this time, or if she actually ran away. Either way, she's missing and I have to find her."

Wallace stroked the skin under his chin.

"What do you say, for old time's sake, you lend me your files on Maddy?" Emma gnawed on her bottom lip while she waited for his response.

"You know you'd have to work this off the books. Your CO finds out about this, and you could be kicked off the force. There's a reason we're not allowed to work cases involving family members."

"Right—but technically, she's not a family member."

Wallace gave her a long look.

Emma knew it was only semantics. She had a relationship with the family, thus she wasn't allowed within ten feet of the investigation.

"I know, I know. It's against the rules. I've already taken a leave of absence from the sheriff's office. Called my sergeant this morning, told him I had some family issues to take care of. I can do most of the legwork on this thing myself, but I might need your help here and there."

"Like how?" He sounded like he was afraid to hear her answer.

"I need you to check Maddy's cell phone." Emma pushed a piece of paper across the table with the girl's number written on it. "Check to see if there have been any incoming or outgoing calls since six thirty a.m. Tuesday morning. If there were, find out which tower the phone pinged off. And check for texts. Can you do that?"

Wallace nodded.

"After this, I'm going check with the school bus driver, see if he even picked her up yesterday. Then I'm going to Maddy's school. I also want to talk to the neighbors, especially the one with surveillance cameras. What's his name?"

"Paul Gleason."

"Right. See if he caught anything on video."

"He's a bit paranoid of cops. I'll give him a call to pave the way. Tell him you'll be stopping by."

"Thanks, Rocky. I really appreciate your help. I've already notified the hospitals to contact me if someone matching Maddy's description is brought in."

"If you uncover anything, hand it off to me. I'll get an investigation started."

Meaning don't go off half-cocked on my own. "I will."

"I'll call my department's receptionist and tell her to make a copy of Maddy's file. You can pick it up in about an hour."

"Thanks again. You have no idea what this means to me. Maddy's had a tough time since her dad walked out and, as you know, she hasn't been dealing with it well. I just hope she hasn't fallen in with a bad crowd. If she did run away, she couldn't have had much cash with her. She won't last long on the streets. And there are far too many guys out there willing to pimp girls like her out."

(48)
HANK FRY

"I said no, Daniel, and that's final."

"But *you* called in sick. Why can't I?" Daniel stood behind the open refrigerator door.

Hank was stooped over, grabbing pancake syrup off the bottom shelf. He was ravenous this morning. "These first few days with Maddy are important." He tapped the fridge door closed with his foot. "I have to see to her training. Go ahead and take the van into work. I'm going to be busy here all day."

He'd gotten lucky with the weather again yesterday. Though it'd stopped raining, the job site was still too wet. Working on a soft bridge embankment was dangerous. However today, the weather forecast had called for sunny skies, so he'd been forced to take a sick day.

"If she's going to be my girlfriend, why can't I stay and help?"

Hank turned away from the kitchen counter. He stepped up to Daniel, moving in close. "If I didn't know any better, I'd say you've started to doubt me. That it? You don't think I know what's best anymore?"

Daniel squirmed under Hank's stare. "I didn't say nothing like that. Only..."

"Only what?"

"When I talked to Maddy last night—"

"You did *what*?"

Daniel took a couple of steps back. "I couldn't sleep. I kept hearing her cry and the couch is all lumpy. I just wanted to see if she was okay."

"I told you to leave her alone, that you weren't allowed to interact with her for at least the first two weeks."

Daniel looked down at his feet. He kicked at the floor with the toe of his shoe. "You said she's mine. I want to be with her." He looked up at Hank. His face was all flushed. A vein bulged in his neck. "You said you got her for me."

I'm tired of being second-guessed by this moron. Who is Daniel to question me? Every day of his pathetic life, I've watched over him. And now, when all I ask for is a little patience, he can't even give me that. I'm sick of always putting his needs first. Where has it gotten me? It's my turn now.

"No," Hank said with a growl. "She's mine. Go get your own girl." His hunger for breakfast had suddenly been replaced with another type of hunger. It was time he taught Maddy the hard lesson of breaking one of his rules. Hank grabbed the keys from the kitchen counter and threw them at Daniel. "Now get out of here, you idiot."

(49)
LILY EASTIN

Forget about putting one foot in front of the other. Lily needed help with something more basic. Breathing. She barely had the strength to pull air into her body. It felt like a gorilla was crushing her chest.

She knew the sensation would pass, but almost wished it wouldn't. If only her body would stop remembering how to breathe, then she could give in to the darkness. The never-ending blackness where there was no pain, no emptiness.

Pills helped her escape for a while. She'd found a few Vicodin Emma had missed while searching the house. But no matter what she took, there always came the point when the haze receded and she was forced to relive the moment of finding an empty house and calling out her precious daughter's name. Lily had broken down, told God if he would only spare her baby, she would go to church, volunteer at the soup kitchen—anything. If only Maddy would walk back through that door.

She was lying on Maddy's bed again. She had a fierce grip on Tiger Lily, Maddy's favorite childhood stuffed animal. Though Maddy said she was "too old" to sleep with the tiger anymore, she hadn't been able to part with him. He'd been relegated to a top shelf—though not so far away that he couldn't be taken down if he was needed. Lily definitely needed him now. With all the pills gone, she had to have something to hold onto. Her sanity was hanging in the balance.

All her life, she'd been preparing for the worst. Preparing for this very moment. The loss of her daughter. She'd naively thought if she could shore up her defenses enough, then when it happened it wouldn't be so devastating. She'd thought keeping Maddy at arm's length would help cushion the blow when it came. But her preparations hadn't been enough. Probably because no matter how much distance she put between herself and Maddy, she could never sever the emotional ties.

She loved her daughter with a fierceness that scared her. Scared her so much she'd erected a steel box to keep her heart safe. Lily hadn't understood how to deal with all the pure, unconditional love she received from her daughter. It was foreign to her, almost painful because she didn't know how to accept it.

A faraway noise caught Lily's attention. She blinked slowly, trying to concentrate on the sound. She turned over onto her side and felt something jab her in the back. When she pulled the hard plastic piece out from under her, she saw it was her phone and it was ringing. She remembered Emma telling her to keep it near, that she would call periodically to update her. Lying back on the pillow, she kept hitting the screen until a voice began speaking.

"What's going on, Lily?"

"Tom? Tom, is that you?"

"Yes, it's me. Why didn't you call me? I had to hear about our missing daughter from Emma Parker, of all people."

"Emma called you?"

"What is wrong with you, Lily? You sound out of it. Are you on something?"

"Oh, Tom. You've got to find her. You've got to find Maddy." Lily started sobbing, unable to say another word.

(50)
MADDY EASTIN

"No more, please," Maddy whispered as she buried her face in her hands when the door opened again.

"I brought you some water, but if you'd like me to leave . . . ?" Hank stood in the open doorway, a tall, clear glass in his hand.

"Yes! I mean no, please don't leave. Sir. I appreciate your kindness and would like to have some water. Thank you."

"Very good. Now that you've learned your lesson for talking to my brother, you can have a drink."

Hank handed Maddy the glass. She bit her lip, holding back her feelings when she saw that it held less than an inch of liquid. She couldn't let her face reflect her thoughts though, or she knew Hank would take the water away. She may not have excelled in school, but she sure learned quickly around here. She knew she had to do everything in her power to stay alive. It was only a matter of time before she was rescued. Everyone would be looking for her and somehow, some way, they would come.

As if reading Maddy's mind, Hank said, "You do know that no one's going to find you, right? The quicker you accept your new reality, the better."

Maddy shook her head, trying to block out his words.

It's not true. No matter what, I have to hold on to the belief that I'll be rescued.

"You need to focus on *me*. Learning what I want and pleasing *me*. I am your only source of food and water. Make me happy, and you'll be rewarded."

Maddy brushed her tongue along the roof of her mouth. She tried to work up some spit, but her mouth was so dry even the one sip of water hadn't helped. If anything, it only made her want more. "May I please have more water?"

"Did I say you could talk?" Hank took the glass away from her and flung it against the wall.

She screamed and tried to shield her naked body from the flying shards.

"Tell me the rule!" Hank hollered.

Maddy's shoulders shook with terror. "I . . . I . . ."

"Now!"

"I am not allowed to speak unless asked a direct question."

"And what happens if you break a rule?" Hank towered over Maddy. She was huddled on the floor, trying to make herself smaller.

"I have to be retaught the lesson until I learn to obey." She berated herself for forgetting, but there were so many rules. It was hard for her to remember them all. For some reason, she couldn't concentrate. She was so thirsty, so hungry, it made thinking difficult.

"Lie down," Hank said.

Maddy crawled over to the mattress pad and laid on her back. Her body trembled. With every step Hank took, her body involuntarily jerked like it was receiving a shock.

He picked a large shard of glass off the floor and straddled her. She knew she wasn't supposed to speak, that to do so would only make things worse, but she couldn't help the mewling sounds that escaped.

"Why are you so scared?"

A question. I can talk.

"I don't want to die."

Hank let out a hard laugh. "This isn't new to you."

Maddy was confused. She didn't understand what he was talking about.

"For someone who cuts her own skin, pain must be a welcome friend." He pointed at the scars on Maddy's calves and stomach.

It finally dawned on her what he meant.

He yanked her right arm up off the floor. She wanted to close her eyes, but couldn't take them off the jagged piece of glass. He pushed the sharp edge against her skin, creating an angry red line from the crook of her elbow to her bicep. Blood droplets emerged from the skin. A groan of pleasure escaped Hank.

(51)
EMMA PARKER

Frustration weighed Emma down. She was getting nowhere, fast. So far, every investigative path she'd followed had led to another dead end. There'd been no sign of Maddy at the Amtrak or Greyhound stations. If the girl left town, she hadn't bought a ticket to do so.

Emma had been pounding the pavement of Maddy's neighborhood for the last thirty minutes when she saw a car pull up to the house next to the Eastins'. A knock earlier at that door had yielded no answer, so she'd skipped it and gone on to see if any of the other neighbors had seen anything the previous morning. No luck yet, but Emma had been keeping an eye on the next-door neighbor's house while canvassing.

An old woman got out of the car and waved to the man in the driver's seat. He returned the gesture and backed out of the driveway.

Emma jogged over to the fenced gate. "Excuse me, ma'am. May I speak to you for a moment?"

The old woman looked behind her. "Me?" she asked, pointing to her chest.

"Yes, ma'am. My name is Emma Parker. I'm a detective with the Hillsborough County Sheriff's Office."

"Nice to meet you, detective. My name is Addie Addison, but you can call me Addie."

"Thank you, Addie. Do mind talking to me for a few minutes?"

"Sure. Come up on my porch and sit a spell."

Emma opened the gate and followed Addie. She slowed her pace once the woman started climbing the stairs.

"Sorry, detective. Arthritis. Don't ever grow old."

"I'll try not to, ma'am."

Emma scooted out the metal chair for a winded Addie and then sat in the seat next to her.

"First off—" Emma stopped midsentence when Addie's front door opened.

A woman peeked her head out the door. "Addie, is that you? What are you doing out here? Oh, I didn't realize you had company."

Emma stood and introduced herself.

"This is one of my caregivers," Addie said by way of explanation. "Go get us some iced tea, Nell."

Emma saw the woman bristle at the order.

"That's not necessary," Emma said. "I won't be here long enough to enjoy it."

"Oh, posh. Nell would be happy to get it. Wouldn't you, Nell?"

The woman went back in the house, slamming the door behind her without a word.

Emma pulled out her notebook and pen, then opened to an empty page. "Your next-door neighbor is missing, a young teenage girl by the name of Maddy Eastin."

"Maddy who?"

Emma pulled out her cell phone and brought up a picture to show Addie.

"Oh, my. How terrible."

"She was last seen walking to her bus stop yesterday morning. When I noticed you standing at your window earlier today, I thought you might have been doing the same thing yesterday and might have seen something?"

"Yes."

"Yes? You were standing at your window yesterday morning, or you saw Maddy Eastin?"

"Both, my dear."

A hum of electricity built inside Emma. "Can you tell me what you saw?"

"I don't sleep much these days. It's often three or four in the morning when I wake up. I get bored since nothing much is going on that early. Oftentimes, I stand at the window and watch as the neighborhood wakes up."

"So yesterday morning . . ?" Emma prompted.

"Yesterday I was standing at my window. I saw the young girl, the one in the picture, walk by my house. Most mornings I see her walk by. Shame she has to leave the house so early to catch her bus. It's so dark out and—"

"She walked by yesterday morning?" Emma said, steering the conversation back.

"Yes. I saw her walk by."

"Then what?"

"A white van pulled up with its side door open. The girl was looking at me and didn't notice the man until he picked her up and threw her inside. The van made a horrible squealing noise driving off."

The humming coursing through Emma's body intensified. "Why didn't you tell anyone?"

Addie thought for a second. "I did. Well, I tried. I sat down to call 911, but when the operator asked me what I wanted to report, I must have forgotten why I called. My memory's like that. Here one second, gone the next." Addie gave a dismissive wave. "Nell found me on the phone and put me back to bed. I hadn't thought about it again until you showed me the girl's picture."

"Can you tell me what kind of van it was?"

Addie seemed to search her memory. She shook her head in confusion. "What kind of van it was?"

"Right. Do you know the make?" Emma tried to keep her patience in check. "Maybe a Chrysler or a Dodge?"

"A Chrysler or a Dodge. Maybe," Addie said.

"Do you remember which way the van was headed when it left?"

"Hmm. Which way?" Addie shook her head.

"What about a description of the man who took Maddy?"

"Who took Maddy?"

Emma scratched her head, confused by Addie's answers. She'd been so coherent just a minute ago. Now she just looked tired. Emma decided to cut the interview short and to talk to her again later. Addie had said she was an early riser. The woman might have a clearer head in the morning.

Nell came out on the porch holding two glasses of tea filled to the rim with ice. "Here's your tea."

"Thank you." Emma took a hearty drink, afraid Nell would throw it in her face if she didn't have any. "Addie here was telling me you found her early yesterday morning on the phone with 911. Did she tell you why she was calling?"

"No. She seemed confused. When I found her, she thought the person on the line had called *her*. I tucked her back into bed, and she hasn't spoken of it since. Why do you ask?"

"The girl next door has disappeared. Did you happen to be looking out the front window around six thirty yesterday morning?" Emma didn't want to say too much in front of Addie, or it might contaminate her eyewitness account.

"No, I'm afraid not," Nell answered.

Emma took another generous swallow of tea and stood, saying her good-byes. Back on the sidewalk, she pulled out her cell phone. This was the tip, the key piece of information that could unlock the path leading straight to Maddy. She just knew it.

"Detective Wallace."

"Rocky, you need to start an official investigation into Maddy's disappearance."

"Whoa, Emma. Slow down. What'd you find out?"

"I have a witness that saw Maddy grabbed off the street yesterday morning and thrown into a white van."

"Wait a minute. What witness?"

"Maddy's next-door neighbor, Addie Addison."

Wallace groaned. "I hate to tell you this, Emma, but Addie suffers from Alzheimer's."

"What are you talking about? She was completely lucid when I talked to her." *At least until the end of the conversation.*

"Tell me exactly what Addie said she saw."

Emma relayed the conversation, then ended with, "I even found a set of fresh skid marks on the road right out in front of Addie's house."

"Think about it, Emma. Addie said she saw a man grab Maddy and drive away in a white van. What does that sound like?" When Emma didn't answer, Wallace said it himself. "It sounds like the exact story Maddy told police when she described her made-up abduction. It was all over the news. Addie could have absorbed the details through any of the numerous television reports or newspaper articles. Alzheimer's patients are notorious for mixing up dates of events. They don't remember timelines like we do. Did she parrot you?"

"What do you mean, parrot me?"

"The day Maddy made her accusation, I interviewed Addie too. I made the mistake of asking her leading questions. All of her answers made it sound like she'd seen the incident firsthand. Luckily though, her daughter was at the house and explained that oftentimes, because of the dementia, Addie repeats back what the person says like it's a fact—hence parroting."

Emma remembered the end of her conversation with Addie. It'd been exactly as Rocky described. "But she didn't do that. She was completely coherent when we spoke." Emma cringed at her half-truth, but she couldn't risk being completely honest if she expected Rocky to get on board with her theory.

"My great-aunt had Alzheimer's for eight years before she passed away," Emma said. "Some days were better than others. Many times, she'd have hours of lucidity before being thrust back into her stupor. I think today was one of Addie's good days."

"Listen to yourself, Emma. You want so badly to find Maddy that you're trying to fit a square peg into a round hole. This is why family members aren't allowed to work cases where they have a personal stake. It clouds their judgment."

"That's not what this is."

"So you're telling me that Maddy makes up a lie about two men in a van trying to abduct her, and then a week later two men in a van really *do* abduct her? Come on. Step back for a moment and listen to how that sounds. What would be your reaction if you were working a case and someone suggested that theory?"

A silence fell between them. Emma knew Rocky was waiting her out.

Is he right? Am I letting my love for Maddy cloud my judgment?

"I know how it sounds, Rocky, but . . . dammit!"

"It's hard, I know, but you've got to hang in there. Tell me what else you've checked into."

Emma ran down her list, updating him on each bullet point. She'd checked into the local transportation options and hospitals, which had been a bust. There was no romantic relationship between Maddy and an online suitor. The bus driver never saw Maddy waiting at the bus stop Tuesday morning. And the school confirmed she'd never made it to first period.

"Somewhere in the ten minutes between Maddy's front porch and the bus coming by to pick her up, she disappeared," Emma said. "How could that happen?"

The sound of flipping pieces of paper echoed over the phone.

"Information came back on Maddy's cell phone," Wallace said. "There haven't been any calls since Sunday. The last text she sent was at 8:17 p.m. Monday evening. A short message to her mother explaining that she was running late. You and Maddy hung out at the mall that night, right?"

"Yes. She was in high spirits and looking forward to seeing her dad the following day. It has been five months since she's seen him."

"What about the dad? You look into him?"

"He doesn't have her." Emma's tone indicated she didn't want to discuss the topic any further. She thought back to her heated conversation with Tom earlier that morning. He'd almost hung up on her after she started reading him the riot act about bailing on his daughter. The only thing that had stopped him was Emma telling him that Maddy was missing. She could tell by his reaction that he'd had no idea. His barrage of questions also told her that Tom wasn't the one who took Maddy.

Emma had suggested Tom go over to Lily's house to wait for word there. She had promised to call with regular updates. Plus, Lily needed someone around right now. Though Emma was worried about her, she had to focus on finding Maddy. Holding true to form, Tom hadn't gone to Lily's, at least not since the last time she and Lily had spoken.

"You can stop by City Hall to pick up the list of phone numbers Maddy's called and texted over the past two months," Wallace said. "And I also wanted to let you know, I gave Paul Gleason a call. He said he wasn't comfortable talking to another cop."

Emma exhaled loudly. She wanted to scream in frustration. "But if someone took Maddy, his security camera would have gotten it on tape."

"He checked the video footage himself and said there were no unusual vehicles in the neighborhood that morning."

"What about Maddy? Did his camera capture her image walking by his house?"

"No."

"No? How could she not walk by the house on the way to the bus stop?"

"Only one answer for that. When Maddy left the house, she turned left instead of right. She walked the opposite way from her bus stop."

Emma thought back to the fresh skid marks she'd found on Maddy's street. The vehicle's tire would have left the heaviest tracks as it accelerated. Once the tires gained traction, the marks would have lightened up. The vehicle that left them would have been facing east, which would have taken it right by Paul Gleason's house.

It doesn't make sense. Do the skid marks belong to another vehicle?

"I'm telling you, Maddy did not run away. When I searched her house, I found money tucked inside her jewelry box. The two twenties I'd just given her Monday night. If she left home, she would have taken them with her."

"Could be an oversight, a lack of planning. Leaving might have been a last-minute decision. Come on, Emma. You know kids these days with their grandiose ideas. Maddy probably hooked up with an old friend and is lying low for a while."

"That's not what happened. I know it."

"I'm sorry. I can't open an investigation with only a skid mark and an unreliable eyewitness statement. Keep digging though. I'm here if anything else comes up."

She wanted to yell at Rocky, to make him understand that something wasn't right. Yet, she knew she couldn't afford to piss him off. Even though he didn't believe her, he was the only one in her corner. She was already taking a huge risk by investigating this herself. If her Sergeant found out, he'd can her ass.

"Okay. I'll call you when I have more."

Emma only hoped she'd find more to call about.

(52)
MADDY EASTIN

Hank threw a balled-up sheet at Maddy. She greedily wrapped it around herself.

"The sooner you accept that this is your new life," he said, "the faster you'll learn your lessons."

Hank pulled at the chain that was snaked through a hole cut in the bottom of the wall. It rattled as the full length of it poured into the room.

He must have unfastened it before he came in.

Maddy had already yanked the chain hard enough to know that it had been firmly fastened to something on the other side.

"I want to show you something." He walked out of the room, chain in tow, leading her like a dog.

She hobbled forward into the living room and saw Daniel standing in the corner, watching them with anger in his eyes. Hank sat down on the couch and grabbed the remote. With his attention diverted, Maddy mouthed the words "Help me!" to Daniel. He looked away.

She crouched down, ready to take a seat on the couch, then felt a jolt of pain shoot through her backside as Hank hit her.

"I didn't say you could sit," he said. "I don't want blood all over my couch."

Maddy looked down at the white sheet—it was already streaked with lines of blood. Many of the cuts had dried, but a few of the deeper ones were still tacky. A noise caught her attention. She looked up and saw the image of newscaster Karl Hurley on the television screen. He was talking about Tampa's recycling plant. Maddy didn't understand what Hank wanted her to learn from this. Then Karl's face grew serious. Her picture popped up in a box in the background behind the reporter.

The police are searching for me!

"Channel 3 News has received additional information about the girl who cried wolf. You'll remember our exposé of Maddy Eastin, the King High School student who claimed two men tried to abduct her from her bus stop on September twenty-first. Another police report has been filed by the Eastin family—this time by the mother, Lily Eastin. She filed a missing persons report. It seems Maddy has run away from home. A Temple Terrace Police spokesperson had this to say, 'We've thoroughly investigated the disappearance of Maddy Eastin and no signs of foul play have been uncovered. She's been classified as a runaway.'"

Karl, who looked like he couldn't care less about the story, continued on: "Police said they would reopen the case if any new information came to light, but this reporter thinks that this newest stunt by Maddy Eastin is just one more cry for help. So Cliff, what's the weather going to be like—"

Hank turned off the TV. "You see? No one's looking for you."

Maddy wiped the tears that had been silently falling while she watched the recorded show. She stared at the one remaining droplet beaded up on her finger, wondering just how much pain a single teardrop could hold.

PART 11

THURSDAY, OCTOBER 1

(53)
HANK FRY

Hank turned over on his side and looked at the alarm clock beside his bed. It read 8:04 a.m.

Holy shit! I haven't slept so late since . . . since I can't remember when. Good thing I texted my boss that lie last night about how my twenty-four hour bug turned into a forty-eight hour illness. I seriously pissed him off, especially after the three-day rain delay, but screw him. I have a boatload of sick days banked. Might as well use them.

Hank brought his hands over his head, stretching like a cat enjoying himself after a nice, long snooze. He hadn't even gotten to bed that late. Must have been the enjoyment of a long hard day of "training" that had tuckered him out. He rolled out of bed whistling a tune he couldn't remember the name of. He pulled on a pair of jeans and left his bedroom, then walked down the hall to the kitchen. Looking into the open living room, he saw Daniel sitting on the floor in front of the couch. Hank could only see the top of the boy's head. He was looking down at something.

"Hey, Daniel. How about I make your favorite? Waffles with chocolate sauce instead of maple syrup?"

He rarely let Daniel indulge because the extra sugar sent him straight into hyper mode, but he figured what the hell. Hank was feeling on top of the world.

Daniel ignored him.

"Hey, Small Fry. Don't be mad at me, I know—"

Daniel finally looked up and held a finger up to his mouth.

"Shuuuuush."

"What's going on?" Hank walked into the living room while trying to scratch an itch between his shoulder blades. "Why do I have to be so—who the hell is that?"

He was staring at a teenage girl lying on his couch. Her hands were duct-taped together in front of her. Her legs were bound at the ankles.

"Quiet. You'll wake her."

"Her *who*?"

"Katie. Says so on her name tag." Daniel pointed at the girl's shirt to prove his point.

Hank recognized the uniform. It was from a restaurant not too far from their house.

"You told me to get my own girl." Daniel puffed out his chest. "So I did."

"Oh shit! Oh shit! Oh shit!"

Hank started pacing in front of the couch. The picture of what must have happened became clearer. He vaguely recalled waking up to a noise sometime after one o'clock in the morning. He'd almost gone to check it out, afraid Maddy had somehow gotten out of her restraints, but then he'd heard Daniel's voice and gave into the exhaustion pulling him back under.

Daniel had stormed out last night while Maddy watched the news report. Once the segment was over, Hank had taken her back to the bedroom to continue her training. Daniel hadn't crossed his mind the entire night.

"What's wrong, Hank? I did it just like you. Now we each have our own girl." Daniel looked down at the Katie, a dreamy look on his face. "She's beautiful, isn't she?"

"You have no idea the shit that is about to rain down on us, brother."

"Don't worry, Hank. You worry too much. Last night when I left, I was mad, real mad. So I decided to go over to Antonio's. Katie waited on me. She was so nice. She looks a little like Maddy, don't you think? Older, but still a lot alike. I knew when she sat down next to me to take my order that she liked me. I waited outside for her, after she was all done working. It wasn't hard to get her in the van. I felt bad hitting her, but I knew if I did everything just like you, it would all work out."

Hank lowered his head, rubbed his forehead with the heels of his hands. "Oh, Daniel."

Antonio's was located in a small strip mall. Even though it was late, university kids were always out and about in that area. There was no way Daniel could have gotten away without being seen.

A noise brought Hank's attention back to the couch. The girl was looking back and forth from Hank to Daniel, horrified. Her eyes looked like they would pop out of her head any minute. If he hadn't been freaking out, he might have found it funny.

The girl's muffled groans struggled to break free from the tape covering her mouth. Exhaled air from her heavy breathing came out of her nostrils, blowing the wisps of blonde hair covering her face.

Daniel talked to her, trying to calm her down. It did nothing to soothe her fears. When he touched her arm, she started flailing.

Hank bent over and yelled in her face. "Stop! I can't think with all this noise. If you don't shut up right now, I'll coldcock you." The girl grew still and her eyes grew even larger.

Hank started pacing again. "What to do? Think of what to do." Should he leave Maddy and Katie, grab Daniel, and get the hell out of Dodge? The cops could show up on their doorstep any minute. It had been seven hours since Daniel took her.

Then Hank thought about all the time he'd already spent training Maddy. He knew he couldn't leave her behind.

Shit!

He was tired of everyone screwing up his fun. First his mom had walked in on him and Rosalina, and now Daniel had to go and screw up his perfect plan for Maddy. Hank had worked out every detail of his plan flawlessly. No one would have ever found her.

Cash. I need cash.

Hank didn't have much lying around, but he thought it would be safe enough to swing by the bank on the way out of town. If the cops weren't at the house yet, they must not know their identities. It surely wouldn't take long though.

But where to go?

Hank frantically scanned the living room, like he'd somehow find the answer written on the walls. Then his eyes fixed on something.

That's it.

"We need to get out of here, Daniel. Now. The cops will be here any minute. We have to grab Maddy and go."

"Nooo," Daniel whined. "Not without Katie."

"She can't come with us. The pressure will be too much if the cops know we have her. Just leave her here for them to find. It'll give us a head start."

Daniel stood up and faced Hank. "It's not fair. Why do you get to take Maddy when I can't have my girl?"

"Stop whining. I won't have it. You'll listen to me, you'll gather your shit together, and we'll leave."

"No! You like her more than you like me."

"Who?"

"Maddy. Ever since she showed up, you've changed. You always ignore me now. You even called me an idiot."

"I'm sorry, Daniel, really. But we don't have time for this right now. Cops will be barging through our door any minute. We'll talk about this in the van."

"I don't believe you. I did everything right. The cops won't find Katie here. You just want me to give her up. Well, I won't!"

(54)
MADDY EASTIN

Maddy awoke to Hank's yelling. She buried her head under the dirty sheet he'd allowed her to keep the last time he left. Sleep had been her only comfort since all this began. Whenever he was gone, she'd fight through the pain and force her mind to shut down.

More angry voices travelled through the closed bedroom door. She couldn't make out the words, but she knew from the tone of voice that something important was happening.

Is this the day Hank will finally kill me?

He had constantly threatened her, telling her that if she didn't please him in the way he liked, he'd snap her neck and find some other girl who could satisfy him.

She told herself to do whatever he said, no matter what, every time he walked through that door. She knew it was the only way to stay alive.

"Stop! I can't think with all this noise."

Maddy jumped at the sound of Hank's voice.

A minute later Daniel's voice said, "Nooo! Not without Katie."

Who's Katie?

Another few minutes went by. Maddy couldn't hear a thing. Somehow she found the silence worse than the shouting. Then the clang of the locks made her jump again. Hank yanked the door open with such force it whacked against the wall. He threw something at her.

"Get dressed. Now."

A sweatshirt and jeans lay in a pile near her. She stared up at Hank, afraid of the look on his face. His eyes were bright, almost shimmering.

They kept darting around the room. She couldn't figure out what he was looking for. She quickly pulled the large USF sweatshirt over her head. When she went to pull on the jeans, she realized she couldn't get them over her feet because of the chain attached to her ankle. But she was afraid to speak because Hank hadn't asked her a question. The painful lesson she'd endured for breaking *that* rule was one lesson she didn't want to repeat. The only thing she could think to do was raise her hand.

"What?" Hank looked at her, annoyed.

"I'm sorry, sir." Maddy coughed. Her voice sounded hoarse from lack of water and disuse. She didn't get to talk much. "I can't put these jeans on with this chain wrapped around my leg."

Hank turned and smashed his fist into the door. He let out an animalistic growl. "Do not move, or you'll regret it like nothing you've ever experienced."

Maddy barely breathed, afraid the rising of her chest would be enough to set him off. He bent down on one knee and put the key in the lock that held the chain around her ankle. When the chain fell to the floor, she fought the urge to rub her leg. She instinctively knew any movement would be the end of her. After Hank stood up and took two steps backward, he ordered her again to get dressed.

When she was done, she rolled up the pant cuffs so she wouldn't trip over the extra material bunching at her feet.

The clothes must have come from Daniel's closet.

Hank pointed toward the open door. "Now go into the living room."

Maddy hesitated, afraid this was the beginning of the end.

Has he finished digging out that hole in the backyard he told me about?

"Don't make me ask you a second time."

Maddy shuffled forward, but shooting pains made it hard to take normal steps. She stopped when she reached the kitchen counter and looked back, waiting for her next set of instructions. Hank walked around her and grabbed a roll of duct tape sitting on the counter. He pulled off a piece and placed it over her lips. When he told her to put her hands together in front of her, she forced her shaking body to comply. He also taped her legs together, and she teetered sideways. With the ease of picking up a bag of mulch, he threw her over his shoulder.

"Now Daniel, I'm going to ask you one more time. Will you come with us?"

"I'm not going anywhere if *she* comes along!" Maddy heard Daniel holler from the room behind her. "You have to choose. Me or her."

Maddy could feel the rage building inside Hank, like heat exploding from his body, ready to scorch her. She watched, upside down, as he carried her into the living room. She craned her neck up and saw what she thought were Daniel's legs. And a girl.

There's a bound girl lying on the couch.

Maddy locked eyes with the girl as Hank opened the door. She knew the terror the girl must be feeling. The only thing Maddy could think of was to memorize her facial features. It seemed the least she could do. Someone should know the girl had been there. Large doe eyes, green maybe. It was hard to tell since one was swollen shut. And long, straight blonde hair that was parted down the middle.

"Just remember, Daniel, I gave you a choice. *You're* the one who's deciding to stay. It's not on me."

(55)
DETECTIVE TERRANCE WALLACE

Wallace patted his cheeks, trying to wake himself up. He took the last gulp of his tepid coffee, even though he knew he'd regret it. Somewhere around eight o'clock that morning, the caffeine had turned on him. Instead of keeping him awake, it had just churned in his stomach like battery acid. Dispatch had called him sometime just after one in the morning about an abduction at a Temple Terrace restaurant just off Fifty-Sixth Street.

"I don't know what's going on around here lately—must be something in the water." Wallace looked around at the six SWAT guys decked out in their black Kevlar equipment. "But we've got an abduction on our hands. Let me get you guys up to speed."

Wallace put his empty coffee cup on the trunk of his car. He leaned back, put a foot up on the rear bumper. "Early this morning, the manager of Antonio's was locking up the place when he saw a man walk up to one of his servers as she was leaving for the night. The guy punched her in the face and then put her in his van. This all happened in the alley right behind the restaurant."

"Pretty ballsy to grab someone right across the street from City Hall," one of the men to Wallace's right said.

"Ballsy or stupid, I don't know which," said another cop.

Wallace held up a picture of Katie Norris. He handed it to the man closest to him, who examined the photograph and then handed it off.

"The manager wasn't able to get a plate number—it was too dark in the back—but a security camera outside the front of a fitness place in the same strip mall captured a white van in the parking lot earlier in the evening. We think the guy cased the joint before he grabbed the waitress. The license plate was traced back to one Hank Fry, address 10309 Hyaleah Road." Wallace looked west, toward Fry's house. He and all the men were congregated in a parking lot at a park about a mile away.

Wallace continued. "When I showed the folks who work in the restaurant Hank Fry's picture, they said he hadn't been in that night, but that he's a regular. A busboy mentioned Hank has a brother, Daniel. We found out Daniel Fry lives with Hank and they often frequent the restaurant together. Two waitresses confirm that Daniel Fry was in Antonio's last night, and that he sat in the missing girl's section."

"Does Daniel Fry have a record?" one of the cops asked.

Wallace shook his head. "He's never been convicted of anything, but about a week and a half ago an officer picked him up on an indecent exposure charge. The guy pulled out his wanker in front of a jogger at the entrance to the trail going through this very park. The lady hasn't pressed charges—yet. I got Officer Topher, who responded to the call, out of bed and grilled him about this Daniel Fry. Topher said the guy seemed harmless. That he'd be surprised if Daniel could have pulled off something like this. Guess he's mentally slow. Daniel gave the excuse that he was only taking a piss when the lady happened to run by. Topher thought Daniel's brother, Hank Fry, would have been a likelier suspect for the abduction. The officer got a weird vibe off the older brother, but nothing he could pinpoint."

Wallace held up a blown-up image of Daniel Fry's DMV photo. "Take a good look at this, men. This is our target. Daniel Fry. And just so you're aware, here's a picture of Hank Fry. The two live together, so when we storm the house we might encounter both. Your team commander will go over the details, but let's take this place assuming Katie Norris is still alive and is being held somewhere in the house. We need a nice clean extraction."

Wallace stepped back, out of the circle, and the team commander, Alex Powell, spread blueprints of the Fry house across the trunk of Wallace's car. Once everyone knew their role, Powell radioed to the SWAT member who'd been watching the Fry house through binoculars across the street.

"Alpha One—report," Powell commanded into the radio.

"Zero vehicles in the driveway. Unknown number of vehicles in the garage. Movement noted at the number-one window. Alpha One out."

"Okay guys, let's play this thing by the book," Powell said. "Be safe, be aware, and be smart." He looked at Wallace. "You can enter after we clear the house. I'll radio when it's safe."

***

Wallace hated this part. Not knowing what was happening, speculating on whether the SWAT team would find Katie Norris and, if they did, whether she'd be alive. He couldn't imagine what the girl's parents were going through. Waiting for the phone to ring, wondering what news the call would bring. Wallace said a silent prayer, petitioning on behalf of Katie. He hoped he'd be able to give the Norrises good news today.

Wallace's radio crackled. "One male has been apprehended, and we found the girl," a voice said.

"Is she alive?" Wallace asked.

Static was the only answer.

"I didn't get that. Can you say again? Is the girl alive?"

"Yes. We found her alive."

Wallace shook the radio high above his head, thanking God for His intercession. He jumped in his car and drove over to the Fry house as fast as he dared. Out front, police cars blocked the road, their lights flashing blue and red. EMTs rolled a gurney into the house. Inside, a

SWAT member stood guard over a girl bound with duct tape lying on the couch. An EMT was checking her vital signs and explaining to her that the tape covering her mouth, arms, and legs wouldn't be removed until they reached the hospital. Once there, doctors could use a special solution to dissolve the glue. Ripping it off now would damage the skin.

The EMT asked Katie questions, and she nodded or shook her head in response. Satisfied that no damage would be inflicted by lifting her, she was put on the gurney and wheeled out. Wallace would catch up with her at the hospital and interview her later, once she was treated. For now, he wanted to check out the house.

The outside of the one-story looked weathered. The paint needed a good pressure washing. Weeds grew in the unkempt yard. It was a stark contrast to the inside, which looked like a furniture showroom. Wallace ran his hand across the dark, cherry-stained wood of the entertainment center. All around the living room, Wallace saw numerous pieces of high-quality wood furniture. He wondered if he would find a wood shop in the house or maybe inside a converted garage.

A SWAT member escorted a handcuffed Daniel Fry into the living room, then handed him over to a police officer standing near Wallace. "He's the only one we found."

"Make sure you read him his rights," Wallace told the officer. "I don't want him slipping out of this one. Take him over to City Hall and wait with him in the interrogation room. I'll be over soon."

Wallace walked from the living room into the kitchen. He scanned the contents of the refrigerator and cupboards. Nothing unusual. Then he turned and froze as he noticed the altered bedroom door—slide locks at the top and bottom, new handle, and the rectangular slot. He opened it and stepped inside, recognizing immediately that the bedroom had been converted into a cell. He saw the thick, heavy chain lying in a pile on the floor, the bloodied mattress pad next to it, and the boarded-up window.

Fury ignited inside Wallace at the thought of what Daniel Fry must have done to Katie Norris. He felt sick to his stomach at the images racing through his mind. Bending forward with his hands braced on his legs, he took deep breaths until the wave of nausea subsided.

Then he noticed two symmetrical lines of blood on the floor, peeking out from underneath the mattress. A corner of the pad had been kicked up—must have happened when SWAT stormed the room. With gloved hands, Wallace lifted the mattress pad off the ground. The message he saw scrawled in red across the hardwood floor chilled him to his very core.

(56)
MADDY EASTIN

A slamming car door brought Maddy back from the blackness. Shooting pain coursed through the left side of her face. The last thing she remembered was Hank parking the van, him climbing into the back, and then pain exploding in her face. She was handcuffed to the a pole again.

The driver's door opened, and Hank sank down on the squeaky seat. "Okay, I've got food, sleeping bags, and all the other supplies I need. What else?" Though Hank had asked a question, allowing for the possibility of a response, Maddy couldn't because of the duct tape covering her mouth. Anyway, it sounded to her like he was talking to himself. "I think that's everything. Now I just gotta swing by Barkley's ."

He started the van and drove for a while. Maddy couldn't tell where they were. The only thing she could see was sky. It was a beautiful blue color, she noticed. The wispy clouds looked like an artist's brush strokes. She had never truly appreciated its beauty until she found herself locked away.

"Shit!"

Maddy cringed. It sounded like Hank had hit the steering wheel with his fist.

"Come on, come on. I gotta ditch this van, and fast."

She tried to tamp down the sudden burst of hope at the thought the police had finally figured out he had her, but she knew how damaging hope could be. It was like a lightness in the soul that made you rise higher.

Unfortunately, the higher you're lifted, the farther you fall.

The van started bouncing more. Her tailbone ached from all the potholes they hit. It sounded like they were driving on a gravel road. Before this, Maddy had never really noticed how every action created a different sound. She'd learned this sitting in an empty room for hours, straining to hear the happenings in other parts of the house just so she didn't feel so alone.

The van stopped and Hank hopped out. Minutes went by—she couldn't tell how many. It was impossible to track the passage of time. She didn't know for sure, but it felt like she'd been held captive for at least a week, maybe more. When the van's back doors opened, she was startled and let out a muffled scream. Craning her head, she could see woods behind Hank's silhouette.

"I'm going to do some rearranging," he told Maddy. "You will follow every command to the letter. Do you understand me?" Hank pulled out a knife from a sheath attached to his belt. "This knife will slice through your skin like butter. If you think last night was painful, you have no idea how long I can keep you alive while inflicting excruciating pain on every nerve ending in your body. So—to the letter. Nod if you understand."

Maddy's round eyes remained transfixed on the long, shiny metal blade. Hearing the threat, her body seemed to nod on its own. She felt her heart jump in her chest. Racing like it wanted to make a break for it. She felt dizzy. Hank was telling her to do something, but the blood rushing in her ears was so loud it made it hard to hear. She forced herself to focus on his mouth to try and understand the words he was saying. She didn't want him to have to ask twice. That was another painful lesson she didn't want to repeat.

"—then you will get in the boat and lie down," he said.

Boat?

Hank jumped in the van and cut through the tape binding her legs. After he returned the knife to his sheath, he took the handcuffs off her wrists. "Now get out and wait for me."

Maddy stepped forward, jagged rocks digging into the soles of her feet. She tried to slyly take in her surroundings. They were parked in front of a garage. A jon boat was angled up against the back of the bumper. For a time, her dad had had a green fishing boat just like it. It had a plastic seat at the front and one in the back, with a space in the middle. Maddy remembered their fishing trips, how the hard plastic had stuck to her sweaty legs as they baked in the sun waiting for a fish to bite. After their fourth trip, she'd refused to go out again.

Dad was always trying to get me to do sucky stuff with him. Fishing, going to baseball games, fixing the car. It was like he wanted a boy but got stuck with a girl. Why was I in such a hurry to go live with him? He was always busy working or making us do what he wanted to do.

"Lie down in the boat!" Hank bellowed. Maddy cowered. "Hurry!"

He held the bow steady, told her not to make it fall since he was already going to have a hard enough time hauling it up into the van with her extra weight in it. She climbed in awkwardly, working to find a comfortable position in its cramped belly.

Wouldn't it have been easier if he'd just handcuffed me somewhere, put the boat in the back of the van, then had me climb in? Serves the asshole right. I hope he pulls something lifting the damn thing.

Hank re-taped her legs together, then handcuffed her to one of the seat legs. With lots of grunting and cursing, he finally got the boat in the back of the van. She saw that it was too large to fit properly, a fourth of it stuck out of the back door. Hank took orange bungee cords and closed the doors around the boat as far as they would go.

Since the back doors didn't completely close, Maddy wondered if she could wait until he was driving, then sit up and try and get the attention of a car following behind them. She ran different scenarios through her mind until Hank suddenly appeared above her and another shot of pain exploded in the back of her head.

(57)
EMMA PARKER

Emma knew she had to get up, had to figure out her next move in the search for Maddy, but she couldn't seem to budge from the couch. She'd been out all night checking the local sex clubs, making sure no one matching Maddy's description had come in—either looking for work or finding it. A girl like Maddy, short on cash and with no place to stay, was susceptible to the influence of the worst scum in the city. After coming up empty, Emma had cruised the known prostitution areas. Thankfully, she hadn't found Maddy.

Then again, I didn't find Maddy.

So just before dawn she'd gone back to the Eastins' house to crash. Lily had heard her walk through the front door and came running from the back of the house. She looked crushed when she saw it wasn't Maddy.

Emma had held her while she cried. When all the tears were spent, Lily grilled Emma on what she'd uncovered, making her promise not to hold anything back. Emma had explained all the different routes she'd taken looking for Maddy, none of them leading anywhere.

Lily had grabbed onto the eyewitness account of her neighbor and wouldn't let it go. "I don't understand?" she said. "If there was a witness who *saw* Maddy get abducted, why won't the police open an investigation?"

"Detective Wallace said Addie is an unreliable witness. Because of her Alzheimer's, he doesn't believe her recollection of the event. Wallace thinks she's confused it with the false abduction claim Maddy made."

"What do you mean? The officer *said* if more evidence came to light, they would look into Maddy's disappearance."

"Lily, they're not going to. The neighbor with the security camera didn't get a van on camera."

Emma's phone rang, bringing her back to the present. She reached over and grabbed it off the end table. She recognized Rocky's phone number. Her nerve endings hummed with anticipation.

"Tell me you got something for me."

"Where are you?" Wallace asked.

"At Lily Eastin's house, why?"

"Do you know where Hyaleah Road is? Over here in Temple Terrace?"

"Vaguely—why?"

Wallace gave Emma the address and a brief description of the location. "I need you to get over here, now."

"Why?"

"Just get here. And . . . Emma . . ."

"Yeah?"

"Don't mention this call to Mrs. Eastin."

***

Wallace was standing in the driveway, waiting for Emma when she pulled up.

"Did you find her, Rocky? Tell me she's okay."

"Hold on, Emma." He grabbed her by the shoulders, stopping her from rushing by him.

She shrugged him off but stepped back, forcing herself to count to ten. Then to another ten. Once she was able to reapply her professional mask, she said, "Why did you call me?"

"There's something I need you to look at. I thought you'd be better equipped to handle it than Maddy's mother. You good?"

"Yeah."

"Yeah?"

"Dammit, Rocky. Just show me."

Wallace led Emma inside the rundown, one-story house. "Watch your step. We haven't finished processing the scene yet."

A tech was hunched over the couch, cutting a long rectangular piece from the seat cushion.

"I've asked CSU to hold off on processing the bedroom until I showed you something. The techs have taken pictures, but that's it. I wanted to see if you could make a positive ID on something I found."

Emma nodded, afraid her voice would give away the feelings churning inside her. She had to keep control—or at least keep projecting the illusion that she was under control—if she wanted to continue being kept in the loop. The worst thing that could happen would be for Rocky to bench her and stop the flow of information.

He pointed the way toward an open door. As she walked through, she gasped, unable to hold back the emotions crashing over her like a wave threatening to drown her. She took in the surroundings of the almost-empty bedroom and nearly collapsed. To regain her balance, she grabbed the door frame.

On the floor, written in lines of blood was **MADY EAS**

"We haven't typed the blood yet, but I'd bet my pension Maddy was being held prisoner in this room." Wallace's voice sounded like it was travelling down a long tunnel.

Emma forced her legs to carry her into the room.

Just another crime scene. Objectively study the room before you.

Wallace crouched over the writing. "This message was scrawled on the floor, then was hidden by the mattress pad. I'm guessing she either didn't have enough blood to finish her whole name or she was interrupted before she could complete it."

He stood up and walked over to the corner of the room. "Watch out, there are some small shards of broken glass scattered around." Wallace pointed at the floor. "This is what I want you to see."

Like the bloody message wasn't enough?

She instantly recognized the aqua shirt lying on the floor. The front had been ripped apart, separating its cat image in two. Emma just kept nodding until she found her voice. "It's one of the shirts I bought Maddy on Monday night."

When Maddy had come out of the dressing room, modeling the shirt for her, she'd asked, "Do you think the cat picture makes me look like a little kid?"

That's what Emma had liked about it. That Maddy was embracing her younger, sillier side. Emma had assured her it didn't, though, knowing fifteen-year-olds strived to look older than they really were.

"Okay, good," Wallace said. "Well, not good," he corrected. "But you know what I mean. Now we can start tracking her down."

"What can I do?" Emma asked.

"Nothing. You have a personal relationship with this girl. I only gave you a call as a professional courtesy, so that you'd know we opened an official investigation into her disappearance. The best thing you can do now is go back to Mrs. Eastin's house and update her. That will give me more time to track down leads."

"What leads?"

"You know I can't go into that." Wallace grabbed Emma by the elbow and led her out into the living room. "Giving you any information would come back to bite me in the ass in a big way."

"Come on, Rocky. You know I'm not gonna go off half-cocked. Use me as a sounding board. Run your theories by me. Maybe I'll think of something that didn't occur to you."

Wallace cocked his head to the side.

"I didn't mean it like that. Of course I trust your investigative skills, but two heads are better than one."

"I have enough heads in on this one. Right now a detective is interrogating the man we found in this house. Others are tearing his life apart, looking for something that might help find Maddy."

"And?"

"Go back to Mrs. Eastin's house and help her get through the waiting. It's the hardest part."

(58)
LILY EASTIN

"Open up, Lily!"

Lily cracked one eye open when she heard pounding. She could make out a voice, but it sounded far away, like she was stuck at the bottom of a deep well. A pit was exactly where she felt like she'd been stuck for the past two days. At first unable to claw her way out, now simply unwilling. She'd only gotten out of Maddy's bed once today and that was because she couldn't ignore the urge to pee.

More yelling. This time Lily could hear her name. She pulled the pillow out from under her and put it over her head, trying to block out the banging noises.

A rattling at Maddy's bedroom window finally drew her attention. She peered out from under the pillow but didn't see anything—the blinds were closed.

If I ignore it, the noise will go away.

More pounding at the window. This time it sounded like the glass might break. She pulled herself up and lumbered across the room. She opened the blinds, then quickly turned away from the bright light.

"Lily? Lily, let me in."

It sounded like Tom. She lowered the arm that had been shading her eyes from the sun and saw that it was him standing outside Maddy's bedroom window.

"I've been knocking on every window. Didn't you hear me?"

Lily shook her head.

"Well, are you going to let me in?"

Before she could answer, he disappeared. With great effort, she made her way to the front door, where an impatient knock greeted her. She unlocked the dead bolt, then turned to go sit down on the couch. She was so exhausted she couldn't even stand up. If felt like lead weights were fastened to each foot.

She heard Tom take a deep breath as he came inside. Lily figured he was preparing himself for the fight that somehow always broke out whenever they were in the same room. He wouldn't have to worry. She didn't have the energy to argue.

Lily laid her head back on the couch and closed her eyes. "What do you want, Tom?"

"What do I want? Are you serious? Don't you know—" Tom stopped speaking. She could hear him take another deep breath. When he spoke again, his soft tone made her open her eyes.

Lily's own breath caught in her throat. Tom looked even more handsome than the day she'd married him. He had a short growth of whiskers covering his face, like he hadn't shaved in a couple of days. A few white hairs were intermingled with the dark brown stubble.

That's something new. So is his hair. He's keeping it long on top—still parted on the side, but he's letting the straight strands hang down loose. It gives him more of an easygoing vibe. Who knows, maybe walking out on his family has been good for him after all. I guess no responsibilities has a way of loosening a person up.

"So I got the first flight I could back into town," she heard him finish. Lily hadn't caught it all, but it didn't matter.

"Are you listening to me, Lily?"

"Yes. You caught your plane and voilà, you're here. Wonderful. Everything will be all better now."

Tom moved closer to the couch. He hunched down on his hindquarters and stared into her eyes. "Are you high?"

"No, I'm not high."

Tom stared harder. He put a hand on top of hers and asked again in a gentle voice that tore at her insides. "Are you high?"

"No, dammit, I'm not high. I don't deserve to be. Why should I get to escape this nightmare when it's my fault Maddy's gone?"

He gave her an incredulous look.

"I told you. I'm not taking pills. Anyway, Emma cleaned the house out."

"So, what? Staying clean is like some kind of penance?"

She shrugged.

"Why do you think Maddy's disappearance is your fault?"

Lily shook her head. She wanted to block out the kind undertone she could hear in Tom's voice. It was so unfamiliar, it made her skin crawl. It wasn't what she deserved. Lily had pushed Maddy away.

Who knows what's happening to my daughter right now, or what she's gotten herself mixed up in? All because she's saddled with a shitty mother.

A part of her was desperate to believe Maddy had been kidnapped. Then her daughter's disappearance wouldn't be her fault.

But the police know the truth. Even Emma probably figures Maddy hightailed it out of here because she couldn't stand to be near me another second.

She didn't blame her daughter. She couldn't stand to be with herself either.

Tom squeezed her hand. She looked at him, blinking back tears. But before she could say anything, he started speaking.

"If Maddy's running away is anyone's fault, it's mine. I left you both alone, and I am so sorry. I don't have any excuses—reasons, sure—but there is no excuse for my behavior these past few months."

He bolted up and started pacing in front of the couch. He ran a rough hand through his hair.

"I hated the person I'd become, Lily. I felt suffocated. I had to get away to get better." Tom stopped moving and looked at her beseechingly.

"Maddy must hate me. That's why she ran away the day I was supposed to see her, right? She's angry that I walked out, that I didn't call. Mad because of the reasons why I left."

"Is that what you think?"

He looked away, embarrassed.

"She has no clue why you walked out on us."

Tom shook his head, confused. "You mean you didn't tell her? I hate to say this, Lily, but I thought you would have poisoned her against me by now. Five months should have been plenty of time to fill her head with stories about my unfaithfulness."

"She adores you, Tom. Worships you. I refused to be the one to burst her bubble. I know what it's like when you find out a parent isn't the person you want them to be." She shook her head. "No. Maddy blames me for your leaving. She thinks my behavior ran you off."

"Oh, Lily. You didn't have to keep up that charade. She needs to know the truth."

"Did leaving help? Have you come to terms with it?"

"You mean being gay? I won't lie. It's been tough. I've had to reprogram more than thirty years of negative thoughts about my sexuality." Tom sat next to Lily on the couch. He took her hand. "I am so sorry for what I put you through. I never should have asked you to marry me. I knew I was gay, had known since I was ten. I thought if I could just make a family, create a life with people I loved, I could shut the door on that part of me. It turns out ignoring my true self was eating me up inside. I know now the ugliness, the hate I spewed on you was just misdirected anger. I despised myself for being gay and unfortunately, took it out on you."

He shook his head, a look of defeat etched into his face. "I'm sorry I left the way I did, severing the ties between me and Maddy. At the time, I thought it would be best to cut off all contact so I could focus on myself. That was wrong, and I know that now. I can't believe I might never get the chance to see her again. To never hold her in my arms and apologize for all my mistakes. What are we going to do?"

When Tom began to cry, Lily pulled him into her arms. Her body invited him in, but the thoughts in her head were cold.

Must be nice to be able to walk away from your life in order to get your shit together. That's one luxury I was never afforded.

Like an old friend, the anger returned. It fueled her, made the sadness retreat. She could feel herself stepping back into that familiar-fitting role, the one she'd started playing as a young girl—mask your feelings, keep a stiff upper lip, put other people's feelings before your own.

I wonder if it's too late in the day to have Dr. Marx call in a prescription.

(59)
MADDY EASTIN

When Maddy slid back into awareness, she thought she might be dreaming. She felt like she was floating. Then she heard the lapping of water and realized she *was* floating, but this wasn't a dream. She was in a boat.

With a large rumble, a motor roared to life. Panic grabbed a hold of her. She had her eyes open, but everything was dark. She raised her head up off the bottom of the boat, then tried to follow with the rest of her body, but a thick material stopped her from sitting up. She realized the darkness was caused by some sort of tarp.

The quick movement brought on a wave of dizziness, so she laid her head back down. She felt like she was going to throw up. The pain in the back of her head thudded rapidly, but it couldn't quite keep time with her heartbeat. She knew she'd gone into tachycardia again. She tried to raise her hands.

If I could just get my thumb into my mouth, maybe I could trick my heart into jumping back into its normal rhythm.

The handcuffs clinked against the side of the boat. There wasn't enough slack.

"One more movement out of you, and I'll throw you overboard," Hank shouted over the noise of a trolling motor he must have attached to the boat. "You'll be gator bait."

Maddy forced herself to be still. She wondered where they were and how long she'd been out. It felt like the boat was increasing in speed. The tarp blew up in the breeze and a triangle of light poured into her cramped compartment. She shivered uncontrollably. Even the sauna-like atmosphere did nothing to help ease her chills. The idea of infection crossed her mind. The cotton material of her heavy sweatshirt had fused with a couple of the open wounds on her chest.

Once her eyes adjusted to the new light, she could see trees. Oaks, pines, cypresses—all bunched together along a bank of water. Then a wooden structure came into view. Maddy knew the landmark. It was the observation deck at Lettuce Lake Park, on one bank of the Hillsborough River. She and her mom had climbed its three-story tower plenty of times.

We're still in town!

Maddy tried to remember the lessons she'd learned while stuck in that little brown visitor's center the day her seventh-grade class went there on a field trip. She'd only been half paying attention, thinking how she'd rather be outside walking along the wooden boardwalk that ran parallel to the river. A game of who could spot the most wildlife was much more fun than learning facts about the river.

Lying in the boat, Maddy couldn't tell if they were headed north or south, but she hoped fate would be on her side and a canoer or kayaker would see them. Then the absurdity of that thought hit her and a bubble of laughter welled up inside.

What would the kayaker do, sternly wave his paddle at the speeding boater racing down the river? No, I'm on my own.

The constant movement of the boat added to her queasiness. She didn't know how many more hits to the head she could take.

Pain. That's all I've felt for days. Physical pain combined with emotional torture and constant terror.

Silent tears fell from Maddy's eyes. With everything and everyone she loved stripped away, she realized that as screwed up as her life had gotten, she was the one who had created all the chaos. She'd taken her life for granted, made bad choices, and had ultimately been hunted down by a predator for it.

All these months, Maddy had looked the other way when it came to her dad's failings, instead deciding to hone in on her mom's weaknesses. When he'd abandoned them, Maddy had thrown tantrums like a child, that's how badly she wanted him back.

He chose to leave. Mom chose to stay. But no, that hadn't been good enough. Why couldn't I see how much Mom cared?

Her mom may have not been able to show love the way Maddy wanted her to, but she demonstrated her love by being there every day. And instead of showing appreciation, Maddy had slammed doors in her mom's face, skipped school, and lied to the police.

The boat slowed.

I just want to go home, MomMom.

(60)
EMMA PARKER

"I thought you were worried that sharing information with me would come back to bite you in the ass," Emma told Rocky. They were standing near his car, outside the Frys' house once again.

Wallace grunted. "Yeah, well, the investigation seems to have hit a brick wall." He rubbed at the gold clip attached to his tie. "I thought that 'two heads' theory of yours might help. So? Do you want to take a look around the house or not?"

"Definitely." Though Emma abhorred the idea of walking into that bedroom again, anything seemed preferable to sitting in between Lily and Tom on the Eastins' couch, waiting for the phone to ring.

Wallace got Emma up to speed on his investigation, providing her all the details she'd asked for earlier but couldn't get out of him. He started with Daniel Fry, then moved on to Daniel's abduction of Katie Norris and the subsequent SWAT team rescue.

"I interrogated Daniel myself. The kid was a blubbering mess. It didn't take long to figure out he's a bit slow."

"What'd he say?"

"That Maddy came to the house of her own free will. He said Maddy's dad had ditched her and her mom was beating her."

"Bullshit!"

"I'd have to agree. It didn't quite match up with the rest of his story or the crime scene. Anyway, Daniel said Hank was training Maddy to be Daniel's wife. That he had to teach her how to serve him properly."

Emma winced at the thought of what that probably meant. To mask her emotions, she balled her hands into fists and dug her nails into the palms.

"I tried to get specifics," Wallace was saying, "but the harder I went at him, the more emotional he became. Finally he lost it and started hitting himself in the head. A doctor's evaluating him now to check his competency level."

"Did the Crime Scene Unit clear the backyard?"

Though the statement seemed cryptic on the surface, Wallace understood what she meant. "Yeah. They brought out equipment, but the dirt on the property hasn't been disturbed. Maddy's not buried out there."

"And you're sure Katie saw Hank Fry leaving the house carrying a girl over his shoulder?"

"Yeah. She wasn't able to make a positive ID, but Katie Norris confirmed the girl had strawberry-blonde hair. She also heard the name Maddy used. We haven't located Hank Fry yet, but a BOLO's been put out on his van."

A Be On the Look Out bulletin would ensure every cop would be searching for Fry's vehicle. If he was anywhere in the area, he'd be found.

As she and Rocky walked into the house, Emma snapped on a pair of latex gloves. "So what are we looking for? Your crime scene guys already went through the house."

"Yes, but let's take a second pass. See if we can find anything indicating a location Fry might hide out in. We have to assume he took Maddy with him." Wallace offered an encouraging smile. "That's a *good* sign. He wants her alive, or he would have left her for dead at the house."

Emma thought of the blood in the bedroom and the nightmare Maddy must have endured, being held captive there for three days. Her knees buckled.

Wallace placed a hand on her arm to steady her. "You okay?"

"Yeah." Emma shrugged him off and walked away, keeping her back to him. She coughed a couple of times, trying to hide the constant rush of emotions hitting her.

Get yourself together, Parker.

She couldn't afford weepiness; she needed a clear mind. There'd be time enough to break down later.

"Let's split up," she said. "I'll take Hank Fry's bedroom first. Stay close though. That way you can fill me in on the list of items removed from the room. It'll help give me a look into this guy's head."

"Sure."

In a loud voice from the bathroom, Wallace said, "For two single guys, they kept the house unusually clean. Especially Hank's bedroom. The guy likes order. You should see his garage. He's converted it into a wood shop. The place is immaculate."

She reached her hand inside the pocket of a pair of pants hanging in the closet. "What else did you find?"

"We removed some hard-core bondage magazines and graphic sex DVDs."

"Young girls?"

"Young looking, but most likely still of age."

Emma kept searching through Hank's stuff. Most of his clothes were casual. Jeans, T-shirts, two pairs of khakis, and one suit. Everything in his closet was arranged by type of clothing, then by color. His drawers were neat—he even folded his socks and underwear.

"Did you find any hidey-holes?" Emma asked. She ran a gloved hand underneath the weight bench in the corner, feeling for anything taped to the underside. Nothing. Since there weren't any clothes draped over the weights or items stacked on the bench, she suspected Hank must have regularly used his equipment. She could visualize him bench-pressing the full 240 pounds of weights, working up an early morning sweat.

"No, we didn't find any secret compartments. All the porn was out in the open. These guys didn't seem too worried about their interests being discovered."

"Any other property in their names? What about parents?"

"Daniel Fry owns no property; the house is in Hank's name. Both parents are dead—mom from suicide and dad from colon cancer. There are no other siblings. Only an aunt who lives up in Michigan. She's been contacted, but says she hasn't heard from the boys in years, not since her brother Earl died in 2002."

When Emma finished searching the bedroom, she moved to the kitchen. Wallace had also finished checking the bathroom and moved into the side bedroom where Maddy had been kept prisoner.

"Hank Fry's room was devoid of any sentimental items," Emma said. "Did CSU confiscate any photo albums or journals?"

"No. We didn't find anything like that in the house. Nothing but a few pictures on the living room wall."

"Any activity on Hank Fry's cell phone?"

"No, he hasn't used it all day. He most likely removed the battery. All calls go directly to voice mail."

"What about bank account activity?"

Wallace came out of the bedroom and stood in the archway of the kitchen. "Yes. The same time SWAT was descending on the Fry house, Hank was emptying his bank accounts. Two thousand in checking. Eleven thousand in savings. When the branch manager asked why he was closing his account, Hank said he was moving. The manager thought Hank's behavior was suspicious. He seemed nervous and in a hurry. When the manager suggested they wire the money to Hank's new bank account in the city he was relocating to, Hank got angry. Told the manager he never was happy with the service he'd gotten at the bank and had wanted to change for some time now. Hank wouldn't even take the suggestion of traveler's checks. The guy wanted cash."

"So the manager knows something's not right but gives him the money anyway?"

"The guy couldn't do anything about it. Hank had all the proper identification. The money was his to do with what he wanted."

She sighed, feeling frustrated as hell. The urge to scream almost overtook her. She wanted to take every dish in the kitchen and smash it against the wall, to tear apart every piece of that monster's handcrafted furniture until it was kindling. Instead, she took a deep breath and asked, "What about work? Is he military?"

"No. He's employed by a construction company. The one that scored the big I-75 expansion bid. Hank's boss said he hasn't been to work since Saturday night, when he clocked in for an eleven-to-seven graveyard shift."

Emma stopped pulling out the plastic grocery sacks from underneath the sink and looked over at Wallace. "He's been off for the last *five* days?"

Wallace nodded. "Sunday, Monday, and Tuesday the job site got rained out. Remember that big thunderstorm? Then Hank called in sick Wednesday and today."

"Was that a normal occurrence, blowing off work?"

"Nope. The boss said he could only remember a handful of times Hank's ever missed work, and that each time it had something to do with his brother. I also talked to Daniel Fry's boss. Daniel works as a bagger at a grocery store. The guy told me Daniel has the mental capacity of a ten-year-old. Hank's been taking care of him since their dad died. I did the math. Hank would've been twenty-one and Daniel only sixteen. That's ten years Hank's been taking care of his little brother. It's a lot of hard work to look after a mentally challenged sibling. Shows some serious devotion."

"Then why did he leave Daniel behind today?"

When Wallace didn't answer right away, she looked over at him. He was tugging on his ear, his lips pressed together in a slight grimace. Shrugging, he said, "Don't have an answer for that one."

"Did either boss report any behavior issues with the Fry brothers?"

"Daniel's boss describes him as happy, outgoing, and a hard worker. Overall, the boss was pleased with his performance. He'd only ever had one problem with him. I read the complaint in Daniel's personnel file, a report made by a checkout girl. She said Daniel kept giving her love notes, leaving roses tucked under her windshield wiper. The attention made her uncomfortable, so she complained. We have a detective interviewing her now."

Wallace left the kitchen and moved into the living room. "Hank's boss didn't have much to say other than that Hank was intense. He also had issues with authority, but the boss put up with it because Hank was one of his best guys. We're still interviewing coworkers. So far nothing's surfaced."

"All these junk drawers are empty. Did you go through everything that was bagged?"

"Yep. Twice. Nothing to indicate a potential hideout."

Emma moved into the living room with Wallace. Empty cans of Mountain Dew littered the tables. A pile of clothes lay in a bunch on the floor. She turned toward the front window and saw the deep pinks and dark purples of another Florida sunset. It was a punch to the gut knowing the sun would soon be setting on another day that she'd failed to bring Maddy home.

She finally tore her gaze away from the window and asked, "Do either of the guys have an arrest record?"

"Hank's clean, but a complaint was filed against Daniel for public exposure." Wallace explained the details relayed to him by the responding officer. "Don't know if it was a purposeful act or an honest mistake. Either way, looks like the complainant isn't going to file charges."

Emma walked over to the pictures on the wall. "Every photograph shows the brothers as adults. You didn't find any baby snapshots, no ugly school pictures?"

"Nope. Those five are the only ones in the house."

"Interesting."

Wallace had shown Emma the DMV photos of the Fry brothers earlier. She knew the muscular man in the pictures was Hank. In one, he had his arm around a thin young man, Daniel, who held up a shopping bag in each hand. It looked like it had been taken inside a supermarket. Emma wondered if the photo commemorated a first day of work. She searched Hank's face, looking for clues to the evil inside him. The only thing she saw was a proud brother beaming into the camera.

Another photo was of Daniel sitting by himself. He was behind the wheel of a vehicle, a set of car keys hanging from a bent finger. It had a blurry quality, probably due to the motion of him swinging the keys.

A third picture showed Hank and Daniel sitting on their couch, toasting soda cans. In this one, she noticed Hank's smile didn't quite match his eyes. He must not have been able to slide his friendly face on quick enough. The camera had flashed a half a second too late to allow him to conceal the cold, calculating eyes.

I'll get you, you son of a bitch.

Emma looked at another framed photograph. "Who's this with Hank?" He had an arm around a beautiful blonde woman. Her cracked smile seemed to indicate an uneasiness at their closeness. "She a girlfriend?"

Wallace walked over. Emma grabbed the frame off the wall and angled it toward him so he could see it.

"No." He chuckled. "She's a TV reporter over at WRTX. Does the five o'clock news." Wallace started humming the broadcast's catchy jingle.

"I thought she looked familiar."

Is it a coincidence that she works for the same station that interviewed Maddy?

Wallace cleared his throat. "What about the side bedroom? Do you really need to see it again? I made a second pass through, and there's nothing there."

She knew she'd been avoiding the room.

Who could blame me? I never want to see it again, but if I don't search every corner of this house, I'll be plagued with the what-ifs.

"Let's go out to the garage first. I need some air. If we don't find anything there, we'll finish up inside."

Emma put the picture frame back on the wall. "Wait a minute. Where was this last photo taken?" She pointed at a shot capturing Hank and a few other guys sitting around a bonfire. An old shack was in the background.

"I don't know," Wallace said.

Emma turned the frame over and slid the cardboard out. On the back of the photograph, in a child's handwriting, was: "Boys wekend at jims fising caben." That familiar jolt of electricity sizzled across Emma's nerve endings. "This is it, Rocky. This place meant something to Hank. To have this picture on the wall, only one of five in the whole house—it had to have meant something to him."

"Or Daniel. But where is the fishing cabin? The guys are surrounded by trees. It could be anywhere. We don't even know if it's in Florida."

"Do you think the lab could enhance the picture? With more detail and some distinguishable characteristics, maybe we could narrow the search area."

"It's worth a shot," he said.

"Why don't you go back to City Hall and run with this? Have your guys track down who Jim is. I'll stay here and keep looking."

"You sure?" Deep worry lines were etched into Wallace's forehead.

She nodded. "If the picture is a dead end, we'll need something else to go on. I'll keep searching. When I'm done, I'll call you. We'll figure out our next steps then."

Emma had to face walking back into that bedroom sometime, and she knew it would be better if she did it alone. Since the moment she'd seen Maddy's message scrawled in blood, flashes of it kept haunting her. Right now they were like pop-up ads on a computer screen—they showed up when she didn't want them, but she could still make them go away. She didn't relish, however, the effect an intense search would have on her. Once she spent time on her hands and knees, studying every crack and crevice in the room, the scene would be forever seared into her mind. But she was willing to live with horrible images if it brought her one step closer to finding Maddy.

(61)
HANK FRY

Hank pulled the throttle back on the boat. He slowed to study the east side of the river for the markers in the trees.

Shit, did I miss it?

The woods looked like they hadn't been disturbed in years. Overgrowth could have obscured the markings.

The weekend he and Daniel had spent at his buddy's fishing shack, Hank hadn't been the one driving the boat. Beers and friendly banter had occupied his attention during the long ride. The only reason he'd even known about the zigzag lines etched into the trees was because of Daniel's incessant questions to Jim. Hank had told the boy to lay off, but Jim said he didn't mind. Daniel was the only one listening to his boring monologue about the different species of birds and indigenous plant life anyway.

Dammit! Everything hinges on me finding this place.

He thought the marker was supposed to be to the right as they entered The Narrows. It was a part of the Hillsborough River that tapered at the north end, becoming extremely shallow and dangerous to traverse.

"Yes!" Hank exclaimed as he spotted the upper part of a line etched into a tree. He'd been right—half of the marking had been obscured by foliage growing up the trunk.

He planned to lie low at the cabin, wait until the heat died down. The police would be looking for him, wanting to question him in the disappearance of the girl Daniel kidnapped. Nobody knew Hank had Maddy but who knew what Daniel would say once in custody? It was too dangerous to be driving on the roads, and there might be an APB out for him, which meant public transportation was out. The cabin was his only option. But if it didn't work out, he'd gut the girl and dump her in the woods. It'd be easier to get out of the city alone.

After Hank maneuvered the boat as close to the bank as he could get, he switched off the motor and jumped into the river. The water only covered the hem of his jeans by a couple of inches. He pulled the motor out of the water, then walked toward the bow. Summoning up all his strength, he yanked the boat up on land. It was difficult to move it through the brush. Heaving and pulling, he finally managed to get it deeper into the woods. He hollered at Maddy through the tarp, told her not to move, then went back to the shoreline to cover up any signs of broken foliage.

Satisfied, Hank walked back to the boat, erasing his steps as he went. He pulled the tarp off Maddy. "I'm going to uncuff you and cut the tape off your legs so you can walk. When you're free, slowly get out of the boat, then wait."

After the girl did as she was commanded, he strapped on a heavy camping backpack with a sleeping bag strapped to the top. Then he put a smaller version of the same pack on her back. He cuffed her hands in front of her once it was on.

He noticed that Maddy looked like she was having trouble breathing, like she couldn't get enough air in through her nose. She swayed, and he grabbed her. With her hands cuffed and the weight of the pack, she would have fallen on her face if he hadn't steadied her.

"What's wrong with you?" he asked, digging his fingers into her arm.

Muffled sounds came out of her mouth.

"If I take this tape off, you'd better not scream. All the rules of training still apply, and I expect you to follow every one of them."

Hank tore the duct tape off Maddy's mouth, enjoying the tears that sprang to her eyes. She stifled the sound of her pain well. Red splotches marked the skin around her lips. She greedily sucked air into her lungs, though it didn't seem to help her catch her breath.

"Don't forget for a minute how easy it would be to dump your body out here. No one would ever know. No one would ever find you. Make sure you keep on pleasing me."

He picked up the two brown paper bags sitting inside the boat and set them on the ground. Then he pulled the tarp over the top, hiding the boat from sight. When he looked up, he saw Maddy with a thumb in her mouth. Her cheeks were also puffed out.

What the hell?

"Quit sucking your thumb and get going." He picked up the bags off the ground and followed behind her. Every once in a while, she would get off course and he'd have to steer her back.

At one point, Maddy stopped and looked down at the bottom of her foot. Hank gave her a good shove from behind and she fell face-first. He saw that the bottoms of her feet were bloody. He hadn't thought to buy her shoes when he went shopping.

In a couple of hours the pain in her feet will be the least of her worries.

He dropped the bags and roughly got Maddy back on her feet. The rough handling didn't help and she teetered, threatening to fall again. He let out a long, guttural howl.

A yelp escaped Maddy.

"So help me, if you don't start walking . . ."

Maddy regained her balance and picked up her pace.

The small, still-rational part of him knew she couldn't help it. With her hands cuffed, if she stumbled, the pack on her back shifted and she had no way to reposition it. Yet that logical part of his brain had all but shut off. With every mile they had travelled down the river, the rage inside him had built.

It's Maddy's fault we're out here in the middle of nowhere. She's the reason I had to leave Daniel behind. Everything was fine until she came along.

Hank couldn't' get his mind off Daniel.

Without me around for protection, how will he cope? Is he safe? Is he being fed? This damn girl bewitched me—that's what happened. Maddy somehow made me choose her over Daniel. If I'd been in my right mind, I never would have put anyone before my brother.

In the waning evening light, he saw the fishing shack up ahead. It was time to teach this girl the lesson of what happened when she tore brothers apart.

(62)
MADDY EASTIN

By the time Maddy reached the shack in the woods, she was practically hyperventilating, the terror inside her constricting her airway. But she knew the pain she'd endured at the house was only a warm-up session compared to what probably awaited her here. She wondered if she would survive to see another sunrise.

They walked inside the four-walled shanty, and Hank went crazy. A wild look overcame him as he pulled at the cobwebs hanging all over the room. He started mumbling something about how the cabin wouldn't do. That he couldn't train her in this filth.

The only thing that had inhabited the place in years was clearly spiders and cockroaches. The bugs seemed to protest when the new occupants arrived by scurrying into their hiding holes. Maddy knew from her own house they'd be back.

"Stop! Stop!" Hank bellowed.

Maddy froze.

"You're making it worse."

She looked down and saw the trail of blood she'd tracked across the dusty floor. The sweat dripping down her brow stung her eyes. She ignored it, refusing to move in order to wipe them dry.

"There's got to be something around here to use to clean up this mess." Hank ran over to the sink and opened the wooden doors underneath it. He reached in and pulled out a bucket. "I'm going outside to the well. Gotta get some water. If the damn thing still works. Don't you dare move."

When he left, Maddy remained in place, only turning her head to look around. One room, about the size of a master bedroom housed everything. Against the far wall, next to the door, was a counter with a sink. Two cabinets with their doors barely hanging on were below, and two doorless cabinets were above. Over her shoulder, she saw a bed in the corner of the room—a bare mattress lying on the floor.

She heard cursing from outside.

Please start.

For her own sake, she prayed the water pump would work.

What if I just ran?

Hank's full attention was on getting water. She could walk right out the front door and have a good two-minute head start. If she didn't leave now, there wouldn't be another opportunity. Intuition told her she'd never walk out of this room alive. If Hank didn't kill her in the next few days, her tachycardia would.

Twice she'd tried the finger-blowing technique to skip her heart back into a normal rhythm, but for some reason it wouldn't work. If she could only stick her head into a sink full of ice, she could also shock her heart that way. She remembered her mom telling her that she'd resorted to that trick when Maddy was a baby.

Her instincts screamed, begging her to make a run for it, but terror and indecision kept her firmly rooted in place.

Where would I hide?

The ground was too flat for a good hiding space. The trees were too thin to conceal herself behind. If she made it to the water, where would she go? The alligators would attack her if she swam for it. The boat wasn't an option as she didn't have the strength to push it into the water—nor did she have the ignition key. Lack of food and little water had kept her barely able to put one foot in front of the other. There was simply no reserve of energy to call upon to make a run for it.

So she stood firmly rooted in the same spot, waiting for Hank to come back. Her feet begged her to sit down, to give them a break, but she refused, remaining locked in place. She would try her hardest to follow all of his rules.

Anything to stay in his good graces.

PART 12

FRIDAY, OCTOBER 2

(63)
DETECTIVE TERRANCE WALLACE

The dominos had finally started to fall. Wallace could feel the momentum rising. He knew the speed with which each piece would crash into the next would increase until finally the last domino fell and he found Maddy Eastin.

He just didn't know whether she'd still be alive when he finally reached her.

That's why he couldn't decide whether he should shut Emma Parker out of the investigation from this point on, or not. He had every right to.

Corporal Rhodes will be up my ass if he finds out I've been consulting with her on the investigation.

But then he thought about what it would be like if the roles were reversed.

What if someone had taken my wife? Could I handle being kept out of the loop? The not knowing is always the worst part. No matter what the situation, a mind could all too easily fill in the blanks. Like a smorgasbord of terrifying scenarios to choose from.

His decision made, Wallace dialed Emma's number.

"Hello?" Her voice sounded bone-deep with exhaustion.

Wallace glanced at his car's dashboard clock: 12:14 a.m. "The BOLO on Hank Fry's van finally turned up a hit."

"What?"

"We got lucky. You know the old fishing village north of Fowler Avenue?"

"No, I'm not familiar with it."

"It used to be a popular place to bunk down and take a boat out fishing on the Hillsborough River, but it's closed to the public now. The owner got too old to keep the place up. It's usually deserted, but the guy's grandson, a USF student, periodically checks on it. He admits his grandson takes his buddies out there to party, but figures it's a good trade-off. Anyway, the kid went out to the cabins tonight and found our white van out there."

"Did he find Maddy?"

"No. The vehicle was abandoned, and there's no sign that Fry even went inside any of the cabins. However, there is an old boat ramp at the bottom of the hill. He could've entered the Hillsborough River at that entry point. It makes sense. The place is deserted—a much better location than the busier boat ramp off Fowler Avenue. If he'd parked on Fowler, we would've found his van too quickly. Same thing with all the other state park entry points along the river."

"That picture on Hank's wall . . . the shack has to be somewhere along the river. That helps, right? It narrows down the search."

"Yes and no. We do have a smaller search radius now, but we still don't know where the place is. There are hundreds of miles of wooded area along the Hillsborough River. With all the dense brush, it would be impossible to search on foot, and a helicopter wouldn't have a line of sight through the thick canopy of trees."

Wallace heard a bang on the other end of the line—no doubt a fist making contact with a hard object. "Don't worry, Emma. We'll find her. The pieces are all falling into place. I'm headed out to the old fishing village now. I'll search the area and get back to you if I find something."

***

"What are you doing here, Emma? I told you I'd call if I found anything." Wallace stood by his car, arms crossed in front of him.

"I can't just sit around and wait." Emma slammed her car door shut.

"Try sleeping then. You look like shit."

Her hair was sticking straight up in thick patches all over her head. Her shirt was a wrinkled mess.

"You sweet-talker." The momentary lightness that had skirted across her face faded with a deep sigh. "Every time I close my eyes, I see Maddy writing on the floor, in blood. Do you have any idea how many possible scenarios have run through my head about the source of all that blood? So no, I can't sleep."

Wallace nodded his understanding.

Emma looked around. Floodlights illuminated the pathways to the cabins and down the hill. "This place looks like a summer camp from a creepy old horror flick."

"I thought the same thing. Wondered when Jason Voorhees would show up." He pointed over to the cabins. "None of the four were touched, but CSU found one set of shoe prints, one set of footprints, and what looks like drag marks made by a boat just over there, down the hill."

Emma walked to the edge and peered over. Jutting out from the bottom of the hill was a narrow, rickety bridge made from a bunch of two-by-fours. A few of the planks were missing. "Doesn't seem like much of a ramp. How could anyone launch a boat off that thing?"

"Not without a lot of difficulty, that's for sure. But a motivated man could make it happen. I went down there. It's more stable than in looks." He stared down at the uneven boards. It looked like it had been thrown together one afternoon by the owner and a couple of buddies after they'd downed a few six-packs.

Wallace couldn't understand the draw of fishing, especially fishing in alligator-infested waters. His wife had tried to talk him into taking a canoe trip up the river once. He'd refused, citing an agreement between him and the wildlife: he didn't trespass on the alligators' territory and they didn't trespass on his.

Wallace's phone rang. As he listened to the caller, his smile widened.

Emma grabbed his arm, but he gave a signal for her to wait a moment. Once he finished the call, he slowly clipped the cell phone back onto his belt holster. He was running the implications of what he'd heard through his head.

Emma tugged on his arm again. "What is it?"

"The next domino just fell."

(64)
HANK FRY

You did a piss-poor job of it this time, didn't you, boy?

Earl Fry's deep voice echoed inside Hank's head again. The constant criticisms and belittling were impossible to tune out.

How many times have I told you, son? To pull off a project this big, you have to plan. Your planning is for shit, and that's why you've found yourself in a big pile of it.

Hank covered his ears, trying to block out the booming laughter in his head.

"Nooooo!" He kicked the bucket, sending it flying into the corner of the room. Water spilled all over the floor. When he saw what he'd done, he shouted and cursed, shaking his fists at the ceiling. He yelled at the girl to clean up the mess. She scurried over and kneeled down to right the bucket. By the light of the lantern, she used her dirt-blackened towel to soak up the spilled water.

They'd been cleaning this shithole for hours and had barely made a dent in the grime. He couldn't stand the smell of the place. It was like being stuck on his family's farm all over again. Clean. This place needed to be clean in order to think, to work, to train.

He cursed Jim Yardley for having let the place go to rot. Hank threw his sponge on the ground as the futility of it all hit him.

Giving up, boy? You gonna be a quitter like your 'tard brother?

"Don't you talk about Daniel like that," Hank screamed.

Oh, come on. You know how worthless he was. That's why you left him back at the house. Good riddance, I say.

"I didn't want to do it!" Hank said.

I'm proud of you, boy. You're a chip off the old block—dumping your moron brother, finding a girl to train. Quit your moping, and let's get back to her.

He didn't want to be like his dad. He'd fought the darkness for fifteen years before it finally took hold of him. Hank looked over at Maddy crouched in the corner. He wondered what was so special about her anyway? She looked like a boy in that stupid sweatshirt. Her hair was all matted down with oil and clumps of dirt. How could anyone be attracted to something like that?

Hank had to start over. Had to get out of town. With twelve thousand dollars, he could start over fresh. A new name. A new girl. He just had to get rid of the one he had.

Right now though, he needed sleep. His father's voice had finally quieted down, and Hank felt heavy. He would lock the girl up tight for the night and then lie down on his sleeping bag. A few hours of rest would make everything better. The morning light. He'd just wait for the morning light.

(65)
EMMA PARKER

Emma knew this was going to end badly for her career. She was no longer sitting on the periphery of another force's investigation. She'd firmly rooted herself directly in the middle of it. Her sergeant hadn't caught wind of her involvement yet, but she knew it was only a matter of time. Up to this point, only Wallace and a couple of crime scene guys knew about her enmeshment with the case. Now the entire Temple Terrace SWAT force was privy to her presence.

Yet none of that seemed to matter. Her job was the least of her worries. Maddy coming out of this alive was the main objective. Emma had to know what was happening, had to know that everything that could be done *was* being done. She wouldn't let any detail, no matter how trivial, fall through the cracks. Not on her watch.

"Gather 'round, everyone," Wallace said as the ten SWAT guys who'd broken off into smaller groups came together. They were all gathered near the Trout Creek Wilderness Park boat ramp east of the floodgate near I-75 and Morris Bridge Road. Floodlights illuminated the 5:00 a.m. darkness. "All of you know most of the details of this case because of the takedown at the Fry house yesterday. Daniel Fry was taken into custody, and because of your quick efforts Katie Norris was retrieved unharmed."

Wallace continued over the ensuing congratulatory banter. "You're here today because we believe the older brother, Hank Fry, has abducted fifteen-year-old Maddie Eastin. She went missing three days ago, on September twenty-ninth. She was originally believed to be a runaway until we uncovered evidence that she was being held against her will in the Fry house. We saved Katie, but were too late for Maddy.

"Hank could have left Maddy at the house and gotten away easier without her. Yet he chose to take her along. But he left behind his brother, Daniel, who's mentally challenged and who Hank has been taking care of for the past ten years. This tells us that the girl is special to him. I'm afraid he won't give her up without a fight."

Wallace fell quiet for a moment to let that last statement sink in.

"Hank Fry's vehicle was found at the old fishing village just a few miles north of the Fowler Avenue boat ramp," he continued. "We have reason to believe he launched a boat from there. Katie Norris told us she saw Hank Fry leave his house yesterday with a girl that bore a resemblance to Maddy Eastin. So we are working under the assumption that Maddy is still with Fry. We have additional evidence that leads us to believe he's holed up in a shack in the northeast quadrant of the woods along the Hillsborough River. That's why we've set up a command post here—it's the closest entry point.

"Early this morning, I interviewed a coworker of Hank Fry's, a Jim Yardley. It took a while to track him down because he took a leave of absence from work to take care of his dad up in Georgia. Anyway, Yardley told me that, years ago, he built a cabin out in the woods. Well, more like a glorified shack. A place to party with his buddies as well as take his lady friends to without his wife finding out."

"How come no one's ever stumbled on the place?" one of the SWAT guys asked.

"Someone may have. Just not law enforcement, or they would have knocked the thing down." Wallace nodded over at a couple of Temple Terrace police officers. "Why don't you elaborate, Kovach?"

"Most of you know us," Kovach said, nodding at the guy next to him. "But for those who don't, Johnson and I are part of a team of two marine units that patrol the Hillsborough River. We patrol as far south as the dam near Busch Gardens, and all the way up north, to this location.

Normally, we're out here making sure everyone is fishing with a license, catching what they're supposed to, and ensuring there are no suspicious characters lurking behind the houses that back up to the river. Every once in a while though, we'll catch some yahoo setting up a campsite, poaching a deer, or net fishing. However, we stay in our boats. So unless the violation is happening along the river's edge, we won't find it."

"You'll be hitching a ride to the entry point with the marine patrol," Wallace said. He pointed at the SWAT commander. "Lieutenant Powell, would you like to take it from here?"

Emma watched Powell spread out a map of the wooded area surrounding the shack Fry was purported to be hiding out in. "You guys know these woods. We've done enough training exercises out here that you should be familiar with the terrain. I want a couple of two-man sniper teams to make their way back to the structure for reconnaissance." Powell pointed at the map. "Be in position by six twenty a.m. That gives you an hour before daylight to be in place. We're going in with flash-bangs at first light. No chopper this time. We can't afford the noise—it might tip off Fry. The forest is too dense to provide us intel anyway. Best to go in on foot."

Powell continued prepping his team, going over every detail of the assault they'd soon be undertaking. He decided which personnel he wanted on the inner perimeter team and which would comprise the entry team. Emma only half-listened. She knew she'd be stuck at the boat ramp for the duration of the extraction. There were only so many rules she could break and charging in with SWAT wouldn't happen. Even Rocky would be stuck there with her, listening to the live audio feed.

Wallace's phone rang, and he stepped away to take the call. The SWAT team finished their briefing and broke off from the circle to start suiting up.

Emma caught the attention of a SWAT guy named CJ. "Can I talk to you for a minute?"

"Sure, what's up?"

She pulled him off to the side and spoke in a hushed voice.

When Wallace finished his phone call, he rejoined the group. "We're all set. Powell, you and your guys ready?"

Powell clapped his hands with a boom, indicating he was all in. "Men—you ready to do this?"

CJ left Emma and went back to the group, adding his own clap to the thunderous sound all the other guys were making. They were ready.

Emma was too.

(66)
MADDY EASTIN

Maddy was ready to jump out of her skin. Every time Hank turned in his sleep, moaned, or made any sound, she startled awake. Then she'd listen to try and determine what noise had caused her intuition to warn her body to be on guard.

Has Hank snuck up on me? Does he have his knife?

She strained her ears, listening. He was murmuring in his sleep again. Maddy couldn't make out the words; she could only hear quiet ranting. His behavior earlier that night had almost terrified her more than her training sessions. She'd never seen him so crazed. While she was cleaning up the water he'd spilled, he had shouted at the ceiling, talking gibberish. She had no idea who he was talking to, so she tried making herself as small as possible.

He eventually threw her down on the ground and duct-taped her arms and legs together. Then he'd stormed over to the far end of the room and laid down on his sleeping bag. Instinctually, she knew he was distancing himself from her. So she remained as still as possible, ignoring the pain of her hunger and thirst, tried to keep the noise of her panting soft. Her chest ached, inside and out. It was becoming more difficult to breathe. She knew the infections and tachycardia were taking a toll on her body.

Oh, MomMom. I miss you so much. I wish I could have one more chance to do things differently. You stuck by me even when Dad didn't. You've always been my biggest cheerleader. You've never given up on me. And for that—

Hank cried out in his sleep. Maddy curled up tighter. Maybe if she was quiet enough, he'd sleep longer. Because the way she figured it, the promise of a new day didn't look too promising.

(67)
EMMA PARKER

"Checking Alpha," the SWAT commander said into his radio. Wallace and Emma were inside the mobile command center at the Turkey Creek boat ramp, listening to Powell check in with the sniper teams. There was less than an hour until sunrise.

"Alpha all clear."

Emma closed her eyes, envisioning the scene like it was playing out in front of her. She knew from this morning's briefing that a two-man sniper team, Alpha, would be taking up a position at the front left-hand corner of the shack—the one-two spot. Another sniper team, Omega, would be at the back right-hand corner of the house—the three-four position. Once they were in place, the cover team would move in to surround the shack, creating an inner perimeter in case Fry made a run for it.

"Checking Omega," said Powell.

"Omega all clear." The men in the field used bone-mic communication systems that enabled them to hear the commander through an earpiece while their words were picked up through a microphone situated across the throat.

"Cover team, move in," ordered Powell.

"Omega here. I have a visual at the number three window. A lone male. No visual on the friendly."

Emma pictured the shack as a square with each side labeled in the numbers one through four. Number one would be the front of the house, and the numbers would rotate clockwise. The number three window was at the back of the house.

"Keep him in your sights," said Powell.

Since SWAT didn't know for certain whether Maddy was in the shack, their directive was to take Fry alive—if possible. If he'd already dumped Maddy's body in the woods, they'd need him if they ever hoped to find her remains.

"Entry team, take your place," Powell commanded.

"Entry team in place."

(68)
HANK FRY

"No! Stop! No!" Hank startled awake at the sound of screaming.

He realized the source of the screams—they'd come from him. With a pounding heart, he looked over at Maddy and saw her right where he'd left her the night before.

It was still dark out. He pushed a button on his watch and the blue, glowing numbers indicated morning would soon be dawning. When he stood up, the cracking noises in his back seemed to tell the story of the night's fractured sleep. He'd been unable to stop thinking of Daniel or having dreams about his dad, so it was no wonder he hadn't gotten any rest.

The sound of rustling leaves outside the cabin caught Hank's attention, putting him instantly on edge. He hurried to the back window and looked outside. About ten feet in the distance, the moonlight illuminated a rabbit darting out of the bush and heading toward another hiding spot.

He turned away from the window and stared at the girl's dark figure lying balled-up on the floor.

That little bitch. This is all her fault.

The entire boat ride to the cabin, he'd fantasized about every slice his knife would make against her pale skin. He'd planned to draw out her death as long as possible. Make it a kind of experiment to see how much pain he could inflict before her body gave out. It'd be useful information to have for when he grabbed the next girl. But the shack had been too filthy. He knew he had to clean the place, or he wouldn't have been able to enjoy any of it. Now he was just ready to be done with it all.

Done with her. Done with this shack. Done.

Hank picked his sheathed knife from where he'd left it, on the floor near the mattress, and moved toward Maddy. He didn't want to wait. He had to kill her now.

He switched on the lantern so he could watch her reaction as the blade sliced through her skin. He sank down to his knees and raised his knife over her face so she could see the imposing weapon.

But instead of terror in her eyes, there was a look of defiance.

Son, don't wait. Kill her. Kill her now! Hank heard his dad yelling at him to slit her throat.

"Go ahead, you coward." Maddy barely spoke above a whisper, but Hank could hear the venom in her words.

How dare this bitch taunt me!

He lowered the knife to her neck, resting the tip of the blade against her throat. He waited to see the fear register, waited to hear her beg him to let her live. Once that happened, he'd slice her from ear to ear.

(69)
EMMA PARKER

Emma could feel the tension in the command center build as they waited for Powell to give the order for the SWAT team to bust down the door of the shack. She forced herself to remain seated and quiet, but all she really wanted to do was give into to her emotions and grab the commander by the shirt and shake him until he finally gave the go-ahead.

What is he waiting for? The team is all set. They're in place, ready to take Fry down. The first light will soon—

"Entry team go," said Powell.

Emma sprang up. She strained, listening to the shuffling of feet and the crunch of leaves through the radio transmission.

"Police! On the ground!" The sound of a steel battering ram splintering the door sounded as the police simultaneously announced their presence. The thundering boom of a flash grenade rang through the audio feed. Pounding boots thudded in a roar.

Then all the noises seemed to mesh together, making it impossible to understand what was happening. Had they found Maddy? It sounded like all hell had broken loose.

"Get on the ground!"

"Knife!"

Pop. Pop. Pop.

Static filled the air.

What happened?

Powell took off his headset. "We lost coms."

(70)
HANK FRY

"Police! On the ground!"

The door burst open and a roar of noise crashed into Hank. An explosion sounded next to him. The blast shook the entire shack and the room filled with smoke. He raised his arms to shield his eyes from the streams of light pouring through the door.

No! This can't be happening. Not yet. I have to kill her first!

"Get on the ground!"

Hank swung the knife down toward Maddy's throat.

"Knife!"

Pop. Pop. Pop.

Hank felt a cold spread through his body. He wondered why he was lying on the floor. His vision blurred, then his dad came into focus.

"Come here, son," Earl Fry said. "I've been waiting for you."

(71)
EMMA PARKER

When Powell announced they'd lost communication with the team, Emma ran out of the mobile unit and down the dirt path to the water's edge. She couldn't afford to fall apart in front of the commander and everyone else at the command post. She crossed the small bridge to the dock and looked down the river to see if she could see a boat returning. Nothing.

Who was on the other end of that gunfire? Has Hank Fry been shot? What was this about a knife? Was Maddy there when SWAT entered?

Not knowing was maddening. She started pacing from one short end of the boat dock to the other.

What am I going to tell Lily? How will I find the words to explain that I failed, that I wasn't able to bring her baby back?

The decision not to tell Lily any of this was going down had been a good one, she knew. Lily would've clung to the hope that her daughter would be rescued. A fall from that high might have been enough to crack her wide open.

The siren of an ambulance sounded in the distance.

Did the shots not kill Fry? Is there a chance he's still alive and can tell us where Maddy is? Did a SWAT member get hurt?

An approaching boat engine rumbled in the distance. Emma wiped her eyes with the back of her hand, trying to clear her vision.

A marine unit slid up to the dock. One of the guys jumped out of the boat and tied the ropes to the cleats. Officer Kovach turned the motor off, killing the engine noise. Emma ducked to the left and right, but she couldn't see around the line of three SWAT guys who had their backs to her.

Who is in the damn boat?

The men parted for CJ. He held Maddy in his arms.

Is she alive?

Maddy's eyes were closed. Her head lolled against CJ's chest. Her hair and feet were caked with dirt. In the filthy, oversize, bloody clothes she was wearing, she looked like a rag doll. Emma couldn't bring herself to ask. For just another moment, she wanted to hold on to hope.

Then CJ nodded at Emma, breaking her frozen state. She rushed over to Maddy and put her fingers against the girl's neck, praying she'd find a pulse. Instead of no heartbeat or even a weak one, Emma was surprised to find Maddy's pulse racing. She practically buckled at the knees as gratitude rushed over her. Then an internal alarm went off.

"Maddy's in tachycardia," she told them. "We've got to get her to the hospital right away."

CJ rushed over the bridge and laid Maddy on a stretcher. EMTs took over, pushing her up the hill.

Emma looked at CJ and mouthed one word—*Hank?*

He shook his head.

Emma smiled.

(72)
LILY EASTIN

Maddy's alive. Maddy's alive.

Lily repeated those words over and over in her head as she walked into the pediatric intensive care unit (PICU). It would help her remember what was most important. It didn't matter what that bastard had done to her or what she looked like. The only thing that mattered was that the doctors said she would live. Even if Maddy was still angry with her, shied away from her touch, Lily could deal with anything—as long as Maddy was alive.

Lily draped herself in a sterile gown and scrubbed her hands. Tom had finished washing a few minutes earlier and rushed off to Maddy's bedside.

"MomMom? MomMom?"

Lily heard Maddy's frantic call. She weaved around Tom and saw her daughter lying on the hospital bed, her face turned away from him, yelling for . . . her.

"I'm here. Don't worry, I'm here."

Maddy held her hands out to her mom, and Lily grabbed them fiercely, locking fingers and pulling in close. She wanted to give her daughter a hug, to grab on and never let go, but she was afraid of hurting her. An IV was taped to the crook of Maddy's elbow and machines beeped, tracking her heart rate. Maddy didn't hesitate though. She pressed in closer, encircling her mom with her one free arm. The two cried together on each other's shoulders.

As Lily wept, she let go of all the anxiety that had built up over the past three days. She realized that her worst fear had come true—but she'd survived. Not very gracefully perhaps, but she was still around to see the end of it.

It was time to make some serious life changes. Get the pill use under control, sure, but more important, get her head on straight. She was tired of living life always waiting for the worst to happen. Because she'd discovered that no matter how much she thought she'd prepared for tragedy, when it finally struck, no preparation was enough. No amount of shielding her heart had made it strong enough to resist shattering.

When Maddy had disappeared, Lily had regretted every moment she'd shrugged her daughter's touch away, every time she'd been too busy to listen. All wasted moments.

She now understood that if she had to lose Maddy, she would prefer to lose her knowing she had loved her with wild abandon than to have squandered their precious time together.

Through a face full of tears, Lily whispered her newfound commitment to change. She wanted Maddy to know she'd do anything in order to become the mother that Maddy had always wanted. The mother that Maddy deserved.

(73)
EMMA PARKER

Emma wanted to be in the PICU room during Lily and Tom's reunion with Maddy, but she knew it was time to take a step back and let them try to heal their family unit. There would be plenty of time for her own hugs later.

She saw Maddy's doctor in the hall and stopped him. Emma knew he wouldn't give her any information because she wasn't family, but it was amazing what the flash of a badge could accomplish. He told her Maddy had been in prolonged tachycardia and that all of her internal organs had enlarged to make up for the heart's deficiency. Another day in that condition and she would have gone into organ failure. Maddy would be monitored in the PICU until the swelling went down and the right mix of medications to control the tachycardia was found.

The doctor went on to talk about Maddy's long-term options for controlling the heart defect, but Emma knew all about radiofrequency ablation from when Maddy was a baby. What Emma said she really needed to know was the extent of the injuries Maddy had suffered at the hands of Hank Fry. The doctor outlined the more minor ones first—like the cuts on her feet, malnourishment, and dehydration—then worked up to more serious injuries, like the lacerations across her chest and stomach. Most had healed, but a few of the deeper cuts had become infected. For now, the doctor was holding off on stitching them up, preferring to allow them to heal from the inside out. If the Eastins were concerned about scarring, they could consult a plastic surgeon.

Most heartbreaking to hear about was the internal trauma Maddy had sustained to her vaginal area. The doctor was still unsure whether it would result in permanent damage. He'd know more after the swelling went down and the tears healed.

Maddy's physical injuries would eventually disappear, but the scars to her psyche would remain forever. Emma hoped all the adults in Maddy's life would be able to come together and surround her in a protective cocoon. Emma knew that meant she would have to take a more active role from now on too. In the past, she'd let her anger toward Lily seep into her relationship with Maddy, and the girl had suffered for it. Emma had abandoned Maddy when she'd needed her most. She wouldn't make that mistake twice.

Emma would, however, make sure Maddy got counseling. She'd also help Lily accept the fact that she needed treatment for her addiction to pills, and somehow she'd make Tom keep an active role in Maddy's life. Emma would be the one to hold them all together if she had to. For Maddy's sake. Maddy—the girl who wasn't her biological daughter, but was the closest thing she had to one.

Now that Hank Fry was dead, Maddy could begin the long trek toward emotional healing. The worst thing would've been sitting in a courtroom and looking at that monster enjoy the recounting of every vile thing he did to her. There was no way Maddy would have made it through a trial, no way any of them could have sat in the gallery listening to her describe every horrific detail.

But then, Emma had known Hank Fry would never see the inside of a courtroom. When she'd seen that CJ had been assigned to the entry team, she knew it was a lucky break. Two years earlier, his daughter had been busted on a drug charge—a charge that never got any further than Emma Parker. The girl was pre-med at Columbia. CJ hadn't wanted his daughter's entire future to suffer because of one bad choice. The girl had never been in real trouble, she just got caught up with the wrong boy on the wrong night.

Emma made sure CJ understood that the moment he forced his way into that shack, he needed to make good on the debt he owed her. His mandate was to find Maddy. If she wasn't in the shack, CJ was to do everything in his power to make sure Hank Fry walked out alive. But if CJ found Maddy inside, the only way Hank Fry should be leaving was in a body bag. She knew the emotional health of the entire Eastin family depended on it.

PART 13
TUESDAY, DECEMBER 1

(74)
MADDY EASTIN

Maddy sat with her pen poised over a blank journal page. The date was the only thing written on it. She thought about what she wanted to say. Her psychologist had suggested a new exercise to help her break through the barrier of negativity she'd been surrounding herself with. Write a passage of only positive statements, a summary of the last few weeks listing the things Maddy was grateful for.

It had been two months since Maddy's limp body was carried through the woods, rescued from the beast who'd hunted her down like prey. And as happy as Maddy was to be home, she was finding it difficult to put those horrific three days behind her.

"Not *behind* you," Maddy could hear her doctor say. "When a feeling comes up, allow yourself to feel it. Ride the emotion out, no matter how painful. It's the only way to release it. If you take your feelings and push them down into a box, keeping them locked up tight, they remain inside you like a disease that eats away at you from the inside out."

The doctor had told Maddy that whenever difficult emotions threatened to overwhelm her, she should try writing about them. It would help her push through the feelings. That's exactly what Maddy had been doing for the past few weeks. She'd already filled two journals writing about her reluctance to leave the house, the jumpy feeling she got whenever she was by herself in a room, and everything else that made her uneasy. Pages and pages were dedicated to her inability to sleep through the night. Every time she closed her eyes, she saw Hank Fry's face hovering over her. She couldn't count the number of times she'd had the same nightmare about a pack of wolves chasing her through a forest.

That morning her doctor had suggested she start a new book, one filled with only positive thoughts. She could still write down her negative feelings in her old journal, but the doctor thought one book should be solely devoted to the good things that had happened since Hank Fry had invaded her life. That way, on particularly bleak days, she could reread her positive thoughts for an emotional boost.

Maddy doodled on the page, thinking of everything that had happened since her mom and dad first came into the PICU. Maddy had travelled a long road to physical recovery. After her organs returned to regular size and her body beat the infection coursing through her system from the cuts she'd sustained, she had a radiofrequency ablation to get her tachycardia under control. The medical procedure seemed to have worked, and she hadn't had any problems since. For that she was thankful.

Her relationship with Aunt Emma had been strengthened. They had a regular Friday girls' night in, and made regular phone calls in between. Maddy was amazed at how hard Aunt Emma fought to track her down and bring her home. How she put her career on the line, willing to sacrifice her own future to make sure Maddy had one. She only wished Aunt Emma and her mom could repair their friendship. But she'd finally realized that even though Aunt Emma had tried to make a go of it, the relationship would never be the same.

Sometimes no matter how much you wanted two people to love each other, they couldn't. Maddy had always hoped her mom and dad would get back together one day, but she now knew that was just a child's dream. Though it was a slow process, Maddy was rebuilding her relationship with her dad. She'd met his new boyfriend and was genuinely glad to see him so happy. At first she'd been shocked at the news that he was gay, but Dad had gotten her to realize it was something he'd known since the age of ten. All those years, he'd just refused to accept it. He also took responsibility for the marriage dissolving, another shocking revelation for Maddy. All this time she'd blamed her mom for running him off, but it turned out she'd been the one protecting Maddy by keeping his secret.

Dad had taken a new job within his same company—one that didn't require so much travel. She was thankful he was around more and involved in her life. He was even helping her with her online courses. Maddy had dropped out of King High School and had enrolled in the county's online school instead. She might go back to public school one day, but for now, while she continued healing, everyone felt this was the best decision.

Her dad had said he'd help her mom out with the bills while she went to rehab. Maddy had known something was wrong with her, but if she were being completely honest with herself, she'd been so checked out and full of self-pity that she hadn't really cared. Maddy felt guilty for not recognizing the signs of drug use. With a lot of coaxing from everyone, her mom had finally agreed to seek treatment, but only in an outpatient program. Since she'd just gotten Maddy back, Mom wasn't ready to let her out of her sight yet. But Maddy thought it might have more to do with her mom being scared that Maddy would never come back after living with her dad.

Maddy recognized that her mom definitely had a long way to go in her healing. She'd spent her life always waiting for the bad to happen, had essentially put her whole life on hold banking on a future event. Maddy couldn't criticize her, though—she'd done the same. They'd both been waiting to live. Maddy had tried to stall life, waiting for her dad to come back home. But life didn't work that way. It went on no matter how much you fought against it.

Maddy's disappearance had changed her mom, for good and bad, but since the journal piece was only supposed to be about the positive, Maddy decided to focus on that. From the first moment she'd seen her mom in the PICU and felt the love pouring out of her, Maddy knew things would be different. With her counselor's help, her mom was learning how to express feelings toward Maddy. The Ice Queen was forever banished, and for that Maddy was thankful.

Maddy thought it was weird how she went from feeling no one cared about her to knowing that all of the adults in her life were super-involved. At times it felt a bit smothering, but with the doctor's help, she was learning how to communicate better and to express her feelings to others.

Maddy lowered her pen to the paper. She hesitated a moment longer, then began writing in her journal.

Only when faced with death can you truly be thankful for life. Only when you're about to breathe your last breath can you be thankful for another gasp of air. Only when you have everything stripped away can you be thankful when it's all returned. And thankful I truly am.

Photo Credit: Ruth Kegel

KELLY MILLER grew up shivering in Illinois but now enjoys the year-round sunshine in Tampa, FL. Her debut novel, *Dead Like Me*, won second place in the best mystery category of the 2011 FWA Royal Palm Literary Awards competition. It was also named a semi-finalist in the mystery category of The Kindle Book Review's 2013 Best Indie Books Awards competition. The Detective Kate Springer series continues with the second book, *Deadly Fantasies*. In Kelly's newest book, *Splintered*, she introduces her readers to a whole new cast of characters.

Visit **www.kellymillerauthor.com** to get a glimpse into the inner workings of her writing life.